COSTS OF LIVING

ADVANCE PRAISE FOR COSTS OF LIVING

Horror has often explored precisely what's terrifying about particular places. The frightening solitude of the woods, the crushing loneliness of an urban crowd, the eerie uniformity of the suburbs. [...] *Costs of Living* is the first collection that I know of which encompasses all of these extremes of experience across a wide swath of space. City, country, and suburb are all explored as terrifying places, proving that there's no place which is safe. With editor Steve Capone's first anthology, Whisper House has announced itself (by scream!) as one of the most promising small horror presses today, and *Costs of Living* proves itself to be an anthology that's very much of the moment and will promise to frighten the ever-living hell out of you— wherever you live.

> ED SIMON, PUBLIC HUMANITIES SPECIAL FACULTY AT CARNEGIE MELLON UNIVERSITY AND AUTHOR OF *DEVIL'S CONTRACT: THE HISTORY OF THE FAUSTIAN BARGAIN* AND *PANDEMONIUM: A VISUAL HISTORY OF DEMONOLOGY.*

A well done, page-turning anthology of stories about home being where the horror is.

> *KIRKUS REVIEWS*

While I devoured every bit of this anthology, I could barely look away [...]. *Costs of Living* is a riveting horror anthology that speaks to our sense of security and comfort.

CHRISTINA PERSAUD AT *ARTICLES OF HORROR*

Whatever your path in life, whatever your story is, there will be tales in this book that will hit you.

BOOKS FOR DECAYING MILLENNIALS

COSTS OF LIVING
A WHISPER HOUSE PRESS ANTHOLOGY

EDITED BY
STEVE CAPONE, JR.

Whisper House Press

Also available from Whisper House Press: *Dread Mondays: A Whisper House Press Horror Anthology*.

Cover by JD&J.

Copyright Registration Number Available from the Publisher

First Printing, First Edition.

Print ISBN: 979-8-9893919-3-6

Ebook ISBN: 979-8-9893919-4-3

Hell is other people.

JEAN-PAUL SARTRE

CONTENTS

FROM THE EDITOR'S DESK

When I publicized Whisper House Press's first call for submissions, I asked for "psychological, suburban, and social horror." I specified further "a focus on the oft-unclear distinction between a scary-enough reality and our less-or-more-frightening imagination, both in personal and social realms." I informed submitters of the proposed title, *Costs of Living*, and offered a few potential interpretations of the theme:

- The Neighbors/HOA/City Council *really are* trying to kill us
- A bad element... is already in the neighborhood
- Why do I feel like everyone is watching me in my new town's grocery store?
- "How can I be sure I am not dreaming?" without the "Oh, it was all a dream" cliché
- Philosophical quandaries run amok in one's mind
- Attic dweller keeps neighborhood watch via security cameras on smart home system starts seeing what they/he/she cannot explain

I figured I'd need to work hard to fill this first anthology and was shocked and gladdened to find that, over the following two months, I received 300 submissions, give or take.

The good thing about receiving that many subs is that I'd have my pick of what I expected would be many high quality stories, and ensuring representation across folkx was thus rendered possible. Therein lay the rub, of course. I'd need to read some 300 submissions.

As a first-time anthology editor, I knew and didn't know what I was getting myself into. I'd heard editing an anthology would be "a lot of work" but rewarding because the thing I produce would meet my own expectations, provided I didn't muck it up along the way.

And here's the surprising (?) thing: at no point was I annoyed at this work. At no point was I dreading reading another submission; rather, I remained grateful. I loved the process. Maybe this is still the view of the naive new guy, but I'm embracing it for as long as that feeling lasts. I have enjoyed every part of this process, and I am proud of what I and contributing authors have created together.

Working with the authors (see "Contributing Authors") was a pleasure. They all submitted to what I'll bet was a more rigorous editing process (including developmental edits, in many cases) than they're probably used to seeing. They expended full effort in editing and revising. Many even agreed to do a totally not-required video interview (find those on our YouTube channel @Whisper-HousePress). They were kind, and they were responsive.

The result is the book you're holding.

If you want to know more about the process, you can find a series of blog posts detailing the publishing process at www.whisperhouse.com. I've called these entries "From the Editor's Desk" because I'm so good at naming things.

I welcome conversation about the learning I've been gifted

through the creation of the *Costs of Living* anthology and hope to pay forward the help I've been given freely by other editors, authors, and small presses (shout out to Collective Tales Publishing and Timber Ghost Press).

———

I believe firmly that stories and the written word in particular are the most important things humans have ever created. These connect us (even those of us who pretty much always feel like we're on the outside looking in) and help us to understand one another's experience.

A last note about what this book is for and what it's about:

This book is what all the best horror books are about: what frightens us. I say this as someone who hates to be scared and puts down books or turns off movies that actually scare him. I do like to explore my fears, though, in controlled ways. I allow vulnerability in doses, as a kind of exposure therapy that never quite scratches the itch of the source of a fear but digs nice and deeply in the process.

A real-life superhero wearing a librarian's outfit once paraphrased to me a quote from Rudine Sims Bishop, describing books as windows and mirrors—showing us more of ourselves or revealing to us the world in which we live. Bishop herself may have thought the contents of this book somewhat disturbing, but I believe the spirit of the thing is right on target.

We are scary to ourselves and to one another, but take heart! Horror is a safe place to explore those fears.

(For content disclaimers, **check the very back of the book**—but you may rest assured that in these pages the dog *will not* at any point die as a prop of emotional manipulation. This move is cheap and will never be something this press permits, dammit. While we're at it, in this super-long parenthetical, please adopt a dog rather than supporting a breeder—our shelters are overcrowded to the point that actual dogs are dying in even our best-intentioned shelters because there aren't enough fosters and adopters out there. For more information, visit your local humane society—if you're in the Mountain West, check out Arctic Rescue. Okay, soapbox rant over. End parenthetical.)

Thanks for reading.

Steve

PART ONE
THE SUBURBS

Something about the suburbs renders them *prima facie* terrifying. That inherent creep factor drives these tales.

INCIDENT WITH THE BARQUELEIGH SQUARE COURT HOMEOWNERS ASSOCIATION

GEVERA BERT PIEDMONT

DEAR MR. STANLEIGH SMYTHE:

AS THE ONLY SURVIVING MEMBER OF the Barqueleigh Square Court Homeowners' Association, it falls upon me to reprimand you for last weekend's unfortunate incident and to levy the appropriate fines. It pains me, it does, to do this so soon after the death of your lovely wife Isabelladonna, not to mention the demise of the rest of the Homeowners Association, the thirteen (13) other neighbors, and those brave first responders. However, our charter requires that we put all reprimands and fines into writing within three (3) business days of any major incident, even if there are over fifty (50) of them.

As Recording Secretary, I had not yet received the opportunity to inspect or process your late wife's application to hold a child-related event on private property before the incident happened. Former President Kraygg Jonsynn assured me the paperwork indicated "a typical children's birthday party with some sort of ponies" and was nothing to be concerned about. Therefore, I was not diligent about its pre-approval. I have now located the unfiled application and I see that Isabelladonna indicated the ninth-birthday party for your triplets, Ashleigh, Kayleigh, and Emmaleigh, included some experimental animals borrowed from your employer (one assumes with permission) called "Teacup Raptors," code-named "Quetzalcoatl," that The Unieda Corporation had specially bred as pets.

Why President Jonsynn believed a "teacup raptor" was a pony, I have no idea. But we have all paid the price for his ignorance and failure to keep to the letter of our HOA code, which would have saved everyone a lot of difficulty had he followed proper procedure. Well, not you, Mr. Smythe, as you knew all along exactly what type of vile creature you were bringing into this suburban oasis—you were never ignorant of anything, except the price you would pay for deceiving the Homeowners' Association. As a consequence of your haste and the former president's mistakes, you have lost your wife, the lovely Isabelladonna, and your triplets are motherless and grieving.

Since the fines associated with this party are so numerous (see attached for the complete itemized list and monetary total), I have reconstructed a timeline of Saturday, the day of the party, based on eyewitness testimony and police reports. Luckily, I was away from the cul-de-sac on Saturday. Otherwise it is likely no HOA board members would have survived the party.

At approximately 1 P.M., the children arrived for the triplets' birthday party. Due to their youth, I cannot identify them by name, but some survived. The various parents dropped off their children and left them with your family with the tacit understanding that both triplets' parents would supervise the party. This oversight incurs the first fine for a failure to have an adequate adult-to-child ratio; you were not at home at 1 P.M. and, even if you had been, the number of adults would have been insufficient to conform to the HOA's policy.

About twenty minutes later, you arrived in a Unieda Corporation van, and this action incurs the second fine—parking an unauthorized commercial vehicle in your driveway, and unfortunately this fine doubles because the infraction took place during the weekend. You then removed three (3) "teacup raptors" from steel-barred cages in the rear of said vehicle. These dog-sized creatures proved to be some sort of horrid bird-reptile hybrid—certainly not the promised ponies that President Jonsynn understood them to be. I learned, from the neighbors who watched through their windows, and from security camera footage, that the flamboyantly feathered creatures wore jeweled collars with matching leashes, and the neighboring children who had not been invited to the party immediately wanted to go outside to play with them. This fact renders these "teacup raptors" an attractive nuisance, which must result in another fine.

The neighbors claim you managed to control the "teacup raptors" for about half an hour while your daughters and their friends frolicked with the ugly creatures, leading them around on their leashes, petting their feathered heads, and even embracing them, apparently not finding them horrible. Although the creatures had bird beaks filled with sharp teeth, you and your wife didn't seem worried, according to reports. Residents overheard you say to the lovely Isabelladonna that you were right not to bring their muzzles because "the muzzles only stress them out." If the HOA had a rule about "teacup raptors," I am sure the lack of proper muzzling would have incurred another fine. In lieu of this hypothetical fee, I have applied a miscellaneous fine.

About an hour into the party, several things happened simultaneously. The pizza delivery arrived, and a sizable group of uninvited neighborhood children broke through the side gates to "get their turn" playing with the "teacup raptors."

(The continued quotation marks indicate my disbelief in

"teacup raptors." That said, nothing with an industrial code name should be playing with children.)

To deal with the pizza delivery, you and Isabelladonna left the children unattended with the "teacup raptors." It's unclear if you realized at that time the neighborhood children had broken through the gates and entered the yard. (I appended a small fine for broken gates and malfunctioning locks and another fine for failure to keep the locks and gates up to HOA code.) The delivery driver, Myq Phranklyn, in a statement to police I managed to obtain, said they saw the children playing in the backyard with "some kind of weird turkey things" and that the kids were very loud and "seemed a bit out of control." They did not realize that uninvited children from neighboring yards were breaking through the fencing. After Myq left the stack of pizzas with you, they departed the neighborhood, not knowing they barely escaped becoming a casualty. The pizza car passed the HOA camera at the gate at 2:11 P.M. (Since Myq was on their phone while driving away, they and their employer were mailed a fine.)

Returning to the children behind your house, Mr. Smythe, you and Isabelladonna discovered the party size had more than doubled with the influx of neighborhood children, and you thus had a vastly insufficient amount of pizza. (A second fine is appended for insufficient supervision of children at a gathering, plus a new one for failure to feed underage guests adequately, which also triggers an automatic call to social services and additional fees.)

The uninvited neighborhood children started yanking on the tails and jeweled leashes of the "teacup raptors," which apparently excited and frightened the animals. All the kids were screaming and fighting over who would get to play with the creatures. The sheer amount of movement overwhelmed your low-budget backyard security cameras, so this escalation is not fully documented (another fine). The neighbors' cameras could not record events clearly over the fences, and eyewitness accounts become confused at this juncture as well. (For the record, I did not fine the neighbors for their camera failures, as each homeowner is only liable for monitoring their own spaces.)

Although I have not (yet) obtained access to your police testimony, it appears you and Isabelladonna decided opening the pizza boxes would entice the children away from the "teacup raptors" and toward the food. However, several of the pizzas had meat toppings—although we could spend all day discussing what is proper to feed growing children, the time and place are neither now nor here—and this choice had a different effect than you anticipated. The "teacup raptors," attracted to the smell of the steaming meat, abandoned the children for the moment and raced toward the folding table spread with open pizza boxes. Isabelladonna stepped between the animals and the table, perhaps to attempt to stop them, and was bowled over by the rapidly advancing "teacup raptors," hitting her head on a paving stone. The "teacup raptors" climbed over her to reach the fragrant pizza with the delicious (to them) meat toppings.

Some children's shouts of glee turned to shrieks of horror upon seeing your lovely, kind wife Isabelladonna sprawled, bleeding and unmoving. Others cried upon seeing the (to them) scrumptious pizza being ruined, torn apart, and devoured by the creatures. Ashleigh, Kayleigh, and Emmaleigh, of course, ran to their mother. After what I can only imagine was a moment of paralysis, you did too. The blow to Isabelladonna's head had killed her instantly, the post-mortem later showed. Her blood soaked into the stone patio around your covered in-ground swimming pool, leaving an unsightly stain you still have not yet cleaned (another fine).

In the short time it took for you and your hysterically screaming identical triplets to realize they were motherless and you were a widower, the three (3) "teacup raptors" finished ravaging all the pizzas on the table but were still hungry. They located a sizable piece of fresh, bloody meat nearby and immediately dug in. Again, I must apply a miscellaneous fine for allowing the creatures to feast upon a human, as our extensive charter simply did not envision such a thing ever coming to pass in our lovely cul-de-sac—plus a fine for possessing a dead animal (person —poor Isabelladonna) in the yard.

The narrative becomes even more confusing after this moment, but I will soldier on, as it would not be right for me to levy fines without explanation.

As you and your daughters tried to shoo the "teacup raptors" off Isabelladonna's gnawed-on corpse, several dozen children raced around the extensive yard, panicking, not thinking to escape through either the broken open side gates or the closed front gate. One boy ran across the in-ground pool and thrashed around on the winter cover, which had collected a few inches of rainwater and leaves (a nominal fine for general untidiness and leaving a breeding ground for vermin). The thin canvas, not rated to hold a child (another fine), split open and dumped the child into the cold, dark, dirty water beneath. No one on the scene seemed to notice.

After you sent Ashleigh, Kayleigh, and Emmaleigh inside for a blanket in which to wrap Isabelladonna's unsightly remains (a miscellaneous fine for having desecrated human remains on your property is against city law, I just realized), the distracted "teacup raptors," now in some kind of blood rage, began chasing the howling children around the yard.

You located a cell phone—determined later to be your wife's— and finally called 911 at 2:46 P.M. (For this, I applied a fine for failure to phone emergency services in a timely manner, and another because you failed entirely to notify the HOA of any of this debacle, either by post as required or by telephone as expected at minimum.)

You completely ignored these other children, whether invited or not, and so I levy a third fine here for improperly supervising minor children under your care—and another for your failure to control the "teacup raptors," although in my reports I had to record this fine as one exacted for "allowing a dangerous dog to be unleashed" three (3) times as there is no option in our charter for whatever the heck a "teacup raptor" is.

By this time, several other residents had called 911 as well as notified the HOA, as well they should have. Those residents whose children had invaded the yard were bursting through their doors on their way to rescue their children from the disaster you had created. No one had attempted to remove the torn cover from the pool to rescue the child, although by that time the boy had surely expired. The next fine is for having a dead animal in your pool since there is no fine in our code for dead children, an oversight perhaps needing rectification.

At 2:55 P.M., four (4) neighbors attempted to enter the backyard through the unbroken main gate connected to the front yard, simultaneous to the pursuit of a mass of hysterical children by what one parent described as "angry mutant reptilian turkeys with feathered mohawks and wearing jewels." The panic-stricken kids detoured through that gate into the front yard and the cul-de-sac proper, and two (2) of the "teacup raptors" followed. One (1) critter stopped to savage the unsuspecting parents, shredding three (3) people with the long razor-sharp claw on its back foot in less time than it takes to tell the tale. The remaining resident made it to the front yard while the "teacup raptor" was distracted with the slicing and dicing—this resident attempted to close the gate. (Fines here include (a) the gate not being locked and (b) also not being structurally sound enough to withhold a direct attack by a wild animal, which I had to record as a miscellaneous fine, and (c) another fine for the allowance of dead animals in the yard [three {3} people] and allowing a dangerous dog ["teacup raptor"] to roam untethered, times three [3].)

In the backyard, you, Mr. Smythe, realized your three (3)

workplace pets had gotten away, and you instructed Ashleigh, Kayleigh, and Emmaleigh to go into the house and remain there, which they did, being very good girls. With the surviving neighbor who had just entered through the gate (later identified as Mr. Jimothee Lipschitz), you advanced into the front yard, past the lacerated corpses propping open the gate.

The police were just arriving at the other end of the cul-de-sac (3:01 P.M.) and giving their reason for being there to the person manning the gate (calling the police for no good reason incurs a fine, but in this instance, I approved the calls after the fact, and I levied no fines for this infraction on anyone who called that day). The police were very slow to arrive—something about an overturned truck and fire on Maine Street, which should not be our problem as Maine Street has its own HOA.

In the meantime, the children had scattered, and the "teacup raptors" individually pursued small groups of them. A child's ragged running speed and random pattern is no match for whatever a "teacup raptor" is, and Mr. Jimothee Lipschitz was dismayed to witness the bejeweled, turkey-like creatures jumping onto kids' backs and taking them down forcefully. All three (3) of the "teacup raptors" were covered in blood, by this time, and looking very bedraggled—and fierce. All this was recorded by doorbell cameras and the cameras of several high-end and attractive electric vehicles approved to be parked in the driveways and street.

Mr. Jimothee Lipschitz ultimately realized his own son was missing from the crowd of indistinguishable, screaming kids; the Lipschitz boy was later located in your pool, Mr. Smythe. Fines levied here include allowing your dog to defecate on other people's lawns and not cleaning it up (again, times three [3], and determined in reference to the "teacup raptors" excreting on Mrs. Plantaine's prize-winning petunias) and allowing your dog to be unleashed on other people's property (again, times three [3], and actually referring to the "teacup raptors"). Rest assured, Mr.

Smythe, several other residents incurred fines for allowing dead animals (i.e. children, in this case) on their lawns.

The other members of the Barqueleigh Square Court Homeowners' Association arrived outside your home at around 3:10 P.M.: President Kraygg Jonsynn, Vice President Carynne O'Shawghniseigh, and Treasurer Kerrynn Jonsynn, from the Jonsynn's residence, where they had been having one of their frequent private meetings to which I was never invited, the ones lasting all night and sometimes all weekend. Someday I'll find out what a "polycule" is, but for now, I must take up the mantle of the presidency. I must shoulder that responsibility because the three (3) of them stood on the Jonsynn's front porch in matching silk bathrobes—perhaps they had been in the hot tub together; it was a regulation-size spa holding up to six people hidden on the Jonsynn's sheltered three-season back porch—surveying what was happening before them. The three of them, standing there open-mouthed and baffled in their matching robes, witnessed dead children being eaten by jewel-wearing turkey things, other children and their parents running and screaming, other turkey things chasing them, a police car crawling down the street, and you and Mr. Jimothee Lipschitz standing on the Smythe front lawn next to an unauthorized commercial van. This seems a good place to add in the noise violation, as well.

At this moment, a "teacup raptor" leapt, soaring incredibly far on its stubby feathered arms, and took down an adult female person in right front of the police car—and then ran off to sully the Papalardos' tiger lilies right in front of their bow window. The police car failed to stop in time and hit the fallen adult, who later on proved sadly to be Mrs. Lipschitz ("Trixybehl"). The autopsy revealed Trixybehl Lipschitz was killed by the police car and not the "teacup raptor," which had wounded her only slightly, biting but not tearing into the back of her neck. I'm not sure I'm allowed to send fines to the police, but I did prepare the unsafe driving paperwork just in case. Our neighborhood, our rules, right?

The police vehicle stopped and then reversed, again driving over poor Trixybehl Lipschitz, which probably did her in. I believe at this time the officers summoned a single ambulance, although they should have summoned the entire fleet, and I did write up another fine for that error, held in abeyance with the unsafe driving fine.

As the two officers, a man and a woman, were attempting to render first aid to the flattened Mrs. Lipschitz, they failed to maintain situational awareness (another fine, again in abeyance) or even inquire about the actual reason they had been summoned to Barqueleigh Square Court. It was not at all difficult for the "teacup raptors" to take down the two officers while they were distracted with administering aid—coming at them from either side in a pincer move, with the third sneaking overtop of the police car, dragging its bloody jeweled chain across the paint and damaging the roof quite a bit. Perhaps if Mr. Jimothee Lipschitz had realized it was his wife to whom the officers were administering aid he might have run into the street to assist... and perhaps been eaten himself... but he did not. It is probably not up to me to fine you, Mr. Smythe, for damaging town property, but I have administered a fine for the scratched paint and the sizable dent in the roof of the police vehicle where the creature leapt onto it. They weigh more than they look, don't they? We must be prepared to handle fines delivered by the police department over this incident, and I will forward any fees onto your account, Mr. Smythe.

The Jonsynns and Ms. O'Shawghniseigh, loose bathrobes unfortunately flapping (some things others do not wish to see get recorded in full color and from many camera angles), dashed off the Jonsynn's front porch toward the police car at 3:16 P.M.

As you, Mr. Smythe, climbed into your unsightly and unregistered Unieda work van at 3:22 P.M., Mr. Lipschitz wandered off, calling for his boy, not knowing little Willyuhm was safe from the jeweled turkeys under the Smythe's pool cover. Safe from everything, in fact, and forever. Well, I mustn't be poetic in this notice of fines; it is, unfortunately, not a work of fiction. The boy was dead in your swimming pool, Mr. Smythe, and you've already been fined for that fact and for related infractions.

The HOA board, minus yours truly, dropped to their bare knees beside the torn-up police officers and the squashed Mrs. Lipschitz. I have to wonder if, as he turned over a dead, macerated cop to locate the woman's radio, Kraygg remembered telling me Isabelladonna's party application specified *ponies*. No pony, no matter how angry or hungry, had ever torn up people the way these "teacup raptors" had done (and were still doing).

Yes, even as all of this chaos transpired, the three (3) monstrous creatures, dragging their fancy leashes through puddles of blood and entrails, continued to attack children and adults. At this point, I'm not sure how many fines to levy and of what type. Dog attack, vicious dog, roaming dog? There are even some fines, far down the list, about committing any sort of crime causing a cul-de-sac resident to feel a need to call emergency services. Plus, of course, all types of fowl are forbidden as pets or livestock per HOA regulations, and these "teacup raptors" resemble angry mutant turkeys in many ways, notwithstanding their sharp teeth and slashing claws.

Although you, Mr. Smythe, did not personally attack anyone, you were both the proximate and immediate cause of all these infractions. Many of these losses cannot be atoned for via fine payments or even apologies; i.e. dead children and predator excrement on prize-winning petunias. And maybe your late, lovely wife Isabelladonna wasn't completely transparent in completing the application for a children's party permit. That's an easy fine, lying on an application for a party. Fines accrue to the household, not the person, so that your wife has since perished is immaterial.

Everything stems from there, doesn't it, Mr. Smythe? The false application for a party with "teacup raptors."

Alas, the three (3) senior members of the Barqueleigh Square Court Homeowners' Association also failed to exercise situational awareness, spending too much time at crucial moments peering under each other's robes and attempting to use the police radio while crouched in the middle of the street over three (3) corpses. Rest assured, I delivered their fines to their households, as is proper. I did not watch the footage after the "teacup raptor" tore these fine community leaders apart, literally and figuratively, as I did not want to see what happened when their robes fell off. Fines for public nudity and public indecency seemed appropriate, however, and these were delivered to their surviving families (including one distant cousin currently residing abroad).

As two (2) of the "teacup raptors" fought over Ms. O'Shawghniseigh's bare left leg at 3:29 P.M., you emerged from that eyesore of a work van with a sports whistle and started blowing it. The piercing, horrible noise echoed up and down the cul-de-sac, evident in every recording. Every dog, cat, hamster, and pet with ears (also babies and toddlers) freaked out, as I understand it, and it will come as no surprise I've levied a fine for each time you blew that whistle for exceeding the allowable decibel levels of noise and also for being a general nuisance.

The single ambulance summoned by the late police officers finally got by the gatekeeper at the mouth of the cul-de-sac at 3:35 P.M., but by then no one needed tending. Everyone at risk was already dead, sprawled in driveways and yards and across rose bushes, half-gnawed (just the good parts, I suppose). The smarter children had hidden inside homes, often not their own (herein lies a conundrum: do I fine neighbors for this occurrence? I haven't decided yet, but I recognize it's improper for adults to consort with other people's children without their parents' permission...so I'll put those fines in abeyance too). The not-smart children received their Darwin awards that day.

You blew and blew that whistle, your face looking fat and red in the videos that showed it, as I made tally marks for each time your lips pursed and your cheeks puffed. The ambulance driver and two-person crew stood helplessly in the bloody street by the police car, gazing at the carnage.

The three (3) "teacup raptors" emerged through the propped-open gate from your backyard at 3:42 P.M. and slinked toward you with their bedraggled feathered heads down, dragging their filthy jeweled leashes. You scratched their bloody crests and shooed them into their cages in the back of the van. No one was paying attention. The surviving neighbors stood behind their screen doors, afraid to come outside, shouting at the ambulance crew in a useless cacophony. The blood and open corpses and what comes out of the dead as they die putrefied the air, springtime or not.

You climbed into the driver's seat of the van and slowly drove away down the street, bringing the three (3) "teacup raptors" with you. At 3:47 P.M., you weaved past the police car with its open doors, the ambulance, and the scattered bodies.

Invented as well is a fine for fleeing the scene of a crime, and then I had to decide how many crimes you were fleeing from. The answer the latter question is: a lot of crimes, Mr. Smythe—a lot. If you hadn't left Ashleigh, Kayleigh, and Emmaleigh inside the house, I don't think you would have returned to face the music, as they say, but you are a good father if not a good neighbor, and you did return home, in your personal vehicle and several hours later. I must report that in so doing you incurred another fine (times three [3]) for leaving your girls without parental supervision—your dead, blanket-wrapped wife doesn't count.

You have thirty (30) days to pay these fifty-three (53) fines, or I will be forced as acting president to place a lien upon your primary residence, 65 Barqueleigh Square, for the full amount of your fines with compounding interest per your Barqueleigh Square Court Homeowners' Association Agreement, a copy of which is attached. I realize you are currently in prison, Mr. Smythe, and Ashleigh, Kayleigh, and Emmaleigh are residing with Isabelladonna's parents in another state—and that 65 Barqueleigh Square is a crime scene that has become a place of public interest and thus a nuisance to your neighbors (one final fine), but none of this is my concern. My concern is for the good of our beautiful neighborhood, and that good requires the prompt payment of all fines.

SINCERELY,

Kharyn Gnewtynn,

Former Recording Secretary, now Acting President of the Barqueleigh Square Court Homeowners' Association, via battlefield commission

P.S. I just noticed on your home purchasing application documents that you are only by a technicality "Dr. Stanleigh Smythe," as you have a Ph.D. in Genome Editing and Gene Therapy. Since you are not a real doctor, I shall continue calling you "Mr. Smythe" in this all and future communications.

THE PHYSICAL IMPOSSIBILITY OF LOVE IN THE HEART OF SOMEONE WANTING

STEPHEN S. POWER

ZOE KEPT HARRY STYLES' LEFT EYE IN A JAR OF PRESERVATIVE gel beside her bed so it would be the last thing she saw at night and the first thing she saw each morning.

It had cost her father a fortune, but it was all she'd wanted for her Sweet Sixteen, and Harry had needed the money for his comeback album and tour. When both became huge successes, Zoe had felt like Queen of the Fans. Harry's queen, too. Daddy had been so happy for her.

Zoe had never imagined another fan would try to steal Harry's eye until she came home early from lacrosse one day and found a woman crawling through her bedroom window.

Zoe shrieked and bolted for her nightstand as the woman slithered to the floor. Zoe got the jar, but the woman got between her and the door. Zoe shrieked louder.

The woman laughed. "No one can hear you. You rich bitches shouldn't live so far from your neighbors. And your daddy should be home more." She set her feet. "Give me Harry's eye."

"No," Zoe said.

The woman wore a black scuba hoodie and yoga pants, off-brand stuff that didn't bulge with a gun or a knife, only sad mom fat. Zoe wished she hadn't left her stick downstairs. She could take her easily. Zoe glanced at the door. If she could reach it—

The woman stretched her arms. "Go ahead. Try. Be sad if the jar broke."

"You wouldn't risk it."

"Didn't have it before. If I don't have it later, what's the difference—for me?"

"It's mine!" Zoe turned sideways and wished she hadn't left her phone downstairs too.

"You don't deserve it." The woman looked around. "No pictures of Harry anywhere. I couldn't believe it when I saw it on your Insta. My walls are covered. And the ceilings. And my chest."

Zoe smirked and patted the jar. "I don't need fake eyes, printed eyes, looking at me when I have the real thing."

Harry's eye jiggled, looking back and forth between them.

The woman scoffed. "You don't care about him like I do. I'd give my eye for Harry."

"I stayed with him the whole week he was recovering."

"So did I—camped in the hospital parking lot." The woman shot out a hand.

Zoe jumped back. "I held his hands. He kissed them."

"He kissed me at a concert, back when we were younger than you. I've seen him thirty times." The woman threw out her other hand. "Thirty-four, if you count One Direction."

Zoe retreated till the bed stopped her. "Really? I've never seen you at a show. Or backstage. But I never sit in the cheap seats. With cheap hair."

"You little shit." The woman slid forward.

"Get out of my room!"

"Not without the eye." The woman flung herself at Zoe.

Zoe turned and stuffed the jar deep into her bedcovers, then slammed backwards into the woman, driving her toward the hall the way she'd work an opposing defender.

The woman wrapped her arms around Zoe's chest. Zoe snapped her head into the woman's nose and kept pushing, but the woman hugged her tighter and chomped on Zoe's neck.

Zoe shrieked, feinted one way, twisted the other, and tore herself free. The woman bent to rush her, but Zoe grabbed her face and planted her thumbs on the woman's eyes.

"I'll pop them," Zoe said. "Like bubbles."

"You couldn't."

"Try me. Get out." Zoe pressed the woman's cheeks with her palms to encourage her.

Instead the woman squatted, loosening Zoe's grip, then stood, getting her own thumbs on Zoe's eyes as Zoe's thumbs found hers again.

The woman said, "What would Daddy say if I ruined you?"

Her thumbs smelled like the rose trellis outside Zoe's window. They throbbed with her heartbeat. Slow. Steady. She'd definitely blind Zoe.

"He'll be home soon," Zoe said.

"He's been in Asia for a month. He's on Insta too."

"And I'm supposed to FaceTime with—"

"Nope, it's study time. On your Google calendar."

"The alarm—"

"Just a sticker on the front door."

"You'll go to jail—"

"I'd crush the eye first, and you'd still be blind." The woman massaged Zoe's eyes. You're getting desperate, sweetie. No one's coming. Mommy's long gone. You're all alone."

Zoe burned. The woman was right. Still, she didn't think the woman could blind her.

The woman didn't think Zoe could either. She hummed the chorus to "Carolina": "She's such a good girl..."

Then the woman said, "Now give me Harry's eye."

"I can't." Zoe started to cry. "I love him."

"Stupid virgin. You'll love plenty of guys. If you're lucky, some won't leave you pregnant." The woman leaned in. "And why love Harry? He's old enough to be your daddy. It's gross."

"He sees me." Zoe couldn't help saying it.

"You, with Daddy's credit card? A fancy car? And new clothes every day? You want to feel ignored, work in a Dollar General. Then you'll see."

"No, Harry sees me. The real me. With every word. With every breath."

"I've watched you for months," the woman said. "There's nothing to see. No wonder your Daddy goes away so often. You're nobody."

"I am not!" Zoe said. "He loves me too. I know it." Zoe jabbed the woman's left eye.

It didn't pop. Or give. It was hard as—

"Glass," the woman said. "I sold mine to a Saudi so I could be in the auction. And replace it with Harry's so I could see the world the way he does. Tell your daddy he shouldn't have topped my final bid." She gripped Zoe's head and—

Zoe plunged her left thumb through the woman's right eye, scraping the socket with her square nail, fluid squirting everywhere.

She wished Harry's eye, safe under the covers, could've seen what she'd done for him.

The woman fell away, gagging, cursing, clutching her face, and staggered into the hall.

Zoe followed her down the main staircase, the pounding of their feet echoing through the three-story foyer, and let the woman feel her way out the front door. Zoe locked it behind her. She wiped off her thumb and hand with her uniform skirt. Then she wrestled her phone out of her knapsack.

She wanted to call her father, but he'd be at his first breakfast meeting. She should call the cops, but what could they do without bothering Daddy? He'd have meetings all day. Her coach would be terrified for Zoe, but useless. How could he understand what Harry means to her? Besides, he was kind of a perv. And Harry, sadly, had long since changed the number she'd gotten off his phone in the hospital.

At least she still had his eye.

So Zoe went back to her room, slammed the window, and, shaking, suddenly exhausted, crawled into bed with the jar. She curled herself around it, kissed the lid, stroked the hard, cold glass and whispered, "I've got you, baby. Don't worry. I'll never let anything happen to you."

WATCHING OVER HER HOUSE
ABBY ANDRESEN

In line to place her latte order, Laura absorbed the familiar hippie vibe of the Deja Brew Cafe. Comforted by the dusty, meandering plants in the windows and the paintings by local artists covering the walls, she imagined Roger were still alive and they still lived just blocks away. And there, as if expecting her, sat Christine.

"Christine!" Laura called to her, stepping out of line with a big wave. Christine was alone at their old table with her coffee—large and in charge—even over her knitting. She looked up from her busy needles and smiled. After paying, Laura made a beeline to Christine's table, latte and cinnamon muffin in hand.

"Hi! I had an appointment over at the clinic," Laura explained. Nothing could have made her happier today than seeing Christine.

"You haven't switched clinics yet?" Christine asked, watching Laura settle in across the table.

"No, not yet," Laura admitted, sinking into her old chair. "Still livin' in the hood in my head. I guess." No, she hadn't switched clinics. Neither had she switched hair stylists, dentists, or nail salons. And whenever she had an appointment, she couldn't help driving by her house, even though she'd sold it last spring, a few months after Roger died.

In fact, she'd driven by her house en route from the clinic to Deja Brew just ten minutes ago. Craning her neck, she'd slowed in front of the cute stucco bungalow as she'd done every few weeks throughout the summer. It upset her to see the mess the new owners were making of the yard. Because they'd done the transaction with the realtor online, she hadn't met them, but she knew they were a young couple named Andrea and Justin Virden. They hadn't mowed the lawn in over a month and the first of the fall leaves were nestling in the raggedy grass. Would they ever bother to rake or pick up the dead branches piling up under the river birch? The geraniums she'd planted last spring in the window boxes were dead, and they hadn't even had a frost yet.

She hoped Andrea and Justin were taking better care of the inside of the house. Christine, who was still probably keeping watch over the house from across the street, would know. A few weeks after the new owners moved in, Christine broke it to her that they were tearing out the textured mocha-colored carpet Laura installed—at no small expense—just a few years ago. Laura couldn't help but feel somewhat violated. The upstairs bedrooms stripped of her cozy carpeting would be hardly habitable. Those floors weren't even finished. How could anybody walk around up there on just bare, cold boards?

"What are you knitting?" Laura asked, looking at the swath of old black and yellow yarn moving under Christine's busy needles. It looked like Christine was repairing a weird pattern of eyes and numbers in the yarn.

"Just a shawl," Christine said over a row of yellow stitches, frowning. Laura was surprised to hear her curse under her breath.

Laura watched, bewildered, as Christine's big face bowed over the needles flashing in her squarish fingers. Where was the benevolent Christine from across the street, the woman who'd left banana bread and egg salad sandwiches on their doorstep when Roger was dying? Laura missed sitting in Christine's lush backyard with its lilac bushes and big elephant ferns. Ironically, everything was in full bloom back there when Christine had her over for a barbecue when Roger was in the ER because of some blood clotting. Christine had reminded her of a Saint Bernard—a rescuing dog like in the old cartoons, brown eyes drooping with compassion, a cask of emergency rum hanging from its thick neck.

She'd been devastated when Christine stopped texting her last month despite sending a flurry of photos from the nature center in her new suburb, including some great shots of deer and turtles and even a great blue heron. Not even a thumbs up emoji came from Christine, who had to know she was Laura's only living connection to the neighborhood—to her house.

Laura stared at the padded dome of Christine's forehead, willing her to look up and invite her confidence. They'd shared so much over coffee on their patios during Covid. Grateful to have a neighbor as a confidante during the pandemic, Laura had opened up about her dysfunctional family, her depression in her twenties, and the ongoing seven-year battle with Roger's cancer.

"So, what's the latest on Andrea and Justin?" Laura couldn't help but ask.

"I haven't seen much of them lately," Christine said.

Laura wondered at that. Christine, sitting like an omniscient Buddha on her porch day and night, knew about everything on their block. If there was anybody to be seen, Christine would see them. If you wanted the latest on anyone—if you needed a house sitter or someone to rake your leaves, or if you wanted to donate extra pet food or garden vegetables or to someone who could use them—you talked to Christine. She exuded the calm authority of a mafia don.

Two puffy late-middle aged women with overflowing knitting

bags swooped over the table, exchanging excited greetings with Christine.

Her knitting group. They met here regularly and sat there nodding and clucking and sometimes breaking into melancholy old folk songs. They were dressed haphazardly, in floppy sweaters and baggy pants, and they had a strange gleam in their eyes as they clustered around Christine.

"Hey, ladies!" Christine said to them with a big smile and a nervous laugh.

"Oh, there it is," cooed the woman carrying the knitting bag emblazoned with purple and orange abstract cats. She squinted at the beat-up piece Christine was repairing.

"Ah, nice—uh oh! Looks like you dropped a stitch there. Pick it up," ordered the old black-eyed woman in a teddy bear and hearts sweatshirt. She peered at Christine's handiwork with a thin-lipped frown.

Christine's forehead puckered in concentration as the women bent over the urgent clicking of her needles. The shawl shook in her hands.

"Ah, okay. Purl. Purl, now!" the black-eyed woman commanded.

"Okay, okay," Christine murmured.

They were joined by two additional excited women, the group now forming a fleshy ring around Christine.

Laura sighed. So much for feeling nostalgic here. She swept up her half-full mug and her crumbling muffin.

"I better get going," she told Christine, waving at her between two wooly heads.

"Okay, bye," Christine said with a distracted nod.

Laura stumbled out of the coffee shop into a sparkling fall day stretching before her, an empty promise.

She had nothing to do that afternoon but to contemplate her cramped condo and the relentless sun streaming through the balcony door. She had no idea where to store the boxes full of household items that wouldn't fit into this small space. The box marked "Kitchen Knick Knacks" in Sharpie caught her eye, and she felt moved to unpack it. She'd packed the curios it held seven months ago when she was numb with grief and newly alone in her house.

She gently unwrapped each piece from its crumpled newspaper. Roger's sister gave them the anthropomorphic salt and pepper pumpkin heads for Halloween years ago. They'd found the rare entwined giraffes at a neighborhood garage sale. The miniature green Fiestaware pitcher—maybe a vintage salesman's sample—they'd discovered at Goodwill. She had no room for them in her new one-butt kitchen, but they'd looked so cute back in her house on their little white shelves.

Laura sat cross-legged over the small collection, imagining herself back at home, chopping and mixing and marinating with the sweet painted faces of her curios looking on.

She knew it was crazy, but she was getting the feeling she needed to go back to her house again, maybe tonight. Viewing it once already today didn't seem like enough. She fought the urge until sundown and then couldn't resist the feeling of her house beckoning. She didn't like driving at night anymore, but as if in a trance she pulled out of her underground condo garage, aimed her Subaru down the exit ramp toward the freeway, and allowed the night to pull her back into the city.

Slowly, she crept along the quiet street past the familiar row of homes gleaming at her as if she'd never moved away, as though she was just coming home from a late grocery store run or from picking up some take out Chinese from New Garden Wok.

Her neighbors must be living their lives undisturbed. The old greyhound couple in the corner house no doubt still walked their rescue dogs every day. Dwight and Annie, the urban farmers with stalks of ripened corn and tomatoes in their moonlit yard, would be harvesting their crops soon. The craggy Vietnam vet who used to wave at her was probably planted in a comfortable old chair in his TV-lit living room.

And there was her house, its porch light calling to her, her antique ceiling lamp glowing through the dining room blinds. She could have taken the precious lamp with her, but she considered it a gift to the house. Hopefully Andrea and Justin wouldn't break it. She slowed, remembering how she and Roger would dine in the golden blush of art deco glass—that is, until the tumor in his hip hurt him too much to sit at the table.

Through the blinds, she could see someone, probably Justin, sitting in Roger's old place. A candle flickered near him on the table. She'd loved having several candles of different heights and styles on the table, turning any dinner into a special event. Somebody, most likely Andrea, moved from the kitchen into the dining room as Laura had so many times, carrying the meal's finishing touches, like lemon slices for the fish or a bottle salad dressing. Mesmerized, she dared pull over in front of the house. She put the car in park and turned off the jazz station.

The dining room blinds snapped open and Laura sank into the driver's seat upholstery. There stood the new homeowner, Justin. They had to know she was out here, peeping—stalking. She almost slammed on the gas and sped off but realized how stupidly obvious that would be. All she could do was freeze and stare, hoping Justin didn't see her. He didn't look as young as she'd imagined. His red hoodie reminded her of the stained Nike sweater Roger wore every day for a few weeks before he died. Actually, she'd seen that big coffee stain under the neck before. In fact, the longer she looked at Justin, the more familiar he became. She recognized the shape of his balding head and then Roger's eyes, large in his tragically sunken face.

"Rog?" she whispered. A chill filled her chest, followed by an overwhelming rush of longing.

He wasn't looking at her. His baleful gaze was focused across the street on Christine's house.

Laura whirled and detected a bulky shape moving on Christine's darkened, screened-in porch. It looked like Christine was in her rocker, watching Laura watching Roger.

"Christine has her telescope out," Roger used to say, urging Laura to keep the blinds drawn at night.

Christine had always lived in her grandma's house across the street and knew the history of Laura's house. At least two men had died there, Christine had said. One had a heart attack while shoveling snow off the roof; he'd tumbled onto the lawn. Another had died a horrible death from untreated AIDS. Christine gave her a ghoulishly detailed account of how she'd watched them carry the AIDS victim's body out of the house on a gurney. Apparently one of the medics had slipped, resulting in an unfortunate spilling of the body onto the street.

Maybe that was why Roger had been wary of Christine. Yet she was solicitous, concerned about the details of Roger's condition and treatment, taking particular interest in his reaction to the punishing chemotherapy and his declining weight. She was too concerned, Laura now realized in a flash of rage. Maybe she'd even gloated over the grim scene of the EMTs wheeling poor Roger, zipped into the finality of a black vinyl body bag, into the waiting ambulance.

Laura shoved open the car door and bolted into the street just as Christine's patterned shawl disappeared from the porch and merged with the murky shadows of her living room. She spun back to her house, but the blinds were drawn again, leaving only the beefy shape of Justin, lumped at the table. She wanted to knock on the door. *And do what? Ask to see Roger?* Or walk across the street to confront Christine. But Christine frightened her now and seemed unapproachable.

She turned off her car and waited in the cooling quiet,

desperate to see what she could see of the couple in her house finishing their meal.

Eventually, the dining room went dark, and the living room blinked to life. Through the blinds she glimpsed flashes of what looked like a football game on their huge TV, its screen much bigger than hers and Roger's, set against the same wall. Vague shapes occasionally rose from the couch and floated away, then returned and slumped back down.

The living room eventually darkened, and Laura imagined Andrea and Justin contentedly retreating up the stairs and padding along the planks to the bedroom. Laura finally rested her head against the back of the car seat. It was almost eleven. Her house and Christine's twinkled at each other. What secret knowledge did their porch lights communicate?

Laura's life had become centered on her nightly drives across town to her house. She'd wait out of the streetlight's glare, sipping iced coffee from her thermos and snacking on trail mix until she tired of Justin and Andrea's predictable pattern. Dinner in the dining room around 6:30 was always followed by television in the living room—usually sports or what looked like a garish sitcom—then lights out around 10:45. She wondered whether she and Roger had been so regimented; how boring for Christine. She'd then fixate on the drawn blinds, willing them to open and again reveal Roger in his red sweater.

Christine seemed to have disappeared along with Roger. The thought nagged at her tonight. Laura searched for movement on her porch, but night after night revealed nothing but a pool of black where Christine's chair would rock. She braced herself for a closer look.

Now standing in the middle of the road and, aggravated by the idea that Christine and Roger had maintained some private, ghostly connection, Laura marched across the street in the eye of the streetlight, strode right up Christine's sidewalk, and stood on her porch. She peered through the window at emptiness. The absence of the rocking chair on the porch made the house seem abandoned. She jabbed at the doorbell and wasn't surprised when no answer came. Through the living room window, she could see the outline of the hallway and wondered if Christine was hiding from her—hiding because Christine knew why Roger had stood at the window that night, looking across the street at her and not at his own wife.

"Hey, wondering where you are," Laura texted Christine. She even tried calling, but she didn't expect or get an answer. She didn't want to risk going around back to see if Christine's car was in the garage. She didn't want to know.

———

Hoping she'd be inconspicuous behind her laptop at a corner table, Laura waited at Deja Brew. She'd had no recent sightings of Christine, but on Wednesday of the second week, the knitting group shuffled through the door.

They settled at their regular table, parked their knitting bags next to their chairs, and got busy with their needles and yarn. Laura was intrigued by a certain intensity in their huddle.

Laura lifted her bulky laptop. Clutching her coffee mug and crumbling muffin in her other hand, she scrambled to a table closer to the knitters, risking Christine walking through the door and catching her.

Laura sat back-to-back with the bossy, black-eyed woman who'd supervised Christine's shawl repair. Fortunately, this woman seemed to be doing most of the talking. Laura could hear snatches of hushed conversation over their clicking needles. They seemed to be arguing.

"It's in the works, all right—the whole ball of wax," Black Eyes hissed.

Laura couldn't help turning around to attempt lip reading and caught the eye of the woman crowned by a mass of gray braids. Her lips formed a nearly imperceptible "o."

The group fell silent.

Laura curled into herself and stared into the cold depths of her coffee. She winced at their chairs scraping against the floor and then peeked at them shambling to a table on the other side of the room.

Laura returned to Deja Brew every day for the next several weeks but never saw Christine or the knitting group again.

———

LAURA ROCKED RHYTHMICALLY on the porch, the old boards creaking occasionally under the chair's oak runners. The spring night was a little chilly, so she pulled her shawl closer. The day had been fresh and sunny. It was the sort of day she and Roger would have been busy in the yard. He'd be putting down mulch under the river birch. She'd be arranging purple and white-budding geraniums in the window boxes.

The Virdens hadn't done any of this yet. The yard still looked trampled by winter. Leaves still clumped together in the grass and on some unsightly bald patches of dirt and exposed tree roots. They needed to re-sod, Roger might say. But the lawn wasn't her main concern.

During the first spring thaw, she bought the house through an online transaction with an "authorized representative" of the owner. She accepted the first offer on her condo and in a giddy rush moved back across town. This house was smaller than hers and Roger's, but it was better than the apartment; she managed to fit a shelf of knick knacks in the space over the kitchen counter. Christine's old house was cramped, but Laura managed to arrange the living room furniture almost like she'd had things across the street.

She'd wave to Andrea and Justin—a husky, moderately attractive young couple—when they got in and out of their silver Honda CRV. Smug in the knowledge they didn't realize who she was, she monitored their lives, especially on weekend nights when she'd rock on the porch with a glass of wine. The couple's shapes through the blinds could have been her and Roger, dining on their teriyaki chicken paired with a light, unoaked chardonnay, settling in front of the TV to watch film noir. The last film noir they watched together was "Double Indemnity," with Barbara Stanwick and Fred MacMurray, now her favorite movie of all time. Once in a while, the couple in her old house watched something in black and white on their big screen. She had to restrain herself from walking across the street to get a better look.

Just last Wednesday, she'd seen someone in red sitting in the dining room. She froze, perched on the edge of her rocker, waiting for the blinds to snap open and reveal Roger in his sweater, looking across the street and recognizing her. It didn't quite happen then, but time was on her side. The porch was her power place, filled with her longing for Roger that would surely reverse whatever demonic spell had been cast over her house. The timelessness of her love would only be matched by her patience.

ONE, TWO, THREE

ROBERT BAGNALL

IT WAS CARNAGE ON THE HIGHWAY JUST GETTING TO Frankie's. There had been a rail accident, a bad one—a freight train derailing within the city, the engine rolling down an embankment into three lanes below. People were injured, maybe dead.

The lunchtime traffic imitated the worst evening rush hour—gridlock, cars inching forward as lanes contracted and junctions closed, drivers jockeying for position, leaning on their horns, pigheadedly not giving an inch. Cars and drivers steamed in unison under a baking sun. Fumes seeped their way into cabins. Tempers frayed. Red-and-white checkerboard ambulances and scarlet fire trucks muscled through, sirens blaring. At the pinch point, policemen in aviator sunglasses frantically waved one lane forward as another growled its disapproval waiting for an upheld palm to drop.

And all the while the radio squawked about a plane crashing minutes after takeoff. No survivors. I could see the ghost of a column of black smoke in the distance against the mountains. Early afternoon anchors speculated whether terrorists were again assaulting the nation, although the smart money was on coincidence. Don't rule out one being terrorism and the other coincidence, a caller pointed out. The grim narrative distracted me as I stared at the same bumper, the same lame bumper sticker, "Horn Broken, Watch for Finger," for over an hour. In the rearview mirror, a bouffant receptionist-type reapplied her lipstick for the fifth—or was it the sixth?—time.

It was almost four when I pulled into my brother's driveway. He was alone, out back by the kidney-shaped pool. Every house here had one, being on the cheap edge of desert land. Dry leaves dotted the water's surface. He was stretched on a lounger, staring westwards to the desert beyond the development, a tumbler at his fingertips, a half-drunk bottle of Jack Daniels within reach.

"Traffic was murder," I complained, taking another lounger and massaging my neck.

"Yeah, sorry about that, Bobby."

"Well, it's not like you did it," I said reflexively, but a note in his voice made me pull up, like a shameful secret you believed long buried has been dug up and quietly thrown back at you.

"Arrive before sunset," he'd said on the phone. It sounded urgent, but not in an excited, you-have-to-see-this way. He'd been oddly grave but also sounded far away as if his mind was elsewhere. He had something to tell me, I knew, and was taking a long run-up. I wanted him to cut to the chase—I faced microwaved leftovers back home as it was.

"There's a train crash and a plane crash. Both here, both this lunchtime. Conspiracy theorists'll have a field day," I said, to fill the silence.

He gave a bitter laugh and kept staring out toward the lowering sun. I'd seen him two weekends before. He was ebullient, spinning sausages on the grill like Tom Cruise in *Cocktail*. He'd learnt a new joke about a chicken and a parrot he was eager to tell anyone who'd listen. Now the domed barbecue was pushed aside, and I was struggling to get a sentence out of him.

He topped up his bourbon and glanced to the open French doors and kitchen beyond. "Grab a glass."

"I'm driving."

He made a face. We'd known each other our whole lives, and I knew that look. It said, "You may think that but you're wrong."

"Do you have superstitions, Bobby?"

"You got me to drive all the way over here to ask if I wear the same lucky boxers every time I watch the Ice Wolves?"

"I had one. Every time I stopped at lights, I'd wait, judge when they'd change, and say to myself, 'one, two, three', and..." He made pistol fingers at an imaginary stop light, sighted, and with a twitch, fired. "And every time—every damn time—the lights changed."

"Was that bottle full when you started, Frankie?"

"I've been doing it for years." He smiled nostalgically. "Never once out of sync."

"So you're perfectly attuned to a traffic light timer. I'll make sure it's in your eulogy."

"I started thinking. What if I wasn't predicting the changing of the lights. What if I was causing the lights to change?"

I twisted around, sat up. Was I witnessing a breakdown?

Glass emptied, he poured himself another finger of spirit.

"Slow down, Frankie. Iris'll be home soon, won't she?"

"I found myself willing the phone to ring. 'One, two, three' and the phone would ring," he said, firing his finger-pistol again. "'One, two, three'—the slot machine pays out. I was *making* it pay out. *Making* it, Bobby"

He looked up at me, eyes bleary and darting this way and that, unable to hold my gaze. Sweat beaded on his skin. His breathing was labored.

"There's your proof, Frankie. If that was true, you'd be rich. You'd get the slots to pay out every time. One, two, three, one, two, three—bingo, you're a millionaire."

He shook his head, like I'd misunderstood the simplest point. "No, no... I can only do it when it lets me..."

"What's 'it'? The universe?"

He slapped me on the shoulder. "Yeah. That's it. When the universe lets me. But now... I've broken through. And I can prove it to you."

My dilemma: play along, or make a pot of coffee and give him a slap? "What do you mean, 'broken through'"?

"I was driving this morning, found myself alongside a freight train..." He raised two fingers, fired. "Plane in the sky..." Another squint, another round silently loosed.

"Frankie. Look at me. None of this is real. This is all in your head. We're going to wait for Iris to come home..."

"Oh, she's home, Bobby. She's lying on the bedroom floor. She's dead."

I spluttered laughter. He'd deadpanned it like a joke, but his stony face said otherwise. My stomach dropped, and I rose to check on my sister-in-law.

"Stay where you are," he slurred with menace and, like the little brother, I dutifully dropped back.

"Shouldn't you call someone?"

"I don't see why. I said to myself, 'Iris is going to have a heart attack on the count of three. One, two, three...'"

How many rounds did he have left in his imaginary pistol?

"Jesus, Frankie. What did you do to her? Did she laugh at you? Did you tell her all this and she didn't take you seriously? I know life hasn't been easy for you, Frank. I know you feel you haven't had the breaks, been dealt a shitty hand, whatever... But this isn't how you solve things."

"I counted—just counted, that's all I did."

"We need to call someone."

"Too late. She's gone."

"We're going to jail, Frankie, if we don't call someone right now."

"You remember Mom always said, whatever happens, the sun will always come up tomorrow." He smiled wistfully and adopted a southern twang. "Don't you worry your pretty head, the sun'll come up tomorra, son." He raised his pistol fingers at the sun.

I didn't like where this was going.

"Sun can't come up tomorrow if I've put it out this afternoon, Bobby." He closed one eye, took aim. "One, two..."

HOODLUMS

KAY HANIFEN

Hello there! Welcome to the neighborhood! As head of the HOA, I'm here to help you integrate into the community, so here's everything you need to know.

All the lawns on Mentone Terrace are mowed on Wednesdays. Trash is picked up on Mondays and Fridays, and the rest of the maintenance is done swiftly and on an as-needed basis. HOA dues are at the end of the month. We take pride in this little neighborhood. Hopefully you will too.

In the past, we've had some trouble with teenage hoodlums. They would loiter in the playgrounds doing their drug deals, skateboarding in the tennis courts, playing basketball, and teaching foul language to any child unfortunate enough to be playing on the playground that day. At least, I assume that there's drug dealing going on. Not to sound like an old fuddy duddy, but teenagers these days have no respect for the community and no desire to keep it beautiful. All they care about is sex, drugs, and that darn rap music.

Do you know what those hoodlums did when I reprimanded them for loitering? They called me a Karen. No respect from the youth of today. You've got a couple children of your own, right? Enjoy it while it lasts, because once they hit puberty, your perfect little angels will become little hellions. Anyway, where was I?

Right, welcoming you to the neighborhood. Aside from that gang, the people here are all lovely, and the neighborhood is perfectly safe. We've made our own little white picket fence utopia out here. Children play outside from dawn 'til dusk without a care in the world.

It's really quite beautiful here, and the people are so friendly. The HOA plans neighborhood get-togethers at least once a month, sometimes more. Eleanor Seaburg hosts a book club every Tuesday, we hold knitting circles at the local rec center, and host cookouts, pool parties, and pickleball tournaments. There's always something to do here. And we look after our own; I can promise you that.

Do you mind if I tell you something? Just between us girls?

Okay, so I've been working on our gang problem here. Most of these hoodlums are from outside the neighborhood. You might have heard about the vandalism at the playground and tennis courts a couple months ago—our beautiful neighborhood marred by lewd pictures spray painted on the court's walls and the climbing equipment. Everyone believes that those hoodlums were to blame—it was their meet-up spot, after all—but I know for a fact that it wasn't them.

It was me.

Don't look at me like that. Desperate times call for desperate measures, right? I decided to take some initiative. The idea came to me when I was driving past them one summer evening. They were on their way to raise hell, terrorizing some other poor family on another street, and I thought to myself, "If only I could keep them out of the park."

You see, the rest of the HOA don't see these gangbangers for the threat that they are and keep telling me to mind my own business. And excuse me, but as board president, keeping this neighborhood safe and beautiful is precisely my business. The nerve of some people! This gang was doing nothing but bringing down property values and terrorizing the neighborhood. They shouldn't be allowed anywhere near the little community we've built for our children.

Then it came to me. I can make the members of the board and the rest of the neighborhood see just how dangerous these hoodlums are. I can get those kids banned from the playground and force them to sell their drugs somewhere else. All I needed was some spray paint.

So, after my husband, Lou, went to bed, I snuck out, feeling almost sixteen again as I crept up to the playground and shook the spray can. I picked a cloudless night, both so that I could see and so that there was no risk of rain washing away the fresh paint.

You have to understand that this criminality completely goes against my nature. I was put on this earth to make it beautiful, not vandalize it. But sacrifices must be made for the greater good. And sometimes, that sacrifice is briefly ruining this beautiful playground with drawings of genitalia and curse words on the tennis and basketball courts.

It worked. Of course, it worked; finally, the rest of our neighbors hated the gang problem as much as I did. The playground was closed down for a couple days while the service we hired power washed the two courts. When these beautiful spaces were ready for public use again, the tennis courts had a lock on them. That way, only those of us who know the password can use them.

When some neighbors with less foresight and understanding protested, I reminded them that this teenage gang problem is why we cannot have nice things like fully public tennis courts. If they had listened to me sooner, then maybe we wouldn't have to take such drastic measures. But no, to those whiners, I'm just paranoid about teens selling drugs and bringing crime to our peaceful street.

By the way, the passcode to get into the tennis courts is in your welcome handbook. It's under "Recreation."

Restricting outsiders' use of the tennis courts was easy, but the basketball courts are a different story. After all, you can't really ban people from an open blacktop. And I think that those teenagers caught wind of me, because my yard seemed to have become the neighborhood's puppy potty overnight. I don't even own a dog, and I had to get a poop scooping service to come by once a week to collect the pet droppings.

What? No, it couldn't possibly have been the rest of the neighborhood letting their dogs use my yard as a public toilet. I'm far too well-respected for such childish retaliation.

Now, I'm not exactly proud of what I'm about to tell you, but I trust you, and no one will believe you if you say anything.

I was driving at night, and I'm not exactly a debutante anymore, so my night vision isn't what it used to be. With the windows down, I heard them playing and causing a ruckus, disturbing the Moth Story Hour on NPR, and I was getting angry. Didn't they get the hint? They weren't the kind of people we wanted here. Them and their filthy mouths and their loud music and their drug dealing. Laughter broke through their ambient noise, and I gripped the wheel hard enough for my knuckles to turn white. They were mocking this neighborhood and all the hard work we all put into making this place beautiful. They were laughing at me, laughing at everything I do for the community to make this a nice place to raise a family, calling me a Karen. My fucking name is Linda!

The boy appeared out of nowhere. One moment, there was a flash of orange as a basketball bounced into the street, and the next, something struck my windshield. It all happened so fast. They say that I accelerated instead of breaking, and maybe I did, but it was only out of surprise and panic. It was an accident. A tragic accident, but these things happen, especially when children are reckless.

He's not dead. I think you should know that. I didn't kill him.

The poor boy might never walk again, and I don't think I'll ever forgive myself for that, but frankly, it's a miracle he survived. I thank God every day for that miracle.

And I think you should know that we haven't had a problem with that gang ever since.

OFF LABEL

JON LASSER

Grace lay in bed flipping channels, looking for a game show or something else to help her chill out. No way could she sleep while Leon, zonked on painkillers, sawed wood like a driver gunning his engine before the Daytona 500. The paramedics had said he'd need rest while the injection performed its healing magic, and oh boy was that bastard husband of hers getting it.

That was just like Leon, wasn't it? She'd taken away his keys after four beers, and he'd still run his pretty green car into a telephone pole, bled out on the asphalt, and somehow ended up lying in bed on cloud nine ripe as a wet dog while she was the one shaking and crying and unable to sleep.

There was a moment after she pulled up to the wreck when Grace had been sure nobody could walk away from something like that. Her heart had skipped a beat. She could never tell anyone how she wondered what the rest of her life would be like if she could move back in with her sister and try college again. Now he was alive and that was all selfish talk.

"VERISPELLIS! One giant leap in medicine brought to you by Awilix Pharmaceuticals," the TV shouted. She flicked to the next channel.

That damned ad seemed to follow her whenever she clicked channels, promising a cure for six kinds of cancer, heart disease, ED. They didn't mention accidental trauma, like Leon's. She hadn't heard of its off-label use until she stood staring down at his tattered body, the paramedics asking if she'd consent to the injection.

She flipped back to the commercial too fast, just in time for its too-fast warning.

"When taking Verispellis, you may experience sleepless nights on a twenty-nine-and-a-half-day cycle and may be confused or agitated during that time. Lost memories and torn clothing have been reported. Be careful when handling Aconitum lycotonum and other members of the Aconitum genus. Do not wear silver jewelry, as injuries may result. Side effects may include tattoo rejection and abnormal hair growth. If you experience a desire to consume human flesh, stop taking your medication and consult your physician."

Truth told, Grace didn't know if she'd be able to spot abnormal hair growth or new rips in Leon's jeans. She didn't put much stock in cannibalism, and she wouldn't know an Aconitum from a Cronut.

The other side effects, though: agitation and sleeplessness on a cycle. On the one hand, between his binges and the dark that so often followed, maybe she wouldn't notice. On the other, maybe she would. Maybe things could get worse, so bad she couldn't not see them, same way she couldn't not see the dents in the wallboard or that moon in the sky, just a sliver now but growing night by night until it swelled up like a black eye.

Grace slipped out of bed, took her purse off the doorknob, and tiptoed the three steps to the bathroom. Leon kept right on snoring. She closed the door behind her, quiet as she could manage, and dug into the purse until she found the syringe. Not a syringe, really. One of those fancy injectors hiding the sliver-thin needle. Just hold the silvery plastic tube's business end against her skin and push the button.

The paramedic—the pretty, young one, had clocked her as soon as she'd bolted from the rideshare to Leon's body. No idea how the blonde had figured it out. She wasn't made up to cover a bruise. Something in her stance, maybe—the way she fawned over him, or the way she hesitated at the question.

After Grace consented to reviving Leon, the paramedic bit her lip and glanced from side to side, making certain the others were looking away. She pressed a second injector into Grace's hands. "You might need this, come twelve days when he wolfs out. Don't wait for the last minute. This week is better than next."

Grace sat on the toilet lid, turning the silvery injector over and over in her hands, worried about those side effects. If she used it, would she even be herself anymore? She stood and checked that her can of Nair was mostly full, then sat down again.

Soon enough Leon would be off the painkillers and pissed as hell about his car, or his now-gone tattoos, or some other shit that'd make him raise his voice. The man simply didn't know how to be grateful for being alive. Maybe he wasn't. But if he raised his hands in anger—whether it was about his ink, his Mustang, or some mistake she'd made in his absence—she'd give him what-for this time. She really would.

DECORATIONS

J.D. SIMPSON

We met under the big oak across from the Millers' place. Hidden in the shadow of its foliage, the four of us could observe our new neighbors without being seen ourselves. It had been a long time since I'd called an emergency meeting like this, but then again, it had been a long time since such an unusual family had moved to our quiet little town.

"What's the verdict, Jerry?" I asked, limping over to lean against the gnarled tree.

"Nothing, that's what." Gerald Price hadn't seen any action since the Gulf War, but he still spoke with the gruff practicality of an NCO. "I got a look into their garage yesterday while they were taking out their trash. They've got nothing, Maurice. No hay bales, no plastic skeletons—not even pumpkins."

"It's still early days yet." Janice Hardin, the school librarian, shook her head. "Plenty of people wait until the last minute to decorate for Halloween."

"Not around here, they don't," Jerry spat, and I had to admit he had a point. "You sure they got the pamphlets, Amy?"

"The town council sends out three mailings every year,

printed on bright orange paper with IMPORTANT INFORMA-TION: DO NOT DISCARD typed in bold on the front page. There's no way they could have missed them."

None of us doubted Amy Chenault: she'd worked with the town council for over twenty years, and if anyone understood these things, it was her.

"They seem like decent folks, don't they?" Jerry squinted at the house across the street as though it were an enemy outpost. In the golden light of the kitchen, Frank Miller was ladling macaroni onto the plates of his two rambunctious boys, Matt and Eli. "I mean, nobody wants a repeat of what happened to those college kids back in '06..."

I winced.

Jerry meant no offense, but we all knew I was to blame for the tragedy of '06. I'd badgered those young people with warnings and reminders all October. Then—when Halloween finally rolled around—they had expressed their irritation with a wild party that dragged on long into the night. They had left their lights on, their music blaring, and even a few windows open...

I shuddered.

"Maurice?" Janice's light touch on my shoulder brought me back to reality. I took a deep breath; the air tasted of apples and woodsmoke.

"It's September 28th. We've still got time, just not as much as we'd like. We need to figure out why the Millers still aren't getting ready for the big night. If there's no change by October 15th, we'll meet back here and plan our next steps."

We said our goodbyes with handshakes and pats on the back. I lingered beneath the tree for a long while after the others left—watching the Miller house. Matt and Eli jumped on their beds upstairs. Sarah wrapped her arms around Frank while he did the dishes, scrubbing stubborn chunks of cheese out of a stainless steel pot.

A quiet evening for a happy, unsuspecting suburban family.

I glanced up at the yellowing oak leaves and whispered a silent prayer: *please God, not again.*

Those oak leaves were as red as blood when we met again two weeks later. The tip of Jerry's cigarette glowed in the rainy gloom.

"I thought you quit."

"I did," he grunted. "But today's a special occasion."

Of course. How could I have forgotten? October 15th was Jerry's daughter's birthday—or it would have been. Kimberly Price had stayed late at her boyfriend's place on Halloween night of '97, then tried to sneak back home after the midnight curfew. It still rankled Jerry that his daughter's deadbeat boyfriend had been the last person to see her alive.

"I had a talk with Frank Miller on Saturday," Jerry said through a cloud of smoke. "I took over a wagonload of my old decorations: wooden tombstones, an inflatable ghost, even a fog machine. When Frank answered the door, I told him I'd noticed he still didn't have any decorations up. I told him I knew what it was like to move to a new town with kids and all their expenses, and that I wanted to help out. I told him everything in the wagon was his for the taking. I even offered to help him set up..." Jerry took a deep drag, coughed, then went on. "Well, Frank didn't like that one bit. He told me his family doesn't celebrate Halloween— not this year, not ever—and I could take my heathen junk right off his lawn."

"The boys said the same thing in different words." Janice sighed. "I overheard them talking in the library last week. They were upset their parents weren't going to let them go trick-or-treating..."

"There's no changing their minds, either." Amy added. "I brought Sarah Miller a batch of my pumpkin cream-cheese muffins yesterday, and she practically slammed the door in my face!"

"Let me give it one last try." I sighed. "If I can't convince them... Janice, can you at least take care of the kids?"

The school librarian nodded.

Fat, hard raindrops drummed rhythmically against the leaves overhead, like a clock counting down to something terrible.

"Of all the towns they could've moved to!" Jerry lit another cigarette and pulled up the hood of his coat. "Good luck, Maurice. You're gonna need it."

The day before Halloween, I was limping up the Millers' driveway with a huge sack of supermarket candy beneath one arm and a plastic cauldron beneath the other. My mouth was dry. My bad leg burned. Everything depended on what happened in the next few minutes.

I rang the Millers' doorbell.

"Yes?" Frank greeted me with a grimace.

I tried to smile back. "Hey, Frank. It's Maurice Healy, from the end of the block? Your boys play in the creek behind my house sometimes. I was wondering... you have a minute to talk?"

"If this is about Halloween—"

"It's not." I held up a hand. "Not exactly. To be honest, it's about your family's safety."

"Excuse me?"

Sarah Miller, eavesdropping from the kitchen, cast a long shadow into the hallway; upstairs, the boys had gone silent at the sound of their father's shouting.

I cleared my throat and forced myself to go on: "The thing is, Frank, October 31st is serious business in this town. And people who don't prepare for it get hurt, or worse."

"Is that a threat?"

"I'm just trying to explain—"

"I think it's time for you to leave."

"All I'm asking is that you leave some candy out tomorrow night. There's more at stake here than you realize, Frank! Please..."

"Get off my property." Frank's voice was deadly calm, but his hands were balled into fists; the conversation was over.

Crestfallen, I lay the plastic cauldron and the sack of candy on the Miller's porch. "I hope you change your mind, Frank. I really do."

When the sun set the following night, I was sitting in my lawn chair behind my own plastic cauldron full of sweets. A jack-o'lantern flickered merrily beside me. In the distance, someone's radio was playing "The Monster Mash." Trick-or-treaters shrieked and laughed in the gathering darkness—

Unaware, for the most part, of what was coming.

By ten P.M., those children were safe behind closed doors—wiping off greasy face paint, changing out of cumbersome costumes, and climbing into slumber-party sleeping bags. While they scared themselves with horror movies and gorged themselves on candy, the rest of us slipped outside, where we followed the instructions on Amy's orange pamphlets to the letter.

Between ten-thirty and eleven, we brought our pets inside, checked our locks, and closed our blinds. We adjusted the masks on our hay-stuffed monsters, re-lit our jack-o'lanterns, and refilled our plastic cauldrons with candy. Any children still awake were reminded to ignore any strange sounds or familiar voices calling in the night—not that they needed much reminding. Even the youngest and most naive among them had heard rumors about what happens in our town after midnight on All Hallow's Eve.

Around eleven forty-five, the temperature plunged. Dead grass hardened into hoary spikes of frost; fog formed in the shivering woods. Soon a hungry mist would come creeping through our empty streets—full of haunting lights, swooping shadows, and gibbering unearthly cries. It was the final warning for those who would listen.

I knew the dangers as well as anyone, but I still couldn't resist peeking through my blinds one last time when the clock struck twelve. I held my breath, half-expecting to find a rotting face or a monstrous yellow eye pressed against the glass. Instead, I was peering into a sea of gloomy fog, broken only by the defiant glow of the Millers' porch light. They hadn't set up any false ghosts or demons to frighten away the real ones, nor had they left out any sweets to sate the fiendish hunger of the things that slither, float, and crawl through our town on Halloween night. Shadowy, emaciated figures circled that lonely light at the end of the street like moths closing in on a flame. I closed the blinds and turned away.

The mist had begun to clear when we met beneath the old oak the next morning, but the tree's branches were still silver with frost. Discarded candy wrappers, toilet paper, and other leavings of the previous night blew past us in a ragged wind. Across the street, the Millers' front door shrieked and banged, swinging hideously on its one remaining hinge. None of us wanted to be the first to go into that lightless house, but after '06, I felt like I owed it to the group.

"Matthew? Elijah?" I called. No response. I heaved my bad leg over the threshold and limped down the hallway, doing my best to ignore the gashes in the drywall and the ominous dripping sound echoing from the kitchen. My only concern was for the two boys upstairs.

Two plastic pumpkins lay overturned in front of the boys' bedroom. Rust-colored, inhuman footprints and ripped-open candy wrappers littered the carpet. Before I could knock on the boys' door, it creaked open just a crack... and a ghoulish, devil-horned face grinned out at me from the darkness. I brought a hand to my chest, cursing my weak heart—

Then I laughed.

"You boys can take those masks off now. It's over."

I held Matt and Eli's hands while we walked downstairs and out of the mutilated house.

Janice's sedan idled in the driveway. She would find the boys a good home, and the town council would take care of the Millers' house—as well as the Millers themselves. I made sure the boys didn't look back as I led them to Janice's car; I didn't want them to see their parents' ragged remains, strung up between the bushes like festive lights. One day too late, Frank and Sarah Miller had finally decorated their home for our town's special holiday.

SHADOWS IN RENOVATION

ELIZABETH SUGGS

Construction noises always remind me of my dead girlfriend Ashtyn.

Ashtyn had loved working on her house.

But that was over a year ago, wasn't it? Now, it was my husband Will's and my home. And Will loved to build, too.

Will knelt at the top of the basement stairs as I swept up yet another of his piles of broken wood and discarded pipes.

Then in the grinding silence came a distinctive baby cry from the bedroom. It was our 6-month-old Lila.

"Evelyn, can you get Lila? She's been crying since I started."

"Well, that's because you didn't start the build until after I put her down for a nap," is what I wanted to say, but I forced a smile and fetched Lila from her crib.

If it were up to me, the house would remain as it always had been, with maybe a few changes here and there, but Will was insistent about upgrades after moving in. It was as if the moment his name was on the deed he felt "inspired" to make "improvements."

I hadn't minded until recently, when he started to work in the basement.

Lila gurgled as I bounced her to one side, but once the noises started up again, her cherubic face went crimson, and her screams echoed throughout the house.

Will stopped. "Can you take Lila on a walk or something? I'll be done soon. I just wanted to finish one last thing."

It was always one last thing, but I didn't say that. Instead, I kissed him quickly and placed Lila in the stroller. We needed cheese, anyway, I tried to console myself. Besides, I didn't have to be next to him, hovering over his every movement.

I shook off the tremor in my hands and pushed Lila down the street.

Ashtyn had been the one to introduce me to this little town, right on the coast of eternity. I often wished she were still here, but at least I had Will. He had been there to pick up my pieces after everything. He was the only one who really understood the impact of Ashtyn's death, but more than that, he was there to comfort me after the rigorous police investigation.

I had been the prime suspect, but they had no evidence against me. And besides, without a body, there was very little they could do. For all they knew, Ashtyn had run out of town.

But she hadn't left. I had found her on the floor of the kitchen, ashen with death and spit encrusted on the side of her face, part of the effects of an overdose on sleeping pills.

I could have told the police about her body, but they would have taken her away, and I knew the last thing she'd have wanted was to be separated from her house and me.

After buying some gouda, Lila and I arrived back home to the sound of hammers on nails, and right then, I was pulled back to a year before when Ashtyn's gray eyes watched me cut through plaster and wood to get into the wall's center.

The construction stopped abruptly, and an eerie silence

enveloped the house—a silence of half-noises, of dripping water, of creaking walls. And then Lila's little gurgle broke through that quiet.

I set the cheese on the counter and picked Lila up, cradling her. She smelled like the summer's heat. And in some ways, she smelled like Ashtyn, though I knew that was impossible.

"Will?" I called, but there was no response.

Something in that absence of noise unsettled me enough to set Lila in her high chair.

Then a low, almost inaudible gasp traveled from the basement. One made of thousands of questions, of red tape, of blood, of police chatter. That gasp could destroy everything for me—for Lila.

I picked up a knife, hid it behind my back, and then stepped toward the basement steps. It was dark, apart from a small light in the corner silhouetting his figure.

"Will, honey, it's time to take a break from your work. I'm going to make your favorite: mac and gouda cheese."

"That's not my favorite," a low voice rumbled from below.

"What are you talking about? We eat it all the time—"

"We eat it all the time because that's what you want. That was her favorite. Right?" He stepped up from the basement stairs and into the light. A deep weariness shadowed his eyes. "And you know what? Suddenly, I don't feel like eating something she liked."

"She has a name," I said, my cheeks growing hotter with each word. I held the knife so tightly against my back the blade pricked at my spine, but I ignored it.

Will chuckled under his breath. In a hoarse whisper, he asked, "It was all an act, wasn't it? You and me."

I raised my chin. "I don't know what you're talking about. I've been a good wife."

He scoffed. "Have you?" He approached Lila and tickled her cheek. "You know, I thought if I could make you fall in love with me, then you'd stop thinking about her." He laughed. "I should consider myself the winner, though. I mean, we're here together."

"You're scaring me," I said. I didn't like that he was so close to Lila. I wanted to snatch her away, but before I could, he'd turned and advanced toward me.

"You loved her, didn't you?" he asked.

"Very much," I whispered.

"Do you love me?" he asked.

Just an hour ago, I would have said, "Yes, of course." But there was something in his eyes I didn't like.

"Answer me!" he spat, veins popping on the sides of his neck and around his temple.

There was only one other time he had reacted so strongly to me, and that had been when I broke up with him for Ashtyn, and it had been Ashtyn who had been there to take the brunt of the attack. She'd always been the stronger one.

I swayed backwards. "Will—"

He grabbed my neck with both hands and squeezed so tight that the only sound I could make was a soft squeak.

I tried to fight him, but he was a bear compared to me, towering tall with biceps the size of my head. He lifted me, causing the tendons in my neck to stretch and pop. Tiny balls of white sprinkled my vision, and I almost dropped the knife then but tightened my hold at the last second.

Lila whined, and I tried to meet her eyes, to remind her mommy was right here—that mommy was okay, but Will's head blocked us, forcing me to stare at his bright blue eyes.

"Please—stop—" I mouthed, but it was no use. He had seen red, and there wasn't anyone to save me now.

Lila wailed, long and low, and I saw a vein pop on the side of Will's temple. He squeezed my neck tighter and thrust me hard against a nearby wall. The impact exhaled the wind out of me and forced the knife deeper into the back of my shirt.

The knife.

If I could just wiggle it free, then maybe I could get him off of me.

He grinned. "It was me who got her to take all those sleeping pills."

My heart skipped a beat, and I tugged at the knife harder, but my back was pressed too close to the wall.

"I'd always wondered what happened to her body. I should have known it was you. You crazy bitch."

He raised me higher. My vision blurred, but my back no longer pressed hard into the wall. I yanked the blade free. It sliced through my skin and I felt warmth run down my spine, but I ignored it, and thrust the blade into his abdomen.

He spasmed, then released me coughing and spitting to the floor.

With the knife still in Will's gut, he stood crooked, metal sticking out of his abdomen and through his shirt and whipped around to face me.

I scrambled away from him, but he teetered forward. He could easily overtake me, but if I could get him to stand over the stairs, maybe I could kick his legs out from under him and force him down.

He needed to take one more step—one more step, and he'd be in front of the stairs.

I narrowed my eyes toward him, waiting.

I stared at his feet.

Come on, take another step. Just one more step.

"Honestly, you two deserved each other," he groaned, then closed the distance between us.

I narrowed my eyes, and kicked him hard in the side, nicking the side of the knife and forcing him down the stairs.

I stood up, screaming, "She has a name!" but my voice was

cracked and ruined from his attack, and I could barely get out two words without coughing.

But even if I had the full power of my voice, Will wouldn't have heard. As I tried to speak, he tumbled down the stairs, thunking into the concrete at the bottom.

He didn't get up.

Lila's sobs rocked the house.

I picked her up, rocking her back and forth. She clung to me with surprising strength and eventually calmed, tucking her head between the crook of my neck and shoulder.

I crept toward the stairs and waited two minutes, five minutes, ten minutes for any sign of Will regaining consciousness. He still didn't move.

I switched on the light, and there he lay, eyes opened wide. Blood squelched out of both the knife wound in his stomach and from his head.

Ashtyn's figure slumped out of the half-crumpled wall, stealing my attention. Nearly a year of captivity, and still she had most of her hair.

I kissed Lila, then set her back down in her high chair.

I descended into the basement, then over to Ashtyn. Her sunken eyes and her dried skin had been eaten away by the myriad of creatures that crept through the walls, but it was her, and she was still just as lovely as ever.

I tucked her remaining hair behind her ear, just like I had all those other times, letting myself imagine for just a moment that we were not in the basement but back in bed, watching the stars grow brighter.

"It should have been us here," I said.

But a part of her was here. She'd always be here, with me. And with Lila.

I kissed her lightly on her decayed cheek, then set her back into the wall, plastering it up just like before. It was quick work.

Most of the plaster and drywall boards were still there. All I needed to do was patch it back together and wait for it to dry.

I turned away from the wall, stepped over Will's corpse, barely giving him a second glance. I was wrong to believe he and I could work. We were just too different, and he was too messy, especially now.

But I wouldn't be cleaning up his mess like a dutiful wife. I'd let the police clean him up. I had a baby to feed.

EVERYTHING IS FINE
ANGELA E. ZOLNER

Linda stepped out of the shower and pulled the curtain closed, so she didn't see the body while she dried her hair. Using the corner of her towel, she cleared a space in the foggy mirror. She leaned in, touched the dark, puffy skin under her eyes, and rubbed her aching throat before pulling her hair dryer and make-up out from under the sink. From a small tube she squeezed a thick layer of concealer and used it to coat the tender skin under her eyes.

After dressing, Linda gathered the laundry. She collected her clothes from the hamper and put them in a laundry basket. From the closet, she pulled her husband's clothes from shelves and hangers and added them to the pile. *I don't understand why he can't use the laundry basket. Was he raised in a barn?* At the door to her son's room, she braced herself and pushed it open. A roiling stench, thick and fetid, overwhelmed her and left her gagging in the hallway. Teenage boys *stink*. She crossed the room and cracked the window, moving quietly to avoid waking the blanket-covered mound on the bed.

Carefully, she eased the dresser drawers open and tossed

clothes into the waiting basket. She flipped on the TV perched atop the dresser. The startup screen for a video game glowed on the screen, the music of the opening credits filling the silence. She closed the door behind her before going down to the laundry room and throwing the load in the washer.

The phone rang while Linda cobbled breakfast together from the scraps of rations she found in the fridge.

"Hello?"

"Oh, Linda, I'm so glad you answered."

"Of course I answered. These phone check-ins are morbid. You know that, right?"

"I know, I know. I'm sorry, we're really worried about you guys, you know? Mom's worried, too. You should call her."

Linda finished cutting up the last of the wrinkly peppers and threw them into a frying pan. They burnt more than fried, the last of the oil having been used making dinner the night before.

"I know, Susan. But we're fine. Bored, annoyed, hungry—but fine." Linda opened the refrigerator and took a carton of eggs off the otherwise empty shelf.

"Hungry? Aren't they bringing you food? On the news they're saying everyone has everything they need."

"Yeah, there's that drop off, but only once a week. I told them at the last one we have a teenage boy in the house, and he eats enough for three people." She cracked the last two eggs over the blackened vegetables. "And laundry detergent. Maybe they think because we don't leave the house our clothes don't get dirty? Seriously, the men in this house stink, even if all they do is lie around." She split the omelet-like concoction and scraped the halves from the pan on waiting plates and put them on the table.

"Hold on a second." Linda put the receiver against her shoulder to muffle the sound as she shouted up the stairs. "Holt, Dan, it's time to get out of bed. Breakfast is on the table." She put the phone back to her ear. "Sorry. Those men sleep in later every day." The pan sizzled as she tossed it to the sink.

"Sammy and Derek said Holt hasn't been online in a few days. They've been trying to finish up some video game quest the three of them are doing."

"Oh, uh... the internet's out. Can you believe it? We're locked in our houses, and the internet goes down." Lina pulled a carton of juice from the fridge door. Would Holt notice if she watered it down?

"Holt can't even do schoolwork." Linda poured the drop of juice into a glass, added some water. "We've been binging old movies all day. Good thing I held on to my DVDs."

Susan's laugh tinkled through the phone line. "How many times have you watched *The Breakfast Club*?

"Only once," Linda's chuckle joined Susan's. "But it's still early days."

Their laughter died away.

"I'll get the boys to call Holt after school and I'll call again tomorrow morning, alright?"

"Alright. Bye Susan."

"Bye."

Linda stood holding the phone for a moment after she hung up, her chin resting on the plastic phone case. She roused herself and called up the stairs again. "Holt, hurry up. Your breakfast is getting cold."

THE BUCKET CLATTERED against the sides of the sink as Linda wrangled it under the tap. Water flowed, swirling and foaming as the soap lathered, inching its way to the rim. Linda stood beside the sink and stared at nothing, her face slack, hands limp at her side. Hot, soapy water lapped over the edge of the bucket and splashed on her feet, bringing her attention back. She sopped up the mess with a towel and lugged the cleaning supplies up the stairs to the bathroom.

Ugh, this place is a disaster.

She scrolled through her phone and selected a party playlist. With music blaring and her foot tapping to the beat, Linda set to cleaning.

The sparkling sink was scoured, gleaming faucets polished. A toilet brush whirred around the shining toilet bowl. A new Ocean Breeze air freshener replaced the spent cartridge. After a moment, she added a second cartridge to cover the bouquet of rot. The bright, beach scent mixed with the fetid air to renew a sickly-sweet concoction. She knelt beside the tub and scrubbed.

A chime rang out over the song. Linda propped the phone against the sink, checked her hair in the mirror, tsked at the bags under her eyes, and answered the video call.

"Dalia, what's up?" Her friend's gaunt face stared back.

"Not a lot. Just wondering what you were up to. Are you cleaning again? Don't you do anything else these days?"

"What's there to do? We've been trapped in this house for more than a month. How're things at your place?"

"Well," Dalia sighed. "It's getting messier over here. I can't seem to make myself do anything. Hank and Eric don't help. They just watch TV and play video games."

Linda snorted. "Yeah. Holt's been playing a game all morning. The music's driving me nuts."

She sat on the edge of the bathtub and scrubbed while she talked. "Maybe we should do something with the other girls. Start an online book club or something." She lifted an arm from the tub basin, wiped the sludge from underneath it. "There's got to be a book we all have. Or maybe we could request something in the drops." She lifted the head, wiped up the pool of fluid beneath it.

Her glove came away with a chunk of hair and scalp. She rinsed it off in the bucket.

Dalia chewed her lip. "Do you have any wine left? Book club is always better with wine."

"Umm," Linda sat up straight, wiped her forehead with her arm. "I might have some gin. Would that do?"

"That'd work." Dalia sat up straighter, a faint smile tugging up her sallow skin.

"Who's left to invite?" Linda returned to scrubbing, lifting a leg, rancid puss oozing over her hand.

Dalia's hands flew to her mouth. "Linda! What is that?" Dalia's voice rose to a shriek, the question ending in a squeal.

"What?" Linda turned and looked at what she was holding in her hand. She blinked slowly. A laugh erupted from deep in her chest.

"Dalia," she dropped the leg and hugged her stomach. "Dalia, it's a... sewing mannequin. I've been cleaning my sewing room. What on earth did you think it was?" She slid from the edge of the bathtub, landing in a boneless heap on the tile.

Dalia hesitated, then let out a nervous chuckle. "I thought...I don't know what I thought. Something crazy."

Linda's belly laugh filled the small bathroom.

"We're all fine here. Everything is fine."

———

LINDA FOUND the breakfast plates still on the table in the kitchen. *You have got to be kidding.* She sighed and scraped the rubbery omelets into the garbage. After loading the dishwasher, she passed through the living room to yell up the stairs.

"Holt and Dan," she announced. "I am not your maid. Please clean up your dishes when you're finished eating."

The repeating tune from Holt's video game was the only answer.

———

The vacuum whirred as Linda maneuvered around the living room, sucking up imaginary dust. The rhythmic motion comforted her. Back and forth. Back and forth. Over and over the same patch of pristine carpet. When the doorbell rang, she switched off the vacuum and wiped her hands on her apron. She plastered on a Stepford smile and answered the door.

On the stoop stood a public health officer, encased head to foot in a puffy white biohazard suit, his face visible through the clear plastic window of the helmet. *This guy again.*

"Hello, Mrs. Whittler. How is everything today?" The same man from last week held a clipboard, his focus on the paper rather than on her. He jotted notes while she answered.

"Fine," she replied. "Everything is fine here. How's the rest of the neighborhood? The Chungs haven't been answering their phone."

The man ignored her questions and took more notes.

"Are your family members available? There's a note that we didn't see them last week." He flipped a page and examined one underneath. "Daniel and... Holt?" He looked at her.

"Uh... Yes, of course. Where else would they be?" Linda straightened, squaring her shoulders.

The man waited.

"They're, uh, upstairs playing video games, in the middle of some kind of quest with my nephews. I've been told not to interrupt. Apparently, it isn't the kind of game you can pause." She stepped back and opened the door wide, inviting the man in. "Did you want to come upstairs to see them?"

He poked the white dome of his head into the house, scanned

the living room then stepped in. The suit shushed as the fabric rubbed against itself. Tinny music from the video game drifted down from the upper level.

Linda moved to the staircase and yelled, "Dan, Holt, Public Health is here. They want to see you." She paused, cocked her head. "Holt! Inappropriate. Dan, deal with that, please."

She turned to the white suit, her cheeks pink. "Sorry about that. That game is his life these days and being locked up is hard on him. He's a good boy, really."

"I couldn't quite make it out over my suit's ventilation," the man replied drily.

"We can go up." Linda grasped the railing, started up the carpeted stairs.

The man glanced around the living room again and noticed the vacuum cleaner. Tilting his clear plastic view screen down at the dusty boots of his suit, he pursed his lips.

"I've heard enough for today." He stepped back through the doorway.

Linda followed.

"Ma'am, we prefer to see all members of the household on these visits—not just hear them. We will return next week at the same time. Please ensure all family members are available." He stepped back and scribbled on the clipboard.

"Yeah. Sure thing." Linda leaned against the door jamb. "I don't suppose you added laundry detergent this time. I'm pretty much out."

"I don't pack the boxes, ma'am." He finished up his notes. "This time next week. If anything changes before then—if any household member begins feeling ill or developing bumps or pustules anywhere on their body—contact us right away. As usual, the number is on the form located inside the supply boxes." The man nodded and turned toward the next house, his biohazard suit swishing down the sidewalk.

Linda stepped onto the porch, reveling in the momentary freedom. She stole a moment in the fresh air and watched the supply truck make its way down the block. It didn't stop very often.

Her boxes had been piled on the side of the porch.

I don't suppose they'd pause their game to help me put these away. She decided the answer was no and dragged them into the house herself.

THE TV FLASHED to life as Linda sat on the couch with a basket of laundry. Faces and nature scenes flickered as she flipped through channels to the news. Items from the basket were laid out on the coffee table, where she folded the soft fabric into tidy packages.

"An update from the quarantine zone: 2,651 people were killed by the virus yesterday, bringing the total to 2.1 million." The news anchor delivered this statement in the same bland way she spoke of traffic conditions. Linda folded another shirt.

"No breeches have been reported and the virus remains localized to the Vancouver area. Scientists are still working to understand where the virus came from and what can be done to stop it." The shot switched to a reporter in a Hawaiian shirt and sunglasses who was reporting on a sandcastle competition from a sunny beach filled with smiling people.

We could use a vacation. I should ask Dan what he thinks about Mexico.

Finished with the laundry, Linda switched off the TV and set out to make dinner.

The Breakfast Club was halfway through its second run of the night when the phone rang. Linda paused the show and answered.

"Hello?"

"Hi, Auntie Linda. It's Sammy. Can I talk to Holt?"

"Sure you can sweetie. Hold on a minute. I'll get him." Linda pressed the "goodbye" button on the phone, put it down on the coffee table, and un-paused the movie. A few minutes later, the phone rang again. Linda picked it up and put it under a throw pillow on the corner of the couch. The phone continued to ring. *Those boys sure are loud.* Linda turned up the volume of the TV.

———

When the movie ended, Linda turned off the lights, made sure the front door was locked, and headed to bed. Along the way, she popped her head into Holt's room to say good night.

The lights were off, and the boy lay under the mound of blankets. The TV was glowing, showing the same screen for the video game it had this morning. The short music sequence played through and restarted, over and over. Her eyes watering from the stench, Linda turned off the TV then moved to the bed.

"Goodnight, Holt," she whispered. Gently pulling back the damp covers, she bent and kissed the decaying forehead, bits of rotting flesh coming away on her lips.

I love you, mom.

"I love you too, sweetheart."

Carefully, she tucked the blankets around the boy and picked a maggot from his hair, the fat white body writhing between her fingers. She pulled the door closed behind her as she left the room.

———

INKY BLACKNESS SWAMPED her vision as her eyes flickered open. Silence pressed on her in the dark. Dan was a loud sleeper. She listened, straining to hear his even breaths, but the only sound to reach her was only her own fluttery exhalations.

She rolled to her side and reached an arm out to Dan's side of the bed, to hug him close like she always did, but felt only the cool sheets on her hot skin. Her mind worked through the implications, stretching through the thick morass of memory.

Foul air invaded the bedroom through cracks around the hallway door, thick fingers of rot laced with Ocean Breeze reaching into every corner. She breathed the putrid scent and listened to the silence. The combination filled her mind, filled her memory, and she remembered where Dan was. Where Holt was.

Hot tears filled her eyes, spilled to puffy skin underneath, and from there, rained on her pillow. Anguished screams filled the empty house.

———

LINDA STEPPED out of the shower and pulled the curtain closed, so she didn't see the body while she dried her hair. She rubbed at her throat, which hurt more this morning than it had yesterday. Squeeze as she might, she could not wrangle a single drop of concealer from the tube. She tossed the container into the trash can and dabbed at her puffy under-eyes with foundation.

The phone rang while she was blow drying her hair. Linda tossed it into the trash can where it joined the empty tube of concealer.

———

THE ROUGH BRISTLES of the scrub brush scraped circles on the tile. Cleaner foamed in the grout and around Linda's fingers. A hypnotic rasp filled the kitchen and filled Linda's mind.

The doorbell startled her and she jumped, knocking the bucket and splashing water across the floor. *Damnit. Who is it now?*

She opened the door to the Public Health officer. Confusion bloomed. "Has it been a week already?"

"Mrs. Whittler, we've received a call from a..." He checked his clipboard. "A Susan Blake, requesting a wellness check."

Movement from the street caught Linda's attention. Spread out in the road was an ambulance and several people, all clad in the same puffy suits as the man on the porch. A pile of black bags rested on the sidewalk.

"I don't understand. Everything is fine here."

"Ma'am, I'm going to have to insist. Can I have all the family members in the living room?" He turned and waved to the suits on the road. Two broke off from the crowd and started toward the house.

"You don't need to see them. Everything is fine."

He took a step forward.

"Ma'am, can I come in?"

"I..." Linda stepped back as the man sidled past. "Dan," she called out. "Come down here."

"I'm going to need you to remain in the living room while we check the house." The other suited men came through the doorway. Linda moved back between the couch and the television, away from the suits and their self-contained sterility.

"I don't know what you're looking for. Everything is fine."

The officers spread out, one starting up the staircase, another moving to the kitchen. The third—the man from the day before—watched her and took notes on the clipboard.

"Careful in the kitchen," Linda called out. "The floor is wet."

She sat on the couch. "This is unnecessary. Everything is fine."

Linda and the Public Health Officer waited. The ventilation apparatus on his suit whirred.

A muffled yell echoed from the second floor, followed by a thump, and then the man in the suit rushed down the stairs, stumbling against the wall.

"What is it? Is your suit punctured?" The officer from yesterday helped him down the last step.

The inner side of the man's plastic view screen was smeared with yellow bile. He moved erratically, stumbling. "He's dead!" He reached for his helmet. "In the bed." He sobbed as another suited man wrestled his hands away from the helmet latch.

Linda rearranged the throw pillows on the couch. Smoothed the wrinkled fabric. Standing, she wandered through the room, pulled a rag from her apron pocket and began dusting the sparking ornaments on shelves lining the wall.

Behind her exploded a flurry of movement. White fabric rustled up and down the stairs, empty black bags brought upstairs. Heavy bundles were carried down and hauled to the ambulance.

"Ma'am," The Public Health officer stood behind her, clipboard dangling from a gloved hand. "I need you to come with me."

Linda moved to the staircase, a potted plant clutched in her hands. A yellowed leaf dropped from a stem, landed on the bottom stair. Leaning over the banister, she called up. "Holt and Dan, I'm doing a load of laundry. Bring down your dirty clothes."

Linda gently placed the plant onto a table. She whispered, "Everything is fine."

JUST CHECKING IN
MICHAEL SUBJACK

"Mom, stop!"

As Bethany pulled back her slightly shaking hands, she was dismayed at how old they looked. Had they been this way for long? They reminded her of her grandmother's hands, which Bethany had always likened to a vulture's claws—a comparison she never dared speak aloud. But while her grandmother had been dead for twenty-five years, Bethany still found herself in the presence of someone birdlike, albeit in a much more appealing way: her daughter, Sydney, reminded Bethany of a parakeet. That admittedly wasn't as true now as when Sydney was little, but some of the traits remained. For one thing, the girl often bore a quizzical countenance, complete with a slightly tilted head, but the look was never accusatory. It was instead sweet and disarming and never failed to make Bethany smile. As her daughter was now navigating her freshman year of high school, said countenance was more of a scowl and was often punctuated with an abundance of eye-rolling, but there were still fleeting moments when she was Bethany's little girl. Her little bird. And right now, her little bird was in the throes of a low-key temper tantrum.

"Will you leave it alone?" Sydney snapped. "It looks fine!"

"It" referred to her hair, a mess of frizz and errant strands. Bethany was an expert at getting it under control, and Sydney had always been happy to let her, though the last time had been the eighth-grade formal several months ago. At Bethany's age, that interregnum was nothing, but to someone on the cusp of fifteen, seven months was a lifetime ago. A lot had changed since then, and while Bethany accepted some of it, most of it was pretty hard to take—particularly some of Sydney's new friends, of whom Bethany did not approve. And of course, that's exactly who her daughter was setting off into the night with.

"It's a mess!" Bethany protested. "You're going out. Don't you want to look nice?"

"I've seen your idea of nice!" Sydney said, pointing at a photo on the wall outside the bathroom.

It was her second-grade picture, which had her in a denim dress Bethan thought was pretty cute then and now. And while Sydney smirked as if the dig were a joke, Bethany couldn't help but feel a little insulted.

Remember who pays for those clothes and takes you shopping to get them, a bitter taste forming on the roof of her mouth.

She watched her daughter preen in front of the mirror, noting her excitement. With the mood jovial again, Bethany thought this was as good a time as any to establish the rules and help put her mind at ease.

"So what's the plan again?" she asked, crossing her arms as she leaned against the doorway.

"Bowling," Sydney replied, her eyes on the bathroom counter.

Bethany told herself that was from the heavy make-up weighing them down and not her daughter being evasive. Did kids go bowling anymore? It sounded like antiquated activity from Bethany's heyday in the early nineties. But then again, things tended to move in cycles. Maybe kids today found bowling retro and kitschy. Weirder things have happened.

"And then what?" Bethany asked, arching an eyebrow.

"Orgy," Sydney said, addressing her mother through her reflection in the mirror. The smirk was there again, and now it was undeniably nasty. Her daughter was trying to get under her skin.

"Very funny," Bethany said. "Tell me the plan again or you're staying in. And I was planning on marathoning *Big Bang Theory*, so brace yourself."

Sydney rolled her eyes and left Bethany hanging as she applied a fresh coat of sparkly lip gloss. She put the brush back in the tube and closed it with an authoritative snap, testing and pushing Bethany, but Bethany remained cool, keeping her gaze casual but unbroken.

Nice try, my little bird. But you're going to have to do better than that.

"We're going to ride around for a while," Sydney finally said. "But not too long."

"And when are you texting me?" Bethany asked, cracking her thumb.

"Nine," Sydney said with a look of distaste, "and again at ten."

"Home by when?" Bethany asked, cracking her other thumb, a gesture that was satisfying regardless of how much it grossed out her daughter.

"Eleven," Sydney replied. "And I wanted to talk to you about that because—"

"No," Bethany cut her off, the one-syllable word as sharp as a dagger. If she knew one thing as a parent, it was that you have to shut down these attempted bargaining sessions almost immediately. Let them whine afterward. Assert yourself, and victory was as good as yours.

Sydney tacitly acknowledged this fact with an agitated huff

and another eye roll. An uneasy silence followed, but before the air could get any more tense, a text chimed on Sydney's phone.

"They're here!" she announced, her face rendered a pale blue from the glowing screen. "See you later!"

She swept by Bethany, leaving behind the lingering scent of Marc Jacobs Daisy. What a waste, considering the company she was keeping. Bethany heard the front door open and quickly slam shut, prompting Toby, their Boston Terrier, to utter a short, protesting bark.

You and me both, buddy.

She shuffled to her bedroom window. The street below was a perfect encapsulation of the picturesque beauty of winter. The pristine snow on the ground twinkled in the moonlight. Flakes floated lazily in the haze of streetlights before joining their brethren on the ground in precise symmetry. The only thing marring this living Norman Rockwell painting was the aging Toyota Camry jittering at the curb, a thick plume of exhaust filling the air behind it like a prolonged fart. Sydney bounded down the walkway like she was about to jump into a limo to head to the Oscars and not bowling with a bunch of ne'er-do-wells doomed for a life of mediocrity.

The driver, a shaggy-haired blond and junior named Ron sported a face that always looked frighteningly vacant. He stared straight ahead while his girlfriend, a trashy sophomore named Tricia, climbed out of the car and greeted Sydney with an enthusiastic hug. Even from her upstairs window, Bethany heard their giggling and high-pitched chatter. Because that wasn't unlike how Bethany's girlfriends had greeted her in her younger years, she relaxed and even allowed herself a slight smile. Their rapport seemed to be genuine, even if Tricia was certifiable white trash. And although he couldn't be seen, Bethany knew that Vince, the other member of their group, was waiting in the backseat. Vince's presence scared her more than anything because he was exactly the sort of boy Bethany would have been attracted to at fifteen. He played guitar and, while not especially handsome, had an aloof quality that tended to drive hormonal and misguided teenage girls insane. As Sydney entered the car, Bethany suddenly had a clear picture of her daughter running her manicured hand over the thigh of Vince's frayed jeans, finding its way inside, where it—

"Stop!" Bethany barked loud enough to earn an appropriate response from Toby.

She gathered her favorite fleece blanket and went downstairs to make popcorn. She didn't end up watching *Big Bang Theory*, but opted instead for *The Office*, taking particular notice of Toby's namesake, who Michael Scott constantly mocked and harangued. Watching it now, she couldn't help but feel a kinship with Toby— something that hadn't existed when the show initially aired and Sydney was a baby who didn't just rely on Bethany but practically worshipped her. As the show was comfort food, Bethany's anxiety subsided somewhat, but that didn't stop her from checking her phone every five minutes. When the time reached 8:58, her anxiety spiked as she concentrated on her phone, desperate for Sydney's first text to arrive.

Up until this point, Sydney's excursions with her friends were largely relegated to coffee shops after school and Tricia's house for movies. She wanted to trust her daughter, but there was a bad feeling extending from Bethany's gut up to her ears, where it spilled out and spun around her like a persistent fly that refused to take a hint. It was 9:01 when the text came in, complete with a picture of a bowling lane, its empty mouth, and a glowing "X" indicating a strike.

"I'm winning!" the text under the pic proclaimed.

Bethany smiled and replied with a thumbs-up emoji—something that wouldn't make her seem too eager or pushy. If anything, Sydney might be inclined to keep the conversation going. She didn't, which didn't bother Bethany much. Her daughter was having fun with her friends, such as they were, and keeping it cool increased the chances that Sydney would text at ten on the dot. Proud of both herself and her daughter, Bethany resumed *The Office*. The next sixty minutes flew by, and as expected, Sydney's next text arrived exactly on the hour. Bowling was over, and they were going to meet some people at Denny's in lieu of driving around, which made Bethany laugh. Some things truly never change. Late-night Denny's runs were practically routine in Bethany's youth. She made for the kitchen, with Toby trailing behind her, for some tea.

Her mood wasn't just good but sparkling now, so she gave her grateful puppy a treat while she brewed a cup of lemon balm. She kept a close watch on the kettle, making sure to catch it just before it started whistling. Bethany didn't like to wait for her tea to cool nor did she have any interest in savoring it. For her, tea worked as a sleep aid and a quick way to warm herself up, so once it was in her mug, it was already half-drunk by the time she got back to the couch for the last ten minutes of the episode she'd been watching. By the time the credits rolled, the tea was gone and Bethany felt downright content.

Bethany made a mental note to offer Sydney a cup of tea when she got back because the trip home would be cold. Perhaps she'd join her daughter in having a cup. If things continued going well, maybe she'd get her daughter's company at the grocery store tomorrow morning. All told, this was shaping up to be a nice little weekend.

———

Barking.

It was distant at first, and a disoriented Bethany's first thought was that she had left poor Toby outside. But then another bark came, this one much closer and definitely inside the house. Toby was safe. With that knowledge, she was free to go back to...

"Oh, God!"

Bethany's eyes snapped open and she jumped to her feet, both knees giving a generous pop that made her wince. That fucking tea. She had fallen asleep, something she wasn't planning on doing until well after midnight when she'd know her daughter was safe and in her bedroom just down the hallway. She checked her phone. 11:30, and no communication from Sydney. Pulse racing, Bethany fired off a text.

"Wgere a e you?"

No response, but Bethany realized something. Sydney was already home and in her bedroom. She'd entered the front door, seen her mother asleep on the couch, giggled to herself, and then crept upstairs. Toby had barked because Sydney had dropped something or closed a door a little too loudly. As true with most terriers, it didn't take much to set him off. With a labored sigh of relief, Bethany climbed the stairs to confirm what she already knew: Sydney was safe and sound. What else could be true?

She reached Sydney's door. Her light was off. She was already in bed but likely not asleep, watching videos on TikTok or exchanging texts with Tricia. She knocked against the heavy wood, producing a slight sting in her knuckles.

"Syd?"

No answer. She probably had her earbuds in. No big deal. Bethany knocked louder this time, sending more pinpricks of pain through her knuckles.

"Sydney? Have fun tonight?"

No response, but then something strange happened. More knocking, but not from Bethany. No, these knocks had a firm, authoritative cadence and they were coming from downstairs. Bethany, still foggy from sleep, tried to make sense of this, but then the pattern repeated, this time in harmony with Toby, who barked and ran toward the front door, his nails scraping and skittering on the hardwood floor. But who would be knocking on the door this late at night? The visitor continued knocking while Toby barked in short, ear-splitting bursts.

"Syd?"

The voice coming from her mouth was no longer the voice of a mother, but one of a frightened child. Now eager for a strict rebuke from her daughter, Bethany swung open the door and turned on the light, finding an undisturbed bed, its blankets, and sheets tightly tucked into the sides with a neatness and precision worthy of the military. If there was one thing Bethany prided herself on, it was a well-made bed. But that was the opposite of what she wanted now. This bed belonged to her daughter, who should have been curled up inside it, her bored face buried in a phone Bethany paid for. The knocks came again, and she wanted to scream. The urge to do so was suppressed by a text that came in. Delirious, Bethany looked at her phone and saw it was from Sydney.

"I'm fine, Mom."

Relief, but still no shortage of confusion, as the barking and knocking refused to subside. Bethany practically floated downstairs, eager to put out whatever fire was at her front door. Her daughter would be home soon, and after a very long talk, they could forget this night ever happened. Bethany swung open the front door to find a morose-looking man in a saggy overcoat standing in front of two equally po-faced uniformed police officers.

"Good evening, ma'am," he said, holding up a badge that cast a dull glint from the warm light of the hallway. "I'm Detective Morris. Are you the mother of Sydney Garrett?"

Bethany tried to speak, but the words stuck in her throat like an errant shard of popcorn.

"Ma'am?"

Bethany's mouth opened as another text came in. And then another. And then another.

"Fine, Mom. I miss you. Love you" and then "Mom, I'm fine. So fine. Just checking in!"

"Ma'am?" the man repeated. "Is your daughter Sydney Garrett?"

Bethany was ready to respond when one more text came in, this one a photo that turned her legs to Jello as she hit the floor in a clumsy heap. With the world no longer making sense, she could hear the frantic voice of the detective ordering the police officers to call for an ambulance. Toby went into hysterics as he pirouetted around Bethany and her phone, which lay on the ground next to her. Through the asymmetrical web of cracks was an image of a leering mouth surrounded by grimy stubble and scabby lips that receded over crooked, discolored teeth. It remained dead center on the screen until it was displaced by one final message:

"Don't be scared, Mom. You'll see me again. Real soon."

A SACRED PLACE

LENA NG

I WAS BLESSED TO FIND THIS PLACE. THE CLAPBOARD cottage, small by some standards, was perfect for my needs. I lived alone and had no need to compromise. I had taken my time researching this location and gathering the necessary funds. The neighborhood seemed quiet and unassuming, and I felt I could fit in without much difficulty. I would bother no one if no one bothered me. My home was a place to put down roots, my safe space, my sacred place. I would take care of it, and through the growth of its value, it would take care of me.

I was tending the garden, planting the bulbs, sowing the seeds, nurturing the grass, etc. when they came bearing gifts. "Welcome neighbor," the pair said—a male and a female if I wasn't mistaken in my classification. They bared their teeth and handed me a container bearing unmoving sustenance. They came from a council called HOA—a ruling class, I gathered. They wanted their entitled respect and to establish dominion. They called themselves John and Margaret. My own name they could not pronounce.

"Why are you here?" I asked. I did not want to make assumptions of evil intentions, but I needed to be prepared.

The teeth quickly retracted.

The male brought out a book, thick and heavy, white, and full of hieroglyphic regulations, typed in small code. I held this book of limits. For these restrictions, and to fund the enforcement of the regulations, I would be required to pay them a monthly tithe.

"Does this country not believe in freedom?" I asked.

"There is freedom, but within boundaries," the female replied. She wore a flowing gown, and her hair was the color of the bare earth. Her eyes brooked no dissent.

"Is this home not my castle?" I asked.

"Hard work and sacrifice are needed to maintain it, for the benefit of you and the community."

I understood hard work and community. As one of my people's first explorers, I came here to help those back home who lacked the necessary resources. Now many light years away, I would not know when I would see them again.

I understood sacrifice as well. Although I would be an eternal outsider, I have sacrificed much to come here. I have offered many sacrifices and was prepared to offer more.

The council members looked at me with weighty expectation. I focused my gaze, and the council members froze. I released my stingers. They would feel no pain. I prepared the altar and said the appropriate prayers.

The house emitted a green glow. A low chanting began, audible only to my frequency. The cosmos thanked me for my gift. It allowed me to keep the remains. I fed the grass the vital red fluid, drained from their bodies. The stems unfurled and their slender green tongues lapped up the liquid life.

The yard's heartbeat drummed against my feet. I put down my roots, their tendrils excavating the land, and raised my hands to the heavens. The house's breath ruffled my hair. I am but a servant to the temple.

SOUNDS OF SUMMER
JESSE ROWELL

I used to know the sounds of a good summer. My lawn chair creaking and sprinklers a' rat-a-tat-tatting above the shouts of children. Insects buzzing. And my voice, languid as a river, calling out to my daughter.

"Alice. Come here, honey. Mommy forgot to put sunscreen on your legs."

My three-year-old skipped over with a wicked grin. No sooner had I started applying the paste to her legs when she spit out a stream of water which hit my shoulder.

"That's the sound a whale makes," Alice laughed.

"Where did you learn that joke, you little stinker?" I tickled Alice under her chin. Sunscreen streaked her neck.

My daughter had begun delighting in practical jokes, yelling "Boo!" at strangers in the mall and hiding inside clothing racks when nobody was looking. I had scolded her severely for both, noting the latter could result in suffocation. The former too, if done to the wrong stranger.

"When's Daddy coming home?" Alice asked as I finished the back of her legs.

"Daddy is off designing airplanes for the future," I answered. Was that a hint of bitterness in my voice? *And why not?* I tightened my jaw.

My husband, Lewis, had dragged me out to bumfuck nowhere to fulfill his career ambitions while my degree in astrophysics languished. Every home here pasteurized to beige, two door garage, Doric columns, repeating itself over and over. He had written our story, suffocated by same-day sameness in the suburbs, sucked into a black hole.

"Big slide," my daughter said. "I want to go on the big slide."

I looked down the street to our subdivision's park. Heat rose off the pavement. I thought I saw a couple of kids hanging off the monkey bars.

"I don't know," I said. "It's getting kind of hot. We should stay near the sprinkler."

The big pout got me every time. So damn cute and earnest, her flush cheeks framed by her bob cut of dark hair.

"Okay," I relented. "Let's go."

The blank faces of each home stared at us as we passed, empty windows for eyes. I realized in the year since we had moved here I hadn't learned any of our neighbors' names. It wouldn't have mattered. If I knew their names I wouldn't have known where to find them, every home looking the same as the next.

Alice threw cedar bark in the air when we got to the park. The children who had been there minutes before had vanished, slunk back into their homes like rabbits into their holes. I sat on a retaining wall and watched Alice dance like an unstable atom, beautiful in her sudden gestures, swaying too close to the edge.

"Be careful up there," I warned.

Not listening, Alice ran down the slide.

I sighed. The heat had pushed me into languor, and I could barely summon the effort to react to much of anything. My mind drifted as the last of the summer bees hunted for something to rub their asses up against, long after the nectar from the blackberry blossoms had been harvested. They will die tonight under the street lights, exhausted as they fall to rest on the pavement.

My daughter stopped playing to look down the street. Maybe her daddy had decided to come home early? That would be a miracle. I craned my neck to look for him. The perpetual absence of my husband: a certainty that should have been written into our wedding vows.

No husband, but a blonde girl—a couple years older than Alice —watched us from a distance. Her hair tied back and wearing a beige shirt that read, "Don't Ask Me," the girl started to shuffle toward the park. Her gait spoke of parents who had an epic row, yelling at her to go to the park while they argued. Lord knows I had been tempted to tell Alice to leave the house on a few occasions, but I never did. The thought of my child walking alone in the neighborhood was too dreadful to consider. It was always a shock to see a neighbor's kid wandering outside alone.

The girl stood in front of me. She looked bent, like a scarecrow. *Maybe she has scoliosis. Poor thing.*

"My name is Lorina," I introduced myself. "We live in the house up on the corner."

Silence. The kid stared through me as if I didn't exist.

"What does your shirt say, sweetie?" I asked her.

The girl didn't answer. I was about to tickle her under the chin, but refrained. Cardinal rule of parenting: do not touch strangers or strangers' kids. Unless they are in danger.

I looked down the street toward the row of homes where the girl had appeared. No parent stuck out their head to check on her. I imagined little heads popping in and out like prairie dogs, or polliwogs in the trifle-truffle bogs. I shook my head. Too much reading Dr. Seuss to Alice at night.

Alice scampered over to the girl, smiling with delight at having a new playmate. She gravitated to older kids. At the mall or the park, it didn't matter. She stuck to them like she'd formed a covalent bond. She'd follow them to their home if she could, and that's when I would have to intervene, pulling little temper-tantrum away as the shared electron, usually a soccer ball or basketball, bounced in the opposite direction, bond disrupted.

Well, let Alice have her fun for now. The older girl will occupy her for the afternoon, and then she'll be easier to put down for a nap.

The blonde girl nodded and grabbed Alice's hand. They bunny-hopped to the edge of the playground where the blackberries grew and they began to pick at them. The girl kept hold of Alice's hand as they picked. Girls were like that—more apt to hold hands, sensitive to each other's feelings. Alice herself had shown this maternal instinct to her dolls, swaddling and feeding them.

They picked their way along the thicket, busy little bees, until they disappeared into a cove.

I drowsed as I watched the dense green undulate like algae-slicked water. Crickets sawed somewhere off in the shadows. A breeze stirred the heat. The neighborhood fell away, turning into golf-green. The sky ran with spectral lines of mercury.

I snapped awake. Had I closed my eyes for a second? The sticky heat, delicious and dangerous, had pulled me under. I looked back toward the cove in the blackberry thicket.

The blonde girl shuffled out, brushing dirt and leaves off her body.

I frowned. Shouldn't Alice be close behind her, following her like a moon in orbital decay? I shook my head, remembering how we had sat on the lawn and watched the moon through my Vivitar telescope. Is the moon falling, Alice kept asking. Yes, I told her. The moon falls toward the Earth, but the Earth runs away.

"Alice?" I called as I walked toward the cove. I squatted and peered inside. Nothing. "Alice?" I called out with more urgency.

"You better not be hiding. This is not the time of day to be joking around."

Alice would usually giggle at this point, revealing her location, but there was no sound. I listened for her voice, looked for her hiding deep in the bushes like a thrush. How did she maneuver past all those blackberry thorns? Alice would howl at the slightest scratch and seek immediate boo-boo attention from me.

I turned and caught up with the blonde girl shuffling up the street.

"Hey, kid," I said. "Stop for a second."

The girl paused and looked up at me with a blank look, her face slouching toward her shoulder like the head of a stuffed animal.

"Do you know where my daughter is hiding?"

Not even a shrug. That same blank look and the same shirt mocking, "Don't Ask Me." An arrogant phrase for a child to wear. For anybody to wear. What kind of designer would think it clever? *A mad hatter delighting in discomfort, that's who.*

She drifted away, an exoplanet sinking into a dying star among thousands of dying stars. I knew if I turned away for a second I would never be able to identify which home absorbed the girl. And maybe that was for the best. I would be tempted to track her down, admonish her, and then have to apologize to her parents.

I ran back to the blackberry thicket. "Alice Liddell," I said through clenched teeth. "Come out here right now."

Nothing.

"Alice, please. You're scaring Mommy."

Glittering snail trails crosshatched the ground and disappeared under the blackberry bushes. I saw something in there. Something waiting behind the diamond deposits of water on leaves. Snapping branches like cracking teeth. A formless fear, almost visible, and then gone.

"That's it," I said. "I'm going home, and you're going to be left here all alone."

I had played this bluff before, walking away when Alice refused to leave the library. She would dash after me, her eyes flush with tears, terrified at the thought of being abandoned. But this time she didn't appear.

I looked helplessly over the homes, wishing a neighbor would peek out and offer to call the police or paramedics, or both. I gauged the distance to our home. Would I be able to find my cell phone in time and run back? Run back before Alice came out of hiding to find her mother gone and descend into full-blown panic? *Her daddy should be here to help me protect her. This is his fault.*

Thorns dug into my arms as I pushed the branches back. How did Alice find her way through this mess? I got down on my hands and knees, fingers sinking into sod.

"Alice," I said, sighing with the heaviness that only a mother can muster. "I'm going to find you in there if it kills me."

I pushed my shoulder through the bushes. The air felt cool inside, inviting and reassuring. I brushed back black moss and slugs. The darkness pulled me in, cool air irresistible against my skin. I crawled deeper. Thorns bit into my back, tore at my flesh, cut my hands. The thing would not let go of me now.

"Alice, where are you?" I whispered, the damp dark muffling my words.

There. A mushroom glowing in the dim light. No. Her white shoe half-buried, the worn tread of its sole facing me. It wiggled as if still attached to her foot. Maybe it is still attached to her foot, I thought. My hands fumbled against the heel as my fingers found purchase around its laces. I pulled. It popped off in time for me to see her foot disappear down a hole.

"Alice!" I screamed. I didn't care if the neighbors heard me now. I wanted them to. I wanted them to rush out of their homes, visages of fear and panic as they ripped open the greenbelt to help me save my daughter from this sinkhole. The homeowners association would be hearing about this, I decided. I'd be bitching up a storm. I'd suffer their counter-accusations of child abandonment as long as I could hold my daughter in my arms again.

I plunged both of my arms into the hole feeling for her leg. I found her ankle and pulled at the slippery wriggling mass. Mud? No. Blood. It covered my hands. Her blood or mine, I couldn't tell, my palms a latticework of cuts. There was too much blood. I began to dig frantically.

The hole opened up like a throat, and I threw myself inside, angling my elbows to keep it from closing over me. I could see her, or parts of her. Dirt poured over us as we fell deeper inside. We fell together, mother and daughter. Buried alive or swallowed into an infinite sinkhole, I didn't know which until I saw her.

She waited for me down there, or a version of her. A clock with no hands. Dark matter pressed against us and I could not see anymore, could not scream anymore, but I was where I was supposed to be in the universe. Next to my daughter as I held her hand.

I used to know the sounds of a good summer. My lawn chair creaking and sprinklers a' rat-a-tat-tatting above the shouts of children. Insects buzzing. And my voice, languid as a river, calling out to my daughter.

IDOLS OF GODLESS MEN
DANIEL LUMPKIN

THE TWO DEPUTIES APPROACHED NATALIE'S CAR WINDOW when she stopped at the gate outside of Jeremiah Anderson's property. The pair wore matching uniforms, hats, and dark sunglasses. Both men used ma'am more as punctuation, it seemed, than formality.

"Can I help you, ma'am?"

"I'm here to see Mr. Anderson," Natalie said. "Natalie Goode."

"Yes, ma'am. You are on the list," the other deputy said. "Can I see your identification? As I check that, my partner here is going to do a quick search under your car and in your trunk—can you pop that open? I'll give you instructions after that. Okay, ma'am?"

Natalie nodded and she watched the first deputy circle around her car with a circular mirror attached to a long stick—it looked like an oversized dental mirror. After finishing the undercarriage check, they popped the trunk, peered through the backseat windows, and eventually both men were standing at her door again.

"Enter through this gate and follow the road all the way up to his house."

"Okay," Natalie said. "Thank you."

But before she could drive off through the open gate, the other deputy held up his hand. "You should know we are stationed outside of his property and aren't permitted on it. If something happens—if you need help—call this number."

He gave her a business card with a phone number written on the back. Natalie half-expected the other deputy to chastise the worried one, to protest he was only scaring her, but both regarded her with blank, serious expressions.

"Thank you," she said, putting the card in her clutch.

"Now, I'm not sure how long you're visiting for or the purpose of your visit," the first deputy said. "He's never had a visitor, so this is quite unusual, but he has strict rules. Power is shut off at seven every night. It doesn't come back on until seven the next morning."

"I don't expect to stay that long," she said, surprised by additional, strange rules, but it was eleven in the morning, which should give her plenty of time.

"Rumor is he doesn't have windows," the other deputy said. "We haven't seen his house behind all those trees, but if it's true and he doesn't have power, You're going into a cave—not a home. You won't be able to see a thing if you're still in there when the place goes dark."

"I'll be gone long before power is cut off," Natalie said, trying to reassure both men.

"Good luck, ma'am."

Natalie drove through the gate and gave the deputies a small wave. The road weaved through thick pines and along rolling elevation until she came to a grassy clearing where, perched atop a small hill, a little wooden cabin with age-stained logs stood. A bright red door stood out between two large windows, illuminated from within.

Prelude I.

"Godless men never stop making gods or declaring they are gods themselves"—something my grandfather always said. We always described Him as a preacher, a pastor, a man of God, but he never had formal education. Besides the Bible, I couldn't say with confidence He'd ever finished a book in his life, but you wouldn't have known it. And He always warned us against making false idols. I held onto His admonition for a long time, until I realized my family had made something of an idol out of my grandfather.

My mother's father regularly struck his adult children for their failures to strike their own children with enough regularity or force. None stood up to Him. How could you? He was God in His daughters' eyes. Our own mothers and aunts clearly weren't blood related.

I seemed to have Him figured out by age nine or so. Chastising a young boy for reading was one of the ways he passed the time.

"Ain't going to find God in anything other than his own word!" My grandfather would say, sitting across the family table from me. If I didn't look up immediately, which I usually didn't, He would smack his palm against the table, making the shaved-down forks and nearly flattened spoons leap up and crash. Once I held up a finger to finish the page. He grabbed my wrist and brought the entire weight of Huckleberry Finn down four or five times. My pointer finger never pointed straight after that.

On my fifteenth birthday, He slapped me for something I'd said or for a glance that curried enough displeasure to warrant a strike. It didn't take much to get Him to that point. I stopped avoiding it. Pain was inevitable. I was the only male in the family besides him. After my mother, all His other daughters produced only daughters. As it happened, He ordered me to dress to match my mother, her sisters, and all of my cousins. Never really thought of it much.

I kicked His bad knee, believing I'd be beat worse than ever before, but He fell. I saw my opportunity. All of that time and all of those beatings... I took my chance. After He was down, I kicked Him a few more times and then reached for something to bash Him with. He let out a sound like a welp from my last kick, like a dog in pain. I wish I'd hit Him with another copy of Huck Finn. There would have been some poetry there. But he'd had Huck burned before I turned ten. I don't even remember what book I grabbed, but it was a book that did Him in. I did Him in with a book, rather, and there was some poetry in that. His blood sprayed my face, and the pages moistened. The room was quiet when it was all done.

Figured I'd read—take advantage of the opportunity. My family hollered, some screaming, some crying, but I didn't hear it the same. The words on the page pulled me in. I know it was the best book I ever read, though I can't even tell you anything about it now.

At one point, I heard somebody rummaging through His overalls. They came up with the key. They whispered that I had done it: I had freed us all. We were free for the first time in our lives, and I basked in my freedom by reading a blood-stained book.

I read, and someone else ran. To do so would have been unforgivable before that moment; someone running would have damned all of us to hell. I'd always wanted to leave, but my mother had always stopped me. But we were free now. The idea began sinking in.

Five years have passed since that day. In that time, I've read more than one hundred fifty books. In fact, people mailed me books after that news interview. The reporter had asked what I wanted to do now that I was free. I said I wanted to read good books for the rest of my life. I had nothing to read, before, and now I've got enough for all lifetimes.

Jeremiah Anderson, Age 20

PRELUDE II.

Dear Mr. Anderson,

My name is Natalie Goode. I write for The Philips County Post. Every morning, except on weekends, I wake up and walk to work. I sit at my desk and write stories. Right now, I'm finishing a story about a Cascade Park dog show—close enough to walk from that gate outside your home. Have you ever been? It's beautiful right now. There were so many different breeds of dogs at this show, and they were all fascinated by each other.

I'm tired of working at the newspaper. I've asked my boss for bigger stories, tougher assignments, but he refuses. He thinks I cannot handle any front-page work. Lately, I've realized I either need to quit or find a story that would prove him wrong. I think yours is the story that proves the world wrong. Reaching out to you will probably get me fired. I don't care anymore.

I know the deputies do a good job of keeping you protected and giving you a quiet life. Most journalists know the rules are in place for your protection. I'm unsure what penalties exist for leaving this letter at your residence, and I figure there's a chance you won't read it—but I owe it to myself to try.

The world wants to know you're okay. Are you okay? What is your life like now? It's been fifteen years since everything happened. Let's do an interview—we'll get through it together. We don't have to talk about your past. I want to discuss whatever interests you. What do you do all day? What do you think about? Do you still read as much as you did last we heard from you? I heard a deputy say people still send you loads of books. I'd love to come to see your collection.

Sincerely,

Natalie Goode

Dear Ms. Goode,

I first want to apologize. Your letter caught me off guard. Unfortunately, due to my past, I'm challenged by events that wouldn't jar most people—like finding a letter at their property gate. When I stumbled across your letter, I believed the man I had known as my grandfather for the first fifteen years of my life had come back to remind me of terrible things I don't want to remember or to put either in this letter or anyone's mind.

I will not press charges.

However, please understand this: the rules protect me along with everyone else. Rules are what keep me grounded firmly in reality. Without them, I struggle knowing what reality even is. As long as that is something you can respect, I will speak with you. I've written to your editor that I will agree to do an interview with you in one calendar year as long as I see he is not only giving you front-page stories but assignments showing your talent. I went through the digital archive and, while I believe you are a fine reporter on fast-food restaurant openings and human-interest stories, I saw your true ability in Judge McIntosh's obituary. That piece was beautiful. Anyone would be honored to have such words written about them.

Your job is secure. I look forward to our conversation.

J.A.

———

Six months into that calendar year, Natalie Goode's front-page bylines with *The Philips County Post* came with such regularity, and were of such high quality, the paper grew in subscribers. Goode broke the story on the county animal shelter's finances and uncovered problems at the jail that had gone unreported for years. This early-twenties college graduate seemed untouchable.

Usually, if one of the ambitious young reporters got too close to a story making county officials look bad, those only had to pay a visit to Editor Victor Hancock to fix their P.R. problem. But after Natalie Goode's arrangement with Jeremiah Anderson came into effect, even the editor's hands were tied. Somehow, Goode had secured an interview with *the* Jeremiah Anderson—a recluse, now, but he'd been the story of the year some odd years ago.

"You gotta get her to pipe down a bit, Vic," Water and Sewage Authority President Ron Walsh had said. "I'm for the first amendment and all, don't get me wrong, but she's got no place trying to come to our meetings."

"Aren't those public meetings?" Victor said, leaning back in his creaky desk chair, looking at the ceiling. The *Post's* editor disliked county officials showing up unannounced, but sometimes their doing so was a sign the paper was doing something right.

"Well, Sure," Ron said. "But that don't mean nothing. You've never had a reporter come in, taking notes at our meetings. Come on, Vic."

"You're going to have to weather this storm for another six months," Victor said. "Be on your best behavior, and I'm sure you'll make it through."

Victor had an ace up his sleeve. He knew it. The girl, as much as her youthful enthusiasm pained him, eventually, she wouldn't be his problem. In six months, she'd either get the story of the year, and it would be picked up for syndication, or Victor would put her back on evergreen and fluff pieces. In that case, he'd expect Natalie's resignation letter within a few hours of word she didn't get the scoop on Anderson. Victor had been an editor for quite some time. He knew she'd leave, and her departure would be fine with him. He also figured Mr. Recluse wouldn't follow through on his promised interview. Jeremiah Anderson, according to just about everyone in town, was a loon of the highest degree.

"What's in six months?" Ron asked.

"She's going to interview *that* Jeremiah Anderson."

"Is she?" Ron asked, sounding impressed by Goode's ability to get such an impossible interview.

"She seems to think so. I'm reluctant to think it'll actually happen, but who knows. She's very persistent."

"I hear he still wears those dresses," Ron said. "Is that true?"

"Could be," Victor answered. "A lot of that is rumor. The deputies assigned to protect him rarely ever see him. Keeps to himself. Reads a lot. He donates many books to the local library—did you know that?"

"Really?" Ron asked, horrified. "My grandson gets books there once a week! Do you think he's gotten any of those?"

"I doubt it," Victor said. "He receives big, thick books. Classics, things about nature, physics—stuff like that—only speaking from what I've been told, of course."

"Okay." Ron sounded relieved. His grandson wasn't interested in those kinds of books.

"Weather the storm for now," Victor told him. "You'll be fine. She's trying to do what she sees as her job and she'll be out of your hair before you know it."

Although he was speculating about this particular case, Victor spoke from experience. Recent college grads didn't remain at *The Philips County Post* for the long term. The paper was a stepping stone for young reporters—to get their reps in and move on to bigger papers or to better opportunities outside of journalism. The work was tough when he started and had only gotten tougher as, across the country, papers thinned their pages and then shuttered entirely.

Although Victor didn't want anyone to know it, he knew deep down he had been wrong about Natalie Goode. She was not only handling the big stories better than he ever thought she could, but her bubbly, spunky personality caught people off guard and resulted in better, more candid quotes for stories. Most people underestimated Natalie, and he was glad to have her for a little while. She would be gone eventually, sure, but right now she was producing award-worthy stuff. This made him look good.

PRELUDE III. [A week before one-year anniversary of letters between Jeremiah Anderson and Natalie Goode.]

Dear Ms. Goode,

I hope this letter finds you well. I usually stay away from the deputies, but I asked them to deliver it to you. I look forward to our conversation, and I hope you don't mind, I have some questions of my own. For now, I have a few requests for your visit next week, and I must stress these requests as quite important.

One: Please do not wear pants or slacks. An appropriate dress is the required attire.

Two: I'm a care-taker at heart. Allow me to take care of you during your visit. If I offer you anything, please accept it without hesitation. If you do not, I fear I will spiral into one of my weeping spells and I will be unable to carry on our discussion.

Three: I have a bad habit. You will notice it. Please do not mention it in anything you say or write about me.

Four: I still call him my grandfather. It is not correct, but I don't like the alternative.

And Five: At the conclusion of our visit, I would like to kiss you goodbye. I hope this is alright. This is the only request that is not required for our conversation to take place.

I look forward to finally meeting you. I have followed your career this year, and out of all the reporters and journalists who have requested to interview me, I sincerely believe you are the right one to do so.

Thank you for your kindness.

Sincerely,
J.A.

———

"You're still gonna go?" Max asked. His look told Natalie he believed she wasn't thinking clearly. They were at his place, a rented room with a kitchenette above a detached garage near town.

"Absolutely," she said, sipping the glass of water Max had poured as she'd read Jeremiah's requests aloud. "Why wouldn't I?"

"Uh, he wants to kiss you," Max said. "You have to wear a dress. What's his bad habit? All of those are red flags."

"I think he's lonely," she said. "You can't judge him though. We can't imagine what he's been through... You don't want me to go?"

"No one who cares about you would want you to do this," he said.

"It's a big opportunity," she said. "I get this story, you know what that could mean?"

"Right," Max said. "The deputies still guard the place?"

"Yeah."

"Alright," he said. He left the small counter near the kitchen sink where they were talking and went to sit on the small sofa he had facing the television.

"You're not mad?" She asked.

"How about I go with you?" He responded. "I'll sit in the car."

"I don't know why, but I suspect Anderson wouldn't be okay with that," she said, shaking her head. "Let's just watch the movie. We haven't had a movie night in a while."

It was true. Max and Natalie had met and started dating their last year at school. Max applied, and was accepted, into a graduate program and Natalie quickly got a job at *The Philips County Post* in town.

"You know what?" He said. "I've got major papers I need to get ahead on. Let's call it a night."

"I just got here. It's not even seven o'clock."

"I'm not enthused about your approach right now. I want to focus on something else."

"Okay," Natalie said, flatly. She was upset, but she wasn't going to be dissuaded from the biggest story of her young career because it was odd. She was ambitious. She was headstrong. She was blind.

———

As Natalie climbed out of her car with her audio recorder and notepad, the front door opened. She noticed it was cracked a few inches as she walked up the front pathway. Natalie stared.

A high-pitched voice intoned, "Just a moment, Natalie," from the other side of the door. The curtains were drawn quickly on the window on her left. A figure passed by the cracked door, and the curtains were drawn on the right window as well. She heard a *click* sound, and the home went dark.

"When you enter, please shut the door behind you," the voice called out to her from a little further inside the home, now. "You may enter when ready."

Natalie opened the door, slowly.

The house had darkened. To her left, an old stove and ice box like the kind her grandmother had kept when Natalie was a child were lit by a single candle. On her right, the house was very dim, but she could make out a silhouette—Anderson—on a small sofa, his back towards her. A small bed rested in the corner closest to her. He faced the wall opposite where she stood. He didn't wave her over. He sat with perfect posture in inky silence.

She closed the door, but before moving, she had to wait for her eyes to adjust.

"Don't be," Jeremiah said, in his high-pitched voice, but then the last word dropped to a much deeper tone. "Frightened."

"I'm not," she said. "Just adapting."

He did not get up to greet or guide Natalie. Once she found she could discern the shape of things, she made her way to an armchair facing him and sat down. After sitting, she started recording.

"Thank you for—" she started, but he spoke over her.

"I've waited for you for a long time," he said, his voice back at the near falsetto tone. "I've waited for this for a very long time."

"So have I," she said. "Where are your books?"

"I do not keep them."

"You give them all to our library?"

"Some," he corrected. "There are other places where they are needed. It depends on the book."

"What is your favorite—"

"I love your dress."

"Thank you," she said. Natalie did not like how the conversation was going, but she figured at some point her dress would come up. It was the newest in her closet. She purchased it earlier that year for Easter Sunday with Max's family. They were very religious—so religious, in fact, they made Natalie not feel irreligious.

"What's the fabric?"

"Cotton."

"I like silk. My mother wore a silk dress. It was her favorite."

"Was it pretty?" Natalie asked. She felt as though she were talking to a child rather than an adult with how he controlled the flow of the conversation.

"Of course, but a dress is only as pretty as the wearer," he said. "Wouldn't you agree?"

"Yes. I've never thought of it like that before."

"Would you like to wear her silk dress? I'd like to see you in it."

"I couldn't," she said.

"I'm offering it to you," he said, his pitch removed from the falsetto tone again. A grave grumbling whisper. A reminder to her of the rules.

"How about at the end of our conversation?"

"Promise." He demanded, again in that whisper.

"Yes," she said. "I will wear it at the end of our conversation."

"Do you like architecture?" He asked, forcing his voice back into the falsetto.

The high pitch of his voice unnerved Natalie. "I suppose," she said. "I've never spent much time—"

"I think everyone needs to love architecture."

"Why's that?"

"It's art and function, intersecting. A building has to serve a purpose, like people do, but when they are beautiful, they serve this function to be seen and adored by the masses. Who is your favorite architect?"

"I don't believe I have one."

"Bertram Goodhue. He's my favorite."

"What is he known for?"

"So many beautiful buildings, but his churches, his cathedrals... You must see them."

"Have you seen any of them?"

"They're in New York, some of them. Have you been?"

"I've been to New York City once," she said. "For a—"

"You probably saw some of his work then, and you didn't even realize," he said, full of pity. "They are so beautiful it seems as though they've always existed. Have you ever seen beauty like that? Something so beautiful that makes you believe it is perfectly impervious to time? I guess that is what truly beautiful things are, aren't they? They're perfection, untouched, unblemished, unstrained by the imperfection of time and space."

"Like the Grand Canyon?"

"I suppose," he said, sounding disappointed with her answer. Jeremiah trailed off, and the house became silent.

"Ask me a question," he said.

But Natalie waited. It was her turn. Silence is one of the strongest interviewing skills a journalist—a good interviewer—can use. A conversation that becomes stagnant—they call it dead air in broadcasting—and it makes people uncomfortable. Most scramble to fill the air with noise. Inviting that noise, Natalie knew, is one of the best ways to direct a conversation.

"I suppose you want to hear about my grandfather," he said without the cadence he'd used when discussing architecture.

"What would you like to tell me about him?"

"I wish there weren't anything to say about him," Jeremiah said. "But I wouldn't be here if that were the case. Neither would you, I suppose."

"How did he meet your mother?"

"He told me God ordered him to collect his brides," inhaling and exhaling deeply as he rubbed his whole face with his hands. "I never heard her side."

"From what I read, they all went willingly. Is that—"

"My grandfather thought about women the same way I think about buildings. He believed all women are born truly beautiful but become corrupted. I think he was trying to uncorrupt and rebeautify. It was a lost cause. That's what he said, anyway."

"How do you think about women?"

"They scare me," he said.

"Why?" Natalie asked. For the first time, she felt like she had full control of the interview.

Quieter now, he answered, "Because of what they might bring out of me."

"Which is what?"

"Him," Jeremiah said, falsetto gone. Jeremiah's voice almost a growl in the darkness.

"Their beauty intimidates you."

"Yes," he said. "Yes, yes, yes."

"That's why you live like this?"

"One of the reasons," he grumbled. "I'm grateful for the community. They make it possible for me to live perfectly protected."

"Many women—many people—think of you as a hero," Natalie said. "You did a very difficult thing and it saved a lot of people needing help."

"That's not why I did it," he said. "I saw an opportunity and acted. It was survival, raw survival."

Another moment of silence. Natalie did not think Jeremiah would listen to her if she attempted to empathize with him. She wanted to but sat motionless a moment more before asking about his life.

"Do you usually sit in the darkness like this?"

"No. I love the windows open, or I sit outside."

"You never leave, though?"

"No," he said. "Judge Mac advised me to stay here on the grounds. Food is delivered, books are delivered. I live in peace. He set all of this up for me. This was his family's land. Did you know that? This was his great-grandfather's cabin. They made it livable for me. Then he asked the Sheriff to have a deputy stationed outside the gate to keep people away. The Judge thought I needed to reset my life, best I could. I set to reading, and I go for walks."

"Sounds like it would get lonely."

"I need loneliness."

"Why?" She asked.

"Never had it, before."

"I want to open a window," she said, getting up.

"Please don't," he pleaded.

"I'm tired of sitting in the dark," she said. "I want to see you."

Natalie got up and moved to the window behind her chair and drew back the thick curtains. She found another window and drew its coverings back as well. She turned. Jeremiah stood at the far end of the house, near the front door.

"Don't be frightened," she said. It was the first time she saw him fully.

He didn't mov, his eyes focused on the floor. He wore a sackcloth, roughly stitched together. His hair lay flat, as it was cut short and combed, and his face was clean shaven.

She came around and sat back down in the armchair and smoothed out her dress.

"I can't," he growled.

"You can," she said. "Please?"

"You're what I'm not," he growled again.

"That's a good thing," she said. "Do you blame them?"

Jeremiah stared at the ceiling now. She could see he was

uncomfortable. She had complete control merely sitting in his home. Maybe he didn't feel it was his home anymore.

"Who?" he asked.

"The town, the people, everyone who allowed your father—"

"My grandfather—"

"to become who he was. Didn't they play a part in what happened?"

"He had a strong, deceiving tongue, and they had trusting hearts. They didn't realize what he had done."

Natalie withdrew a piece of paper from an interview she did a while ago, after she had struck up a friendship with the retired Judge Damien McIntosh.

"What's that?" Jeremiah asked.

"A quote from the Judge from an interview I did with him. He asked me not to publish it until after his death. I held onto it. Just listen." She read.

We had no idea why the man, the wonderful pastor from television would move to our small, isolated community. He told us he was merely doing as he was commanded to do. We loved that. He told us he was starting a new church for the entire town. We loved that. He told us his church would be sending people out as missionaries, on their own missions and they would build their own churches. He was giving our children a godly life, or so we thought. We were blind. The young women he sent never left. They had elected, in private and secrecy, to stay with him forever in his home. In darkness. They would give him children and they would fulfill the prophecy he believed God had given him. It was all a terrible mistake. Nobody questioned him. We were all fooled. Terribly and tragically fooled. That's why we set up a trust for the boy, specifically. The girls were all babies, really young, they weren't going to remember. Some weren't even born until after they all escaped. But Jeremiah was older. Much older and from all he told me and told the lawyers and everything, it falls on us a little bit. We didn't think to question anything. We all looked like fools. The whole community.

"When did he say this?"

"We had several conversations before he died," Natalie said. "He was very helpful for this."

"He talked about me?"

"Not at first," she said. Now she was standing, the light behind her illuminating her dark hair, giving it an auburn glow. She removed her round glasses and then her flats. Her hair was bundled up in a bun, but she released it and it draped over her shoulders and down her back.

"Look at me," she commanded.

He glanced up at her as she reached back and released the button on her dress. It fell to the floor.

Jeremiah fell backwards against the wall and slid onto the floor. It was as though he could not bear the sight of such foreign flesh, unmasked and unprotected from the world. Jeremiah could not speak. He struggled, gasping for air.

"Godless men never stop making gods or, in fact, declaring they are gods themselves," Natalie quoted the words of their father. "It was his second attempt at our species when he made god from bone, from rib. The proof of God is the ability to create new life from nothing."

"His ideas have corrupted your mind," Jeremiah wheezed, his body seizing and convulsing under the sheer weight of his lacking, his weakness, his faults. He always knew yet had refused to believe that his father had been right all along. The prophecies. The visions. It had all been real. Jeremiah deserved death for getting in the way of God.

Through the windows, the sunlight burned brighter than it ever had. Natalie's body was not only bathed in bright white light.

She was light herself, transformed fully into what she always was. He had to turn away. He'd fallen short before his god and wasn't prepared for a death that seemed imminent but didn't arrive.

Her eyes were white. Her hair was white. Her skin was white. Everything burned a righteous pale white fire. It all burned through her, in her, and became one bright shining truth around her.

JUST BEING NEIGHBORLY

JORDAN KING-LACROIX

It was weird when our neighbors swung by to tell us we were the first Jews to live in the area. At least, that they'd met. They saw us putting up our mezuzah and thought it was really neat, a quaint little curio. When they asked what it was and we told them, they cooed like they were seeing some antique from the distant past.

The Harrisons stood at the door looking like a set of people out of an ad from the USA in the 1950s. Although suburban Adelaide —specifically the Adelaide Hills—is different enough from the version in 1950s America, some of it looks exactly the same. White-picket fences and everything.

Daniel Harrison was tall, probably just over six feet, with close-cropped blond hair styled in a neat swish across his head. A dark green jumper was tied around his shoulders, sitting like a cape on top of his salmon pink Polo Ralph Lauren shirt. The one with the big logo, not the little one, so you could be sure it wasn't Lacoste. He introduced his wife—shorter than he was, about five foot two—as Belinda, also blonde. They had two kids, a boy and a girl—of course—thirteen and fifteen, Riley and Tamara.

"Just thought we'd say hi," Daniel said, flashing perfect teeth. "Welcome you lot to the neighborhood."

"It's a great place to live," Belinda said. "We hope you'll love it here. The school is nearby and the kids just love it.'"

"When they're not complaining about homework!" The two laughed, seeming too in-sync.

I was used to the sounds of shouted arguing from the neighbors at our old unit, so I had no idea what other kinds of normal looked like. Our old place was a small block of about twelve units, all compact and built of yellow brick from the 1970s. We were right on the main road, so the yellow bricks were smeared with black from all the exhaust dust.

The only reason we'd been able to move to the Hills was because Mum got a good job with a big salary advance. She could work from home and make her own hours. It was a lot more money than her old job, so she could afford to move us to a new place. She'd always wanted to live somewhere nicer, somewhere fancy, and so here we were. No more exhaust dust for us.

"If you need anything, just pop on over," Daniel said. "We try to look after each other in our little area."

"We know our little area can seem a little intimidating at first," Belinda said. "But really everyone's very nice. Don't let the size of the houses fool you! We're all really down to earth."

"There's a Church barbecue every other weekend," he said, but then stopped himself. "Well, I know you lot don't go in for Church, but you'd be welcome all the same."

"All God's creatures," she said, smiling with all her shiny teeth.

Adelaide was known as the City of Churches because of early residents' attitudes towards religious freedom and tolerance. Although nowadays, and probably even back then, it's pretty white and Christian. We had the white part down—at least, as far as anyone could tell—but definitely not the Christian part. Mum is Ashkenazi Jewish—or, as she liked to joke, "potato Jewish"—and

Dad was Iraqi Muslim. He died not long ago. I don't like to talk about that.

We'd always lived around lots of Buddhists and Muslims and Jews and other sorts. We had a few Mexican Catholics living next to us once, but they didn't speak much English and we didn't speak any Spanish. They left after only a couple of months anyway. This was our first time living in an area that seemed to be overwhelmingly and actively Christian.

"Feel free to wear your little hats if it would make you feel more comfortable," Daniel said. "I don't know what they're called."

"Oh, they're so darling, those little hats," Belinda said. "And those side-curls, whatever they're called. So cute."

My mum thanked them and said she would think about it, but right now we had to start unpacking and setting up the house. The neighbors smiled and nodded and said goodbye and God bless us and went away.

"Yikes," Mum said when she'd closed the door. "I think we're about to be invited as the token Jews to a lot of stuff."

I laughed. Mum was really funny. Even after Dad died, she stayed funny. A lot of it was probably just for me, but I knew she liked to laugh her way through troubles anyway. We made each other laugh.

"They were kinda weird, right?" I said.

"Yeah," Mum agreed, heading into the kitchen to continue making lunch. "But they were just being neighborly. Trying their best to, anyway."

"It's really different from Kilburn," I said.

"It is," she said. "But different isn't bad. Just something to get used to."

We sat on the living room floor—we hadn't unpacked everything from our rented moving van yet—and ate sandwiches. The bamboo floorboards were nice. I'd never seen that kind of thing before.

"Why don't we go to one of those barbecues?" Mum asked, staring out the big window.

"At the church?" I asked. We'd never been to church. I'd been to Temple with Mum a few times—just the High Holy Days and a few bar mitzvahs and weddings—and to the Mosque with Dad a bunch. I'd only ever been inside a church twice in my life: once when I was in primary school and we had scripture classes, all the Jews—all two of us—were in "non-scripture" but at the end of the year, we still had to go to the big Catholic mass; and the other time was for my classmate's granddad's funeral. It was a Greek Orthodox affair.

"It could be fun," Mum said. "Eat a few sausages, meet some new people."

"Sing a few hymns," I said.

We laughed.

"Seriously though," she said. "You'll be at a new school—a grammar school—and it might be good to meet some people beforehand. Don't you think?"

I shrugged. "Sure," I said. "I don't mind."

Mum smiled. She looked like she had more to say, but then didn't. She had a lot going on and she was doing her best. I was just glad she seemed happier than she had in a long time.

It turned out there was a church barbecue that weekend. Daniel and Belinda were sure to let us know about it. They would be going, along with their kids, and it would be a good time to chat with people from the neighborhood. Lots of the kids I'd be going to school with would be there.

"I might even bring my little hat," I said, smiling.

Mum shot me a look, but smiled and said we would be there.

"Don't be mean," she said, when she was getting us ready. 'These people don't really know anything about us, or anything outside of their bubble it looks like."

"I know," I said. "But man, how hard is it to learn the word yarmulke? Or kippah?"

"It's not," she said, laughing. "But they probably never even thought they'd have to. Their whole lives are just church barbecues and, uh," she paused for a moment, "well, other stuff, I'm sure."

I grabbed my yarmulke—I wasn't going to wear it, I just wanted to have it on me in case one of them asked about it—and we headed off. The church was a little red brick building with no pomp or circumstance about it. There had been a little modernist extension added on sometime in the last decade or so. A little sign out the front read, "Glenalta Baptist Church."

"Baptists?" Mum said. "Huh. These guys had Presbyterian or Episcopalian written all over them."

The interior hadn't been updated since the 1980s—lots of powder blues and beiges. We had to go through the main hall to reach the back where we could hear the sounds of people chatting and kids playing.

"Here we go, into the breach," I said.

"It'll be fine," Mum said. "Remember to use some of your Jew magic on them."

"I've got my tiny hat. Nothing can stop me now," I said.

Out the back, Belinda and Daniel immediately greeted us and introduced us to the minister. He was an older man, bald on top, with a ruddy face and skin cancer removal scars on his nose, cheeks and forehead. He said his name was Luke.

"Welcome," he said. "We welcome all sorts here. No one is turned away."

"We didn't burst into flames when we walked through the door," Mum joked. "So, everything must be okay!"

There was a beat before everyone laughed. The laugh felt real, but also rehearsed. it's hard to explain.

"Oh, it's true what they say," Minister Luke said. "Jews are funny!"

Another round of chuckles, but Mum and I just kept silent smiles on our faces. Our eyes met and she seemed to be saying, "They don't know any better."

Riley and Tamara approached to greet me. There was a certain wariness in their movements, but they invited me over to hang out with the other kids. Although I was a little older than Riley, at seventeen, I went over. It looked like all the school kids were hanging out together, regardless of age.=

"You're the first Jew we've ever met," one of them said. He had a shock of red hair.

"Happy to be of service," I said.

"I thought you guys had horns?" Red Hair said.

"I—" I started.

"He's just being a dick," Tamara said. "John is always being a dick."

"It's true," John said. "It's kind of my thing."

They didn't seem so bad. Normal kids. Normal, albeit very sheltered. None of them seemed to listen to any of the music, read any of the books or watch any of the TV shows Mum and I did. Most of them seemed to be signed up to the Christian version of Netflix and Spotify, although they sometimes looked up "taboo material" online.

"That's how we've managed to watch most of the Marvel movies," Tamara said. "We all huddle together in someone's basement and watch YouTube uploads of them."

"Wild," I said. "Well, if you want to watch, you know, actually good versions of them, you can just come over. We have a good collection of movies and are signed up to a few different streaming services."

The looks on their faces. I swear, you'd think they thought I was the Messiah.

The food was good. They'd bought special non-pork sausages because they'd heard we were coming. Mum thanked them but said we didn't keep kosher, and that it wasn't necessary to trouble themselves for next time. They looked almost disappointed. If we'd kept kosher, she said, we wouldn't have come at all, this being in a church and all. That perked them up.

The event went for most of the day and the sun had set by the time we left. On the drive home, I told Mum the other kids seemed all right.

"See?" Mum said. "I told you."

"It's weird how under a rock they live, though," I said. "It's like they don't know anything."

"Different values," Mum said. "It takes all sorts."

Mum had also gotten to know the neighbors and they seemed like nice people.

"I think we should make an effort to go a few of those barbecues, just while we're settling in," she said. "Be good to have something active to do in the community."

"Yeah," I said. "I'll still miss Lai-Foong's family get togethers, though, with those homemade sweets."

"Oh, and the roast duck," Mum said. "Well, looks like we're getting Chinese food tonight."

The only Chinese place in the area was, in a word, terrible. Everything was thick and sweet and gluggy. Nothing had any spice to it, even the ones marked with multiple chili peppers on the menu.

"Okay," Mum said. "I guess we'll order Chinese from a little further afield than this."

"Please," I said.

The next day, there was another knock on the door. It was Daniel and Belinda again.

Hi," Mum said. "What's up?"

"Well, it's just a small thing," Daniel said.

"Itty-bitty," Belinda said.

"Our kids—and some of the others' kids, for that matter—told us your son had invited them around to watch movies if they wanted to," Daniel said.

"Uh-huh?" Mum said.

"Well, we keep a tight lid on things around here," Daniel said. "In our little area."

"For their benefit," Belinda said. "You know."

"Okay."

"Well, it's just that," Belinda looked from Daniel to Mum.

"What Belle is trying to say," Daniel said, "is we'd appreciate it if you, well, if you'd be open to perhaps keeping our kids away from all that sort of taboo material."

"Oh," Mum said, leaning against the door jamb. "Like not letting them watch films where the rating isn't suitable? G and PG only, that kind of thing?"

"Ideally," Daniel continued, "not even PG. We're trying to bring the kids up right."

"We all are here," Belinda said. "You know, everyone doing the best they can."

"Of course," Mum said. "I get that."

"Right," Daniel said. "So, nothing PG."

"I'll do my best," Mum said. "But you know how kids are. If I go to sleep, I can't control what they pull out of the movie collection or bring up on streaming."

"You could parental lock the system?" Daniel said.

"Or better yet," Belinda said. "Unsubscribe."

The three adults looked at each other and then Mum laughed. "Don't tempt me, I've thought about it."

"Kids need more time outside anyway," Belinda said. "And we can give you the details for a good, wholesome streaming service."

"I appreciate that," Mum said. "But I think we're okay. And I'll pass on the message that he's only to watch G-Rated stuff with your kids. But kids will be kids, you know?"

There was an awkward pause between them.

"Right," Daniel said. "Okay."

"Our kids are good kids," Belinda said. The look on her face was like she hadn't meant to speak.

"They are," Mum said. "But you must remember what it was like when you were kids. Getting into your parents' stuff, watching stuff you weren't meant to, all that."

"We're all just trying to look out for each other," Daniel said. "That's all."

He put his hand on Belinda's shoulder. She cast her eyes to the floor.

"Right," Mum said. "Well, if you'll excuse me, I've got to make lunch."

The two left and Mum closed the door. She met my eyes and performed a big, exaggerated sigh.

"Well, that was weird," Mum said.

"It takes all sorts?" I said, waggling my eyebrows at her.

"City of Churches," Mum said. "Let's put a little distance between us and that, hey?"

"Read my mind."

The next day, during recess, I was sitting with Tamara and John on the steps to one of the demountable classrooms.

"Don't worry about them," Tamara said, gesturing at some kids giving me the side-eye at school. Although she was younger than both John and I—it turned out John was my age and in most of my classes—she hung out with us a lot. "They just get all their thoughts from their parents. People talk around here."

"I'd noticed," I said.

The allure of watching 4K non-Christian films had kept John and Tamara, and by extension Riley, by my side. they'd heard their parents talking about their little visit to my place and I had confirmed it.

"Haven't other people moved here who weren't as, ah, conservative as everyone else?" I asked.

"A few," John said.

"What happened to them?"

"They don't," John started and then went quiet.

"They don't live in the neighborhood anymore," Tamara said.

They came over for movie nights. Although Mum tried her best to exclude the more extreme of our movie tastes, stuff the neighbors really wouldn't have wanted their kids to see, she couldn't catch us every time. They practically begged me to show them something exciting.

"Come on, man," John said. "Literally anything that isn't fluffy animals being best friends."

"Something better than Marvel," Tamara said. "I wanna see a blood splatter!"

We stayed up late and I showed them their first ever MA15+ movie. They loved it because of course they did. Riley would come along too, sometimes. Thirteen is just too young to really hang out and be friends, though.

One night, Tamara and John were over and I was about to show them 300. I didn't tell Mum that's what we were watching, but it was late and she was asleep. She called going to be before we did giving herself "plausible deniability."

That's when we heard a crash from downstairs. Mum and I met at the top of the stairs and descended slowly, not sure what to expect. John and Tamara stood by the railing and watched us, faces white with fear. A brick lay on the floor amongst shattered glass. There was a dent in the bamboo floorboards.

Another crash exploded behind us.

The door swung open and people in black fatigues and masks entered. They grabbed us and wrenched black bags over our heads. My mum screamed. As we were being dragged outside, I could have sworn I heard Tamara say, "That's a shame."

WHEN THE BAG WAS REMOVED, I was alone. The room was dark. A single light shone down on me from above. Tight bindings secured me to a hard chair. Someone behind me shifted into my field of view. A sinking feeling filled my stomach. I wanted to both cry and scream, but I found I couldn't do either.

The man crouched before me, placing his hand on my arm. Light fell across his face.

"Hello there, son," Minister Luke said, sounding almost sad.

"What's going on?" I yelled, struggling. "Where's my mum?"

"She's in another room," he said. "Getting a talking to by my associate, Brother Daniel."

"What the hell is going on?"

"Now, now," he said. "Don't go invoking Hell so lightly. It's all too real and you'll end up there if you don't change your ways."

"What are you talking about?"

"Your ways are not our ways," he said. "And you'll repent, or you'll die."

My blood turned to ice in my veins.

"You see, child," he continued. "We try to keep this neighborhood nice and clean and proper. We're just trying to be neighborly. It's what's best for you."

There was an echo at the back of my mind of Mum saying the Harrisons were just being neighborly, that everyone was trying their best.

"Let me go," I said. "Let me go!"

"If you take the Lord Jesus Christ into your heart," Minister Luke said, "you'll be free to go. As will your mother if she does the same."

"You can't do this," I said. "You can't!"

"We can," he said. "It's what our little area has always been about. Little Riley turned you in, like a good boy should, for what you've been showing to those poor other kids. Trying to drag innocents down and damn them with you. That Riley, he's a good boy, a real soldier of God."

"What?"

"If you refuse to be saved," he said. "We'll ensure you don't live in this neighborhood anymore."

I don't need to go over what happened in that room. They're blurry memories now, for the most part. The only thing you need to know is that I came out of that room and still live in the neighborhood. It's a nice neighborhood. We keep it clean. Our little area. Years have gone by, and I do my fair share of hosting backyard barbecues for church fundraisers.

There are some patched-over screw holes on our door frame where the mezuzah used to be. And my mother? Well, we just say she doesn't live in the neighborhood anymore.

THE GEESE OF BRONSON BOULEVARD

TYLER JOHN KASISHKE

You skip down Bronson Boulevard's wide, paved road. Hand in hand with Charlotte, your bellies bloated and full, you cackle and honk, projecting your presence, your satisfaction, to the entire neighborhood as you approach the final house of the night.

Every home on Bronson Boulevard is immaculate and sprawling, each one a mini-mansion perched upon a hill overlooking the road, carefully positioned at the center of a two-acre lot. Some owners have cleared the wooded lots—putting in pools and tennis courts—while others have kept theirs untouched, electing for the feeling of seclusion and tranquility.

It's an ideal summer night: sky clear and speckled, breeze light and cool, cicadas and crickets orchestrating a wonderful tune to your weekly outing with Charlotte.

Rich, blackened mush drips from your orange beak. Crumbs and splotches of ganache trail down your white feathered neck, down your checked tweed suit—along your suit's arms and spotting both pant legs. In your free hand, you hold the previous home's offering: a generous piece of chocolate cake, moist and layered with raspberry filling.

And though the fine offering makes your mouth water, you fear it will not be you who will enjoy this delectable delight tonight.

Bronson Boulevard is the safest neighborhood in Newbridge County. The number of 911 calls made each year can be counted on one hand, the number of crimes committed even fewer. Most residents haven't lived here long enough to recall the last violent crime that took place many, many years ago. And those who have been around that long are growing old, their memories fogged and fading.

You remember it all too well.

And though you can't say how many times it has come to that, the number far too high to track—you were here long before the streets were paved and this land was called Bronson Boulevard—you remember every single one.

The land has been manipulated over the years, yes—many times built upon, then torn down, then built upon again—but the people who reside here haven't changed a bit. They flock to this land. They're the kind of people who spare no expense for themselves. They think they've worked hard for their money, are entitled to every penny, and so think they can spend it however they want. And they can... with one exception.

The last home on Bronson Boulevard rests where the street ends: a quaint cul-de-sac nestled against a mature wood. As you approach the steep driveway, you crane your long, hooked neck to get a look at the doormat. You find it barren, and your mood sours. You feel a hiss crawling up your throat, but hold back the fury.

Get a closer look. Better be sure.

Bronson Boulevard is in the Portstown School District where the test scores are highest in the state, and the baseball, football, and soccer teams make deep playoff runs year after year. Graduates are well prepped for, and always get accepted into, respected universities about which their parents can boast to their friends.

The neighborhood is equidistant from the country and the city. It's a short ride to apple picking in fall and blueberry picking in summer. Just a jaunt to the ice rink in winter and botanical gardens in spring.

But there's a cost to living on Bronson Boulevard. There's a cost to peace of mind, prestige, and convenience. There's a cost to luxury.

And though the cost isn't much—what you're asking for *isn't* much, has *never been* much—grave penalties await those who fail to comply.

They've called you many things through the centuries: gods, spirits, demons, angels. Each name fit in some respects and not in others. Once, you and Charlotte were mortals. What a different life that was—one of luxury and greed. The details are hazy, but you and Charlotte weren't much different from the residents of Bronson Boulevard back then—that is, until that fateful night when the common folk stormed your manor. With the thrill and anxiety and rancor of revolution in the air, you were both swept up in the night's festivities. Stolen from your home, you were tarred and feathered.

Then they took your heads.

At some point that night, you became you.

Now bound to these lands, you and Charlotte have always asked one thing of the privileged, the elite. To keep them in check, to keep their *greed* in check—to never let what happened to you happen again. It hasn't always been the same. It started out simple: a tithe; a percent of one's income; the simplest form of devotion, really. But that quickly became rather boring. So you moved onto finer things—gems, jewelry, heirlooms. Anything that would glimmer and sparkle in the light—anything that caught the eye. You sometimes think Charlotte misses these offerings the most. She's always had expensive taste.

Centuries passed, and somewhere down the line, you ended

up with cake. Not just any cake: chocolate cake. Money and jewels showed devotion, yes, and these were pleasing to the eye, but food gave you flavors and textures and variety. Chocotorta and Wuzetka. German Chocolate Cake. And oh, how you love a slice of Sachertorte.

And you try to be reasonable. You issue warnings. Have an escalation process. Because it's true: human memories are fickle. Distractions happen from time to time. Just last week, you gave out two warnings: one to the Dobsons and another to the Johnstons.

The Dobsons should have known better. But they're cheap. Everyone on Bronson Boulevard is cheap, really. No matter how much they have, it's never enough. And they are so wary to give.

That's where you come in.

They all fork it out for their new BMWs and Escalades, their tennis courts and swimming pools, each of their children's golf carts for cruising the neighborhood. They fork it out for their lawns, no questions asked, spraying pesticides weekly to prevent dandelions and mosquitoes. They run sprinklers daily to ensure lush, green grass. Small crews equipped with zero-turn mowers and weed whackers come out weekly to manicure lawns like golf courses.

But two neatly plated pieces of chocolate cake, once a week?

It's too much for some of them, apparently. Last week, the Dobsons's cake was surely mass produced, probably on clearance weeks past its sell-by date. The sponge was dry and crusty. The frosting, chalky. Both pieces sat on a flimsy paper plate.

You were happy to find their offering today, though: devil's food cake plated on fine china. Charlotte's favorite. The broken window, the returned cake, must have sent the message clear enough.

Cheap fucks. Just where did they think they lived?

The Johnstons, however, had just moved to the neighborhood.

Last week was week three. They got a pass in weeks one and two. But they should have known by week three.

They were certainly warned by the neighbors, probably had gone through the progressions: suspecting crazy neighbors suffering from dementia and a fairy tale, neighborhood kids inventing stories, and community-wide practical jokes.

So you smeared their windows with the Darlings's molten chocolate cake.

Sad, to waste cake on that. The Darlings really had outdone themselves. But you and Charlotte made the most of it—had fun with it, even. That hot chocolate made for perfect smearing. Front windows and back, second story and first. Don had elected not to park in his four-car garage that night, so his Audi got a nice coating as well.

As you walk the sloped driveway approaching the Johnstons's doorstep, the final stop of the night, rage—red and hot—boils over.

You let loose a loud, lingering hiss.

The doormat is empty: no plates nor cake for the fourth week in a row. You snap your head to Charlotte, your newsboy hat falling to the ground.

Large tears well in Charlotte's beady eyes. A low, hollow noise escapes her throat. Mournful. It's setting in that she, too, will not be eating the raspberry chocolate cake cupped in her right hand. The tears trail down her hooked neck and onto her matching swing dress.

Another long, drawn-out hiss slips from your throat, and you begin barking hysterically, marching toward the front door, Charlotte in tow.

You've given them grace periods, issued warnings. You can excuse, on occasion, errant memories and misplaced priorities. Even disbelief—let them see you if they must, if that's what it takes to believe.

And Don Johnston has seen you. You'd looked straight into

those stupid cameras posted around his house—like it's a fucking military compound—when you and Charlotte smeared lava cake on his windows.

But what you cannot excuse is deliberate noncompliance. Disrespect. This greed makes you hot with anger. Well, you will give them reason to comply tonight; they will never make such a foolhardy mistake again.

If they do, it will be their last.

As you approach the front door, motion-activated flood lights illuminate the concrete front porch. The impressive oak front door, stained to a burnt orange, is sandwiched between two large picture windows. You and Charlotte stand at each, looking inside the home. You both begin tapping your beaks against the panes in slow, deliberate motions.

Tap, tap, tap.

Your taps are firm, rhythmic, in unison—until you both can't control yourselves, until your pace is rapid and your force is excessive, manic. You tap until you hear commotion inside the house, lights switching on, until you can see an adult frozen in the foyer.

Then you stop, but just for a moment, just so they can see your silhouette in the window. So they can see the shape and size of your body, how similar it is to their own, how perfectly it fits those large windows. So they can see your small, oval head. So they can see your sickled neck.

After a moment—a moment to stun, to shock—you shatter the glass. Charlotte works in perfect harmony, shattering her glass pane as well.

Across the foyer stands Don Johnston: a forty-something-year-old man. He's tall—about your height—and muscular, with a receding hairline.

"Get out—Or I'll shoot."

Man's weapons have never harmed you. They never will.

Don loads slugs into the shotgun's magazine and cocks the weapon. "Mary, call the cops."

Go ahead. Call the cops, Don. Tell them a pair of geese people broke in because you didn't offer them cake. Tell them you just couldn't spare the funds or the time. You can't help but laugh a little, a hollow honk escaping your throat.

"We don't owe you anything. Everyone in this neighborhood has lost their damn mind."

Oh, Don. But you owe us everything. To live in such luxury, peace comes at a cost. And that's our job—to keep the peace. To keep you in check.

"Get the fuck out of my house," Don warns.

His voice quivers as he talks. He's never seen anything quite like you before. No one has... until they do. You are a sight to behold.

You rush the man.

Don fires, but it's useless. He begins to retreat, stymied by shock and the ineffectiveness of his trusty shotgun. You tackle him to the tiled floor.

The wife and children are screaming, the dogs whimpering and whining as Charlotte hisses at them, hunched over and ready to strike. She backs them away so you can deliver your message in terms Don will understand.

You shove one hand into Don's mouth and pry it open. You stuff the slice of cake inside, pushing it down his throat, as far as you can go. At first, he tries to pull your hands away, but then he just bucks, violently trying to dislodge you along with the cake in his esophagus. But the weight of your body is enough to keep him down, so you can honk and hiss and spit into his face—so you can stuff his throat.

Charlotte hands you her piece of cake.

Try as you might, you're only able to get a small portion of Charlotte's cake into Don's mouth—his mouth and throat are full, won't take anymore. So, you smear the remaining cake—sponge and frosting and raspberry jelly—around his face, up his nostrils, in his ears, filling in the gaps until his kicking slows, his resistance wanes.

Then you relent, get up. Hearing the man gasp for air, choking out cake, you exit through the shattered window.

Hand in hand with Charlotte once again, frosting and crumbs smeared around your beaks, covering your hands, you stroll back down Bronson Boulevard.

Next week, there will be cake—there had better be cake. Otherwise, you'll not show such restraint. There is but one cost to living here, and that is satisfying you and Charlotte, the Geese of Bronson Boulevard.

PART TWO
CITY LIFE

If Hell is other people, then the most oppressive level of hell is The City.

CREEPY CRAWLY
SAM WELLER

THE FIRST TIME I SAW IT, I HAD BEEN IN THE APARTMENT FOR about a month. I was in the kitchen washing dishes when I noticed something small, dark, and freakishly fast roto across the dirty and chipped vinyl floor. I turned quickly and gazed down. It was some sort of long, tawny-colored insect. Hairy. Like a centipede, with more than a dozen legs. I'd say it was an inch-and-a-half in length but appeared to have antennae and back legs that made it considerably longer. It freaked me out, the way it moved so fast.

I went to step on it, to squash it out of existence, but it immediately shifted direction when I came at it, like it saw me, or, to be more precise, it sensed me.

It scurried along the kitchen floorboard until it came to a tiny hole in the wall, a hole the size of a pencil eraser. It crawled in and was gone.

The next time I saw it, I was reading Dante's *Inferno* in bed, smoking a cigarette. I know, it's stupid to smoke in bed, but what can I say? Nicotine is more addictive than heroin. I come from a family with a long history of addiction. My need for a cig fix is a far cry from Mom's Oxy dependency or Dad's daily fifth of Jack.

Dragging on my smoke, inhaling deeply, I watched the insect on the wall above my dresser, near the ceiling. Maybe it wasn't the exact same creature I had seen previously in the kitchen—maybe it was just one of the same species that hid somewhere behind the plaster walls of my old, crappy Chicago apartment building. Maybe it was part of a vast syndicate of insects residing in the darkness, behind the walls, amongst the joists, the nails, the dust and insulation—only coming at night. But I had this weird feeling that it was, in fact, the very same freak of elongated nature I had first seen in my kitchen.

I dragged on my Marlboro Red and exhaled. Smoke spiraled towards the ceiling light. The elevated train passed outside, rails screeching, acrid electricity snarling, as it skirled the curve a block away. I laid there and watched the thing. It barely moved. Only its antennae twitched. Ever-so-slightly. It knew I was watching it. It was aware of me. My ex-girlfriend once said I was on the "Druid Spectrum, or something." I was in tune with nature. Who really knows? She was a user, so her judgment was slightly clouded. She dated me, after all, right?

The creepy insect stayed there on the wall for five minutes, then ten, not moving. I lit another cigarette. I decided this bug needed a name. I ran several through my mind:

Harry (too obvious).

Godzilla (too derivative).

I settled on "Dante" because of my current reading material.

Dante moved. He scampered about six inches along the wall.

I extinguished my smoke in the ashtray on my bedside table and decided I'd had enough. This thing didn't need a name.

It needed to die.

I climbed out of bed and picked up a copy of the *New Yorker* from the floor. I rolled it up like a police baton in my hand. The creature's antennae twitched a little faster. He was on to me. He knew he was being hunted. I was going to have to go full-ninja with this operation if I was going to rid my world of its filth. This thing would no longer torment my existence.

I stood in place, in my boxer shorts and Motorhead t-shirt, and waited. No movement, full Zen. The insect didn't budge either. He could play the Zen game, too, apparently. This was a staring contest I wasn't going to lose. Minutes ticked by. I was Chuck Norris, Ralph Macchio, David Carradine. It was a total bad-ass Buddhist-warrior, Jedi Knight, Avatar-state moment.

I took a barely perceptible step closer.

Antennae twitched again.

I took another step. Slowly. Pausing. Barely breathing.

Another step towards the wall and the beast. I stood now just feet away from being positioned to swat this thing out of existence.

Another step. He moved a few inches along the wall. He knew I was there, edging ever closer. I tightened my grip on the rolled-up magazine. I was only going to have one shot. This was my moment.

I breathed gently out of my nostrils. Focused. Closed my eyes. Visualized the thing on the wall.

My eyes serpented open, and then, I made my move.

Wham!

I swatted the rolled-up *New Yorker* against the wall like an angry cop's billy club.

The hairy beast was hit. Stunned. But this had not been a direct strike. My Chuck Norris moment was incomplete. I had failed. The thing dropped from the wall, flailing to the floor. He quickly regained his faculties and bee-lined along the dirty white baseboard. He was damned fast. I tried to squash him with my bare foot but missed. The insect found its tiny, pencil-eraser sized hole in the floorboard, darted inside, and was gone.

I didn't see Dante for two weeks. I began to wonder if maybe my magazine strike had injured him and the creature had gone into its hole in the wall and died a slow, grueling, miserable death.

In bed one night, I awoke and reached for the glass of water on my nightstand. As I sat up to take a drink, I was instantly aware that something was wrong. Something was in my mouthful of water, thrashing about my gums. I quickly spit the liquid back into the glass.

There was Dante. Floating in the water.

He had likely been perched on the lip of my water glass and when I drank from it, he washed into my mouth. He probably flossed my teeth with his legs while he was in there, the bastard. After spitting the water back into the glass, he was floating about, and, amazingly, desperately crawled up the side, and literally leaped away onto my nightstand, down the wall and was gone.

I had almost ingested Dante. He had been in my mouth. The thought disgusted me. It was revolting. It angered me, too. I was hereby one hundred percent convinced that this tawny, hairy, specimen of insect grotesquery and all-out evil was out to get me.

Shortly after that, one evening after my shift at the local record shop, I was down in the basement of my building doing laundry. The basement of my apartment is dimly lit, a single 60-watt bulb on the ceiling with a pull chain, like some secret interrogation room in the catacombs of deepest Moscow. The basement is unfinished, musty, with two coin-operated washers and dryers for tenants. There was a large, stiff pair of men's size 44 tighty-whiteys on one of the dryers that had been there since I moved in.

As I poured liquid detergent into the washer, I felt a presence. Dante.

Sure enough, there, sitting in a basement window alcove, that fucking insect was watching me. That fucking twitcher. He had grown, too, he was now bigger. How is that even possible?

"I'm going to kill you soon, you know that, right, Dante? Are you ready to die?" I said, calmly.

He just sat there, decidedly unafraid. Unfazed.

"I'm going to trap you under a glass and find a way to burn you with my cigarette lighter. Slowly. End to fucking end, you Goddamned nuisance. You fucking tormenter."

Antennae flickered.

I put quarters in the washing machine. Pushed the coin mechanism in. Ran my laundry and quietly went upstairs to my apartment. Now was not the time for death. Nope. That would have to wait until just the right moment.

More weeks passed. No sightings of the beast.

At night, I had trouble sleeping. I was anxious. Waiting for Dante. Worried he might crawl out and onto me while I slept. I would have taken some Xanax, but I wanted to be alert for his arrival. I regularly stayed up and waited like a sentry. Night after night. Keeping vigil for the arrival of the thing.

One night while sitting up in bed, I looked up "centipedes" on my phone and found Dante's class.

"Ciliophora."

There were more than 3,000 different types of these fuckers. Dante was a "House Centipede," lauded for actually hunting other insects like roaches, moths, and spiders. Science said they served a predatory purpose. I was part of that purpose. Dante simply saw me as just another hunt.

To prove the point. One night, I finally fell asleep (reading horrible *New Yorker* fiction is better than a couple Zambian tabs, let me tell you).

I awoke to a feeling. Something on my forehead.

I bolted upright. Sure enough, there he was. When I shot up, he fell from my face, on to the bed, and sprinted like Jesse fucking Owens across the comforter, down the side of the bed and into his little hole in the wall.

I had a weird existential realization at this moment. We both lived in a hole-in-the-wall. And if you really look at it, in one way or another, don't we all?

"I'm going to kill you, Dante," I said. I was now speaking aloud to a centipede. My life was utterly fucked. I was utterly fucked.

Normalcy. That's what I needed. Normalcy. I met a woman at a coffee shop who was cool. She had multiple piercings on her face and pink cotton candy colored hair. She was named Callisto, after one of the moons of Jupiter. I invited her to my place. We ordered Chinese carry-out and watched a movie.

Sitting on the sofa, I looked over at her for a moment and was mortified.

There was Dante crawling through Callisto's pink hair.

She quickly sensed the thing, noticed it, stood up, spilled her wine all over the floor, and screamed.

"What the fuck?!" she said flicking at her hair. The insect dropped to the floor and ran off.

"That's Dante," I said.

She glared at me. "You have a name for that thing!?"

"He fucks with me often," I said.

She continued to glare in silence, then, finally: "You're sick." She grabbed her phone and her purse and marched out the door.

End of date.

Foiled by Dante.

That was it. The war had to end. I had to go Hiroshima on this creepy crawly creature from the seventh ring of hell.

I shot some mega-toxic bug spray into the little hole in the wall. All along the floorboards. I dispensed the entire damned can.

I decided to wait up most nights, catching sleep in fits and starts. I was feeling agitated, sleep deprived, but also focused.

One night, as the elevated train screeched by outside, I was in bed, sitting up, waiting... waiting... waiting.

And there he was. Dante. Longer than ever. Tawny. Twitching. He had emerged from his fumigated hole in the wall, still alive. He was there on the floor, facing me, undeterred.

I swung my legs from my bed. We stood six feet apart, Dante.

and me, facing one another. Both waiting to make a move, an old west gunfight.

Slowly, I went into the *Karate Kid* "crane pose," standing on my right foot, left foot raised from the floor, arms umbrellaed above me.

Breathe. Slowly. In. Out. Breathe. In. Out. Heartbeat slowing. Mindfulness.

And then I acted. I sprang at Dante. Catapulting off my right foot, up and across the six-foot expanse, arching upward, upward, then, reaching the zenith, coming down, down a slow-motion death pounce, Dante contemplating his move. I came down towards the centipede. He twitched right, now left, but I adjusted, mid-air. Descending ever downward, my right foot landing firmly on the hardwood floor, like Neil fucking Armstrong's moon boot in lunar dust. I landed on Dante.

I ground my barefoot into the wood for good measure, like I was extinguishing a cigarette. I could feel Dante's lifeless mass, first in its death throes, then, suddenly, immobile, stuck underneath the sole of my callused foot.

Slowly, hesitantly, still unconvinced he was gone, I lifted my foot, held my ankle in my hand, and upturned it to look. There he was. On the ball of my foot. Squashed. Flattened like interstate road kill. Fully eliminated from the universe. Destroyed. Annihilated. Gone. Forever.

Goodbye, twitcher.

Dante was dead.

I went to bed that night and slept more soundly than I had in months, my mattress and pillow suddenly all baby's breath, cumulus cloud, mounds of Jet-Puff Marshmallow.

As I slept, and I wouldn't realize this until it was far too late, a stream of dozens—maybe hundreds—of House Centipedes armied out from the little hole in the floorboard. Coming for me.

THE SCREAM
MELISSA BOBE

THE TRANSFORMATION SURPRISED HER. IT WASN'T SO MUCH the change that was unexpected as its occurrence on an unremarkable Tuesday in August. She would have thought a becoming might fall on a more dramatic date. But what did she know about the dramatic, really? Before the change, she'd been just like everybody else.

She'd descended into the station, thinking (as she had the first time she'd been there, and every time since) that it felt like a descent into some dead poet's hell: Dante or Homer, but less classical, more modern-day budget-film dystopic. The station was hot, strangely dark in the way of stone rooms lit by fluorescent bulbs, with a shadowed glare chipping away at the mind, humming mechanically so as to be an undetectable, droning erosion.

And then there were people. It was not noisy; it was mundanely busy, that quality that leaves one unaware of constant bustle, of aural chaos. Such places become soundless in their sheer excess of sound. Bodies perpetually moving on all sides and wherever she looked, such that her vision blurred and she saw nothing just as she heard nothing, excess eliminating detail. And there were too many people.

As she stepped into the main hall of the concourse, she was flooded on all sides by stoic faces pouring from where she wanted to go and parts elsewhere. They spoke not at all because words hinder haste, but they existed as a cacophony: of footfalls, of the brushing of bodies zipping past and lightly sliding against one another, of the swish of thighs grazing and sticking in the crush of sweat accumulated in a warm, overcrowded train. Those who lived by and set the pace of the city comprised the first wave, but they were not the only bodies competing for existence.

Those awaiting a longer road home shuffled erratically, seeking direction to escape the city. Unaccustomed to the constant, hurried flow, they became a hindrance, the ilk of which one might encounter in tourist traps and theme parks: bodies unpredictable and deadly in their slow, confused progression, so many jellyfish forming a lethargic horde uniform only in its arbitrariness.

And there were too many people.

The scream started slowly in her abdomen. It gestated, growing in detail and definition before deciding to emerge, mature and ready to separate from its parent body. She felt her mouth open, felt the jaws that cradled it stretch, crack, unhinge. She would have wondered at the lack of pain, but before she could, her body seemed to fold in on itself. It was as though she'd been gutted, all the unneeded organs sucked away, leaving only what was necessary to birth her atonally extended offspring: lungs, lips, throat, diaphragm. The scream seemed to drain all blood and pulsing motivation from her limbs. She was rooted to where she'd stopped in her tracks (unfathomable!), the most grievous act one could commit in such an endlessly buzzing hive. Her gaze lifted within her bloodless countenance to rest on that dull stone ceiling; she felt the cool white infinity of bulbs erasing all else from her vision. She released the demon born of a claustrophobic, inexplicable rage she'd never known she'd harbored.

A child tugged at his elder sister's hand.

"Just ignore it," she said as they continued down the corridor. When the little one gave her another tug, she sighed. "That's what you become when you can't anymore."

THE CUSTOMER IS ALWAYS WRONG

TIFFANY MICHELLE BROWN

"This toast is cold," the man in the bowtie says.

It's been all of thirty seconds since you plucked the bread from the industrial toaster and delivered the order to Table 9. You watch a pat of butter slide across one of the craggy slices of rye. If you reach out and stick a finger in the bread, you'd feel its warmth.

But you can't do that. It would be a health code violation. And when the man complains, Deb will reprimand you. You've been trained to defer to the customer, and you'll do just that.

You plaster on your work smile, genial and accommodating. "I'm so sorry. Let me take care of that for you."

The man holds up his hands as you reach for the dish. His cufflinks wink in the brash, artificial lighting. He's overdressed for a late breakfast in a cheap diner. "I'd like it remade, please."

"Of course. I promise I'll get you new slices of rye. Fresh and toasty." You'll squirrel away the sent-back bread in the waitstaff cubby, eat it cold during the lull between lunch and dinner so it doesn't go to waste.

"No," the man says, his voice quiet, water over stone. A small smile dances across his lips. "I'd like the kitchen to remake the whole dish."

"But the toast is on the side," you say reflexively.

Shit. Deb is liable to double your prep work if she hears you talking to a customer like that. You know she's tucked away in her office working on financial reports, but you sneak a glance around the dining room anyway. Blessedly, she's nowhere to be seen.

Regardless, you need to change tack. You lacquer your tongue with honey. "Is there something wrong with the chilaquiles?"

You know the answer to this, because Roy is working today, and the man is a bona fide magician in the kitchen. The tortilla chips are fried to perfection, topped with a vibrant rojo salsa, fresh cilantro, cotija cheese, and two sunny-side-up eggs, their yolks ready to burst at the mere suggestion of a fork tine.

The rye toast the man ordered—on the side—sits on a separate plate. The butter has dribbled off the bread and pools on the white china, a sad puddle of oil and separated milk solids.

"They won't be warm by the time you get back," the man says with the tiniest shrug of his shoulders. His demeanor remains calm, unbothered. "I want to enjoy everything together."

You wait for him to tell you he's joking. Any second now, he'll plunge a fork into the egg yolks and paint his lips yellow.

The moment never comes. You simply stare at each other, a standoff you're designed to lose.

"Sure," you say, drawing out the word as if you're drunk. You stare intently at a sprinkle of cotija cheese as you collect the plates from the table, unable to meet the man's gaze. You've done nothing wrong, yet embarrassment flares in you like a falling star.

You deposit the untouched chilaquiles in the employee cubby. It's not what you'd planned on eating during your break, but you don't have the heart to toss it.

You print a new order ticket and send it around the metal

carousel to Roy, power-walking away before he can ask you about the repeat order. His memory is impeccable. He'll know the chilaquiles were sent back, and you don't have the energy both to console him and placate the customer. You need to regain control of the situation in the dining room. You'll make it right and move on.

Ice tumbles into a clean pitcher, and you fill it to the top with water. You count to thirty, give the vessel a stir to disperse the chill, and then head back into the dining room.

Your timing is spot on. The man's glass is half empty. You sidle over and ask if he'd like a refill.

The man finds your eyes and smiles. It's genuine. Appreciative. "Thank you."

"My pleasure." You don't spill a drop and offer him a toothy grin. You're good at this. He'll see.

You have a plan: anticipate his needs, give him attention, and make it personal. You hope excellent service will warm him to you. A customer is less likely to send food back if they like their server, right?

You return to the back to grab a bite of the discarded chilaquiles. The once picture-perfect eggs are cold and congealed. The tortilla chips are a little too soggy now, so the texture of the dish is off, but it tastes great. You chew, swallow, and wash your hands.

Roy is at the flat top, cracking eggs. It's time for toast. You watch the bread trundle through the conveyer, the coils flaring red like brake lights. These slices need to be just right—not too blond, not burnt. The bread is the optimal shade of brown when it emerges. You immediately put the slices on a plate and under the warmer. They will not get cold.

"Order up!" You burn your fingertips snatching the plates out of the pickup window, but you're so focused you barely feel the pain. You motor into the dining room, a green tray hoisted proudly on your shoulder. The man is waiting patiently, his hands clasped and resting on the tabletop.

"Here you go!" You serve him quickly. Steam curls up from both plates. There's no way he can claim the dish is anything but piping hot.

The man looks down at his meal. He smiles, and his eyes crinkle.

You did it! He's pleased. Another happy custom—

"These eggs aren't sunny-side-up."

The statement is a cold animal burrowing into your stomach and dying. You're suddenly freezing despite the ancient heater pumping stale, warm air throughout the diner.

You scan the plate, worried that Roy accidentally placed an order of over-hard eggs on top, and in your haste, you didn't catch the error. But the whites are slick and shiny. The yolks quiver, ready to succumb to any type of pressure. You've never seen a more immaculate serving of chilaquiles. Roy did everything in his power to make sure this plate wouldn't be sent back.

And yet, that's exactly what this man wants.

He's looking at you, expectant, and you realize you've misjudged him. Goddamn, you were so very wrong. Distracted by the bowtie and the show of false propriety, perhaps.

You're used to placating people who regularly overstep boundaries and take advantage of the customer-server power dynamic. Church groups that reek of faux-righteousness and demand the world of you, only to leave the paltriest of tips. Men who ask you if you're a single mother after ordering a Coke, like it's a perfectly normal question to pose to a stranger. Diners who don't contest any aspect of their meal until the bill has arrived, shamelessly seeking discounts at the eleventh hour. Even the guy Deb kicked out for masturbating in the booth in the corner was better than this, because his intentions were at least obvious, albeit disgusting.

This man, in his carefully pressed suit and bowtie, had seemed harmless. But he's not. He's a liar grinning at you as if you should be grinning, too. You've unwittingly entered an insidious game of chicken. He's not going to ask for what he wants. He expects you to offer it. The unspoken presumption crackles in the air between you with the fervent energy of an active power line.

You want to draw a mustache on the man in ketchup, something with exaggerated curlicues. Facial hair befitting a villain, because that's what he is. A slippery, seemingly well-mannered villain.

Your gut clenches and releases. Your silence is unprofessional, but you're afraid you'll word-vomit if you speak too soon. Adrenaline makes your heart thrum, so you have to concentrate and perform some throat gymnastics to keep your voice from becoming shrill. "Would you like us to make this for you again?"

"Yes, please." His eyes suddenly look small and beady. Snake eyes. "I'm in no rush."

And you know he isn't lying. Not now. He'll stay here all day toying with you, if you let him. Asshole.

The plates are anvils, and you struggle to lift them from the table. All the while, you're aware of the man's smile proudly displayed mere inches away from your own face. You hold your breath, not wanting to breathe the same air as him.

You need reinforcements. You go straight to Deb's office and knock. She takes one look at you clutching a plate of chilaquiles, seething, and invites you in. You try to keep your explanation as devoid of emotion as possible, but your voice is scratchy and breaks a couple of times. This is in no way, shape, or form Roy's fault, you explain. He's provided delicious food, and you've done everything you could as a server. It's the customer. What should you do?

Deb stands and straightens her blouse. "I believe you, but let's try this again, shall we? I'll assist and make sure this customer leaves happy." It's not the response you were hoping for—you wanted her to kick him out—but Deb clearly has her democratic manager hat on. Honestly, you'll take whatever help you can get.

Per Deb's request, you submit a new ticket. You give Roy an I'm-sorry-dude expression as you pass the slip of paper to him through the service window. Deb watches the line cook as he prepares the chilaquiles for a third time. She never interferes or asks him to remake something, and you aren't the least bit surprised, because again, Roy is good at his job. It's the asshat in the dining room who's screwing everything up.

Deb toasts the rye herself, and you don't mind one bit. You want your manager to have every ounce of ammo possible. She's in this with you now, thank God.

When the order's up, Deb loads a clean tray and nods. You've discussed this. You'll deliver the food to maintain a consistent customer experience. She wants it to appear normal, like you're willing to do whatever you can to make him happy. It's cringe-worthy at best, but you're complying, because what else can you do?

When you exit the kitchen, the dining room has transformed into a stage. You're the timid ingénue, framed by light, expected to act and speak and move through the world in a choreographed way. You put your work smile on, but it feels crooked. Your legs tremble. Somehow, you make it to the table.

Deb is only a booth away, observing. With a practiced hand, you set down the plates.

"Third time's the charm," you say, a little too brightly.

The man makes you wait. He looks at you, his weasel-like smile as casual as ever. The crinkles by his eyes seem darker now, deep chasms you could easily fall into. You imagine fire and brim-stone and the smell of sulfur.

He licks his lips. "These chips are stale."

His words set off something inside you. It scrabbles against your stomach lining, aching to be released. You feel it throttling up your throat, its merciless claws puncturing your larynx, and yet... there is no pain. Only sweet adrenaline and this intense desire to act. You realize that cold animal you left for dead in your belly has roared back to life. And she's angry.

She lurches forward and crawls over the tabletop, nails scratching against Formica. Spittle flies from her lips. A bottle of ketchup feels like a bomb in her paw. She tears open the cap with her teeth, assumes a predatory stance, and squeezes. A stream of sugar-laced tomato sauce rips through the air and hits the man squarely in the face.

He doesn't flinch. He continues to smile, even as the assault continues and he is drenched in red.

When the bottle is empty, you collapse onto your hands and knees atop the table, gasping. You're aware of Deb yelling, but you can't make out her words. You don't care what she's saying anyway. You only care about him. About his reaction.

The man's white bowtie is slathered in red goo. Some of the ketchup found its way into his mouth, so it looks like his gums are bleeding.

He's still smiling that fucking smile. He wipes a dab of ketchup off the shoulder of his ruined suit and slides it into his mouth. He picks up the discarded condiment bottle and studies the label. He levels his gaze at you.

"This ketchup isn't organic."

IF I GO MISSING
SUMMER ALEXIS

PATTY OPENED THE BINDER AND STARTED ON HER NEW project.

HOW TO GO MISSING: A Plan in 4 Steps
   Objective: become an object of desire

- Step One: research common factors in
  disappearances of women like me.
- Step Two: replicate as many factors as
  possible.
- Step Thee: inebriation.
- Step Four: do not resist.

SHE FELT PRETTY good about her plan. Patty meant to do everything her parents and the policemen who visited her school always told you not to do. She would wear revealing outfits, drink too much, and leave her drink where someone could put something in it. Patty wanted to become wanted, as she hadn't felt something like desire directed toward her since high school when men would catcall from moving cars. She'd never admit it for fear of being viewed as unfeminist, but she missed that attention. Those stares scared her, but they also made her feel seen.

Patty knew when the moment came she'd welcome it with open arms.

In the bar that night, Patty drank her fourth or fifth alcoholic cider and scanned the room. She'd been on this mission for weeks, but she'd had no luck so far. It was becoming frustrating. She took so much time to consider her location, her outfit, and what she had told Jack.

Patty needed to be wanted and missed and cared about. She wanted to go missing.

She didn't want to run away from her life. She lived a good life with a loving husband and cute kids who only annoyed her half of the time. But she'd grown bored.

On the news she'd seen the faces of beautiful women who'd gone missing—women with more handsome husbands and cuter kids. The husband of such a woman would cry and tell everyone everywhere how their wife lit up a room and what a doting mother she was and how she was his soulmate.

Patty wished for that kind of love from Jack but suspected she'd need to do something extreme to get it. She didn't want to die and had no desire to hurt herself, her family, or to leave her husband. She wanted to be important.

Patty was one of dozens of mothers and wives in the suburbs who all looked similar in light-blue denim jeans and flowing blouses. They all read similar magazines on how to look younger than their already young average of thirty-one years, and they all absorbed fashion tips and made their way to the local strip mall where they bought identical clothing from the same store. Patty's chemically lightened hair fell to the middle of her back, and she spent mornings heating up the flat iron and then the curling iron, the first to straighten it and the second to give her hair slightly lopsided waves in her naturally wavy (but not wavy in the way she wanted) hair.

Of medium height and slightly lower-than-average weight, Patty intended to keep herself as average as possible. She enjoyed fitting in and being one of a hundred in their neighborhood. She and Jack had been high school sweethearts, and she became pregnant a month after graduation. They married, and she gave birth to their twins prematurely. Jack had gone on to work for his father's construction company, which paid well for minimum effort. Patty had thus never needed to work. Her parents raised her to be a housewife and a mother to one girl and one boy, and that's what she did. She never aspired to anything more or less than just what she'd become.

That is, until news started spreading that an uncharacteristically high number of women fitting the neighborhood mold—one Patty matched—were going missing. Whether it was due to the tendency of news agencies to focus on women from her neighborhood who looked like her or because Patty sought out these other women's stories, she didn't know.

With the increased circulation of rumors grew the suspicion that if women just like her were disappearing from bars and sidewalks, she might be desirable to someone out there, too. Patty had the sense this possibility should frighten her, but it did not.

It wasn't that she wanted to be stalked and killed, but she couldn't imagine how much someone would have to want someone else to stalk them and kill them. While she never felt undesired by her husband, Patty knew Jack would never have violent outbursts. The mere idea of the heat of such obsession lit a fire in her abdomen. If she were to announce to Jack she was taking the kids and leaving him, he would say, "Okay." He probably wouldn't argue or yell. He was too soft, too kind. While she had friends whose husbands were loud and even scary at times, Jack had never been like that. Most likely because nothing was ever denied to him, life always fell into place, and he was always peaceful and content.

Patty hated him a little.

After being consumed with news stories of the missing beautiful women day after day, Patty began fantasizing about what people would say if she went missing. She was a wife, a mother. A solid presence in her neighborhood book club. Patty made the tastiest gingersnap cookies you ever had and had been homecoming queen in high school. She had one of the top SAT scores in her school, though she decided not to go to college. And Patty was beautiful by traditional standards. But was that all? When she thought about how little her homemaking accomplishments looked compared to those of that nurse who'd been taken from the hospital parking lot, Patty's own status angered her. If she were to go missing, her life would be as important as that woman's. Patty was more attractive than her, anyway—nurses never wore makeup.

So, she began to plan.

Patty went to the craft supplies store and filled her cart with a three-inch binder, the expensive heavyweight scrapbooking paper, those little triangles you put on the corners of pictures, and page protectors. She bought everything she could think of that would help her represent her whole life in that binder.

When she returned home, Patty got to work.

"If I Go Missing," she wrote in bold block letters on the front of her binder.

Patty had examined the Missing Person posters of the women whose stories she had been following that week. The O.R. nurse she decided she didn't like was a white woman, 5'6" with light brown hair and blue eyes. That woman weighed in at 140 pounds and had a butterfly tattooed on her arm. A white stay-at-home mom was five-foot four and blonde with brown eyes and a mole on her chest and weighed about 155. A green-eyed teacher, also white, stood 4'11", boasted a scar on her lip, and barely tipped the scales at 120. A Mexican pianist was among those missing but Patty mostly ignored her story, finding her case annoying for reasons she didn't want to think about. *I'm not like her.*

In her binder Patty titled each page with a new category of information:

    HAIR AND EYE COLOR

    SCARS AND BIRTHMARKS

    CLOTHING SIZES

    MEDICAL HISTORY

    RECENT PHOTOGRAPHS

    LOGIN PASSWORDS

    IMPORTANT DOCUMENTS

    HAIR AND BLOOD SAMPLES

Patty pored over the news articles for other types of information she'd need to include She took close ups of her eyes and hair color as well as the scars and birthmarks all over her body. She noted her weight and clothing sizes and every medical incident she'd had. She included some of her favorite photographs of herself so that if she were to go missing the police would use a good picture of her on the Missing Person flier. She wrote down her email username and password along with other website logins. She photocopied her social security card, birth certificate, her driver's license, and her passport. Last, she plucked three hairs from their roots and pricked her index finger to bleed on a piece of gauze. She added all of this to the binder.

Patty was satisfied. She felt powerful knowing that if she ever went missing, this binder would bring her back. She imagined Jack going to the police station and telling them, "Look! Patty knew I would be so lost without her. She thought of everything. Use this to bring her back to us." As she imagined it, he'd wail and tear at his clothes, only realizing what he'd found in a wife and woman until Patty was gone.

The satisfaction only lasted so long. Her IF I GO MISSING binder began taunting her.

"You're not interesting enough to kidnap," it said to her. Was "kidnap" the right word? Patty wasn't a kid, so maybe "abduct"? That was another word often used with children, while these women simply went missing. There was never any indication of foul play until they turned up dead. But Patty didn't want to die— she wanted to be noticed for something other than being a wife and mother.

In their house, Patty was irreplaceable. She knew where everything was, how every major appliance worked, the family schedule, the recipes. Jack really would be lost without her. Out there in the "real world," these skills she'd trained her whole life to master didn't do Patty any good. Maybe she wasn't interesting or important enough to kidnap.

Patty sat on her bed, knowing the sheets she had just pulled out of the dryer would wrinkle under her weight, and stared at the photograph of Jack and her on their wedding day. She needed a plan, so she began her list.

It wasn't until she stumbled home from her fourth unsuccessful trip to a dive bar in cutoff jean shorts and a skin-tight black tank top that she began to consider what she previously had not let cross her mind.

No one wanted her.

Not the men who had ridden in on motorcycles. Not the off-duty cops who drank beer like water. Not the seedy men with armpit stains who she honestly found revolting but would be willing to accept as captors. Not one man who'd crossed her path during the month she had been getting dolled up. Not Jack. Not one.

What was it about her that they didn't like? Did she reek of desperation? Did they only want someone who was unsuspecting?

But that was the thing: every woman was suspecting. Every woman since birth had been told she had something men wanted and needed to be protective of herself because even a second's dropped guard would mean being taken.

Patty had worn clothes showing too much skin, drunk more than she ever had. She'd left her drink on the bar counter and slurred loudly, "I'm going to pee—watch this please" to no one in particular. The cup had been empty—not otherwise tampered with—when she returned.

The morning after her latest bar night, she clicked through news stories about the women again, finding that new ones had gone missing since she'd created her binder. Some had been found partially decomposed. One was thought to have fallen and injured herself during a hike. Patty didn't live an interesting enough life to have an accident like that. There were only so many places the housewife traveled.

She had told Jack she was joining a book club and would need Friday evenings to herself to discuss this or that book. He hadn't asked her where or with whom.

The more she looked at the photograph of the woman who had in fact been murdered—brutally too—the more she thought she was prettier than that woman. Her highlights were fresh and her makeup evenly applied. Who had chosen these unflattering pictures of this woman?

Patty flipped through her binder, ripped out pages from her previous plan, and went back to the drawing board.

She'd plan a new way to go missing. If this one failed, she'd need to take things into her own hands.

One way or another, Patty would be noticed.

THE HUMMING REFRIGERATOR IS ALMOST PURRING

KATLINA SOMMERBERG

The morning after your boyfriend took the cat and moved out, you trip on—not Biscuit weaving between your legs—a vine growing from beneath the refrigerator. The end is coiled around a cabinet handle; the entire plant hangs, suspended in the air, to avoid the chilly tile floor. You step over it as you set the kettle and grind coffee beans.

You drop six eggs into boiling water. He's not here to smell the noxious farts; you can eat as much protein as you want. Crying and gulping burned coffee, you stumble outside into the sunshine. No time to grieve on a nine-to-five.

After eight hours of herding lawyers and studying for the bar exam as an underpaid secretary, you stop in the townhouse's foyer to rip off your heels. You stomp into the kitchen so loudly your neighbor's dog barks.

The vine has a twin. Blue flecks gleam on their leaves like broken gemstones. Velvety soft, the tendrils reach out and wrap around your fingers. The squeeze is a perfect imitation of a friend's physical comfort: what you've been craving all day while forcing a smile at work. Your knees liquify. As you cry, you lean against the refrigerator's plastic door and imagine the hum is a purr.

Biscuit's was louder. Your lap is cold and empty where she should be curled into the crook of your knee.

Your ex made it sound so reasonable to split the physical objects based on who paid for what, with your name on the lease and his on the veterinary bills, but you bottle-fed Biscuit. You realize shared love encapsulated by shared pain is why your parents stayed together—to raise you—while their marriage deteriorated.

The doorbell startles you. You hurriedly wipe away snot—is he back?—until your phone flashes a notification containing a photo of groceries set beside your snail statue flashes on your phone screen.

The groceries are easier to drag inside than you expect. He always complained about the weight of milk and meat. You pick up a cantaloupe and jostle it around, poorly imitating his carping. The vines approve; their leaves caress the rough rind, tracing the outline of a jack-o-lantern, and you run with the idea.

Your knife slices off the top on the first try. You exchange the blade for a spoon and shovel out the melon's guts, alternating between dumping the stringy seeds in the trash and consuming the orange flesh. The crunch between your teeth is so satisfying, you don't mind the bland and unripe taste. Sticky juice drips from your mouth; you imagine it's his blood.

You eat it down to the rind. The empty shell resists your attempts to crush it to a pulp.

Instead, you carve a Halloween grin into its skin. You place it next to the french press before shambling to bed.

His song wakes you up. You smash the alarm off and—with your eyes foggy and crusty—swipe through your phone's settings to change it to a breakup single.

After kicking on slippers, you waddle into the bathroom. The sticky film of cantaloupe juice washes off in the shower. You laugh because your shampoo smells exactly like the summertime jack-o-lantern.

You're pouring the first cup of coffee when you realize the carved melon is not on the counter. Not in the cabinets or refrigerator, either. The number of vines has doubled.

As you drink your second cup and wonder, a leaf tickles the arch of your foot.

Your laugh cuts off short. Secret eating and foot massages—they're an offshoot of him.

Leaves slip between your toes. You hop up to sit on the counter. A vine follows your foot, so you kick at it and miss. Your heel cracks the refrigerator.

All four vines thrash in asynchronous panic. One entwines your ankle and squeezes.

The vines slam the refrigerator against the countertops. The knife block topples, and the knives kling-klang into the sink.

You grab the closest hilt and swing it down like an ax.

The vine releases to dodge; the knife's edge chips on the tile.

You slash at the flailing vines. They're evasive, despite their aimless thrashing. But even when you hit one, the cut isn't deep, and the vine is undeterred.

After tossing the knife in the sink, you squat in front of the refrigerator. The vines lash at your face and shoulders, but it's no worse than walking into a tree branch. Scooping them up, two in each hand, you pull, but they're stuck under the refrigerator.

Weight on your heels, you lean backwards and heave.

The refrigerator slides an inch.

You heave again; it slides further forward.

When it's twelve inches out of place, the vines hang, limp, in your hands. You squeeze. Then they squirm half-heartedly. The blue flecks in their leaves have muted to a dull navy.

You drop the vines. They rest on the eggshell-littered tiles.

The vines' four green tendrils point lines from you to the refrigerator's vacant floorspace. Their roots are entangled around black and orange fabric. Pressed against the corner rests a filthy plushy. There's familiarity in its round shape and pink oval ears, so you climb onto the counter and lean down so far you have to brace your hand against the floor, and you pluck it from the grime. Calcium shards dig into your palm as you study the horse-hair whiskers.

Biscuit's favorite toy, vanished the day you adopted out her littermates.

As you blink back tears, you refocus on orange fabric wedged under the refrigerator. You toss Biscuit's toy onto the counter and drag out the ugliest Halloween sweater. It must be the only thing your ex left.

You bring the sweater to the kitchen window. The vines reach for the sunlight, anchored by roots entwined in the thread. You pinch a vine's root and yank.

One vine strikes at your ear. Unsalvageable. You toss the sweater and all in the trash and tie a knot so tight the vines can't escape the plastic.

While you carry the garbage to the dumpster, you pull out your phone and call the local animal shelter. You're available again to foster.

Yes, you can take a litter today.

THE STAIN
MICHAEL ALLEN ROSE

ZACK LEANED OVER THE TUB AND PULLED THE PLASTIC FREE of the bath bomb with his fingernail. The scent of coconuts filled the air, accentuated with a spicy hint of citrus. "You put the lime in the coconut and drink it all up," he sang to himself as he dropped the sphere into the running water.

The calcium carbonate started fizzing, and colorful tentacles began leaching from the ball. Zack stood and stepped into the tub, then lowered himself into a sitting position. He leaned back and turned off the faucet with his toes, sinking into the steaming hot water. His muscles relaxed into the heat.

Zack loved baths. They represented a time when he could be alone with his thoughts, without distractions, and luxuriate. He reached outside the tub to pick up his current read, carefully putting his bookmark on the far edge of the bath mat. He was a tub reader, and proud of it. In the nearly forty years he'd been reading in the bathtub, Zack had only dropped a book into the water twice. The odds remained in his favor.

He settled in and opened the paperback. It was engaging enough. Some science-fiction story about a space colony taken over by zombies. He skimmed the page. The most brazen character, a hot-shot space-jockey type, was getting the survivors into trouble with his hubris. He'd made a deal with some outlaws, and, of course, they were in the process of screwing over the crew, putting them in mortal danger. Zack's colleagues were a lot like this crew. At work, he'd often find it was their efforts sabotaging them, over and over again. This sad fact was one of the many reasons he reserved an evening or two every week for a bath.

His eyes breezed over sentences, tripping over words. He blinked hard and shook his head a bit. The water was so warm, and the heady scent of his favorite boozy fruits surrounded him and delighted his senses. He rarely fell asleep in the tub, and especially not with a book in his hands. Some part of him remained alert enough to panic, and he would gasp and twitch with a hypnic jerk, the way bodies sometimes do just before drifting into sleep.

He followed letters in spirals, like navigating a maze, and finally realized he had been reading the same paragraph repeatedly, without comprehension. Zack closed his eyes, took a deep breath, and re-opened them. Yes, he'd skimmed page sixty-four three times and couldn't remember anything he'd read.

Something was distracting him. His attention lifted past the edge of the page and up toward the ceiling. He allowed himself to focus. There, he noticed the stain for the first time.

The stain was barely a centimeter wide—just a dot, really. Zack might not have noticed at all, chalking it up to a floater on the surface of his eyeball, had the ceiling not been painted so bright a shade of white. The dot contrasted starkly with the paint surrounding it.

"Huh," he muttered, staring. It wasn't a fly or a gnat, taking a break on his bathroom ceiling, as it didn't move. The task of scrubbing the bathroom ceiling moved up one notch on his long list of things to do around his apartment, between cleaning the outside of the living room windows and polishing the kitchen faucets.

Zack went back to his book, but his water had become tepid. How long had he been lost in ambient thoughts? The point of taking a bath was to stop concentrating and allow the mind to wander, but he couldn't track the last few leaps his brain had taken.

Briefly, he wondered if his long-standing rule about not falling asleep in the bath had been broken, and his hands had somehow conspired to remain in possession of his book. No, his concentration was just shot. He looked around the bathroom and took time to note other tiny details he wouldn't normally observe: the color scheme of the tissue container, the fonts on his bottles of shampoo, the weft of the carpet on his bath mat. He peered over the side of his tub and reached out to place his book in a safe place beyond the splash zone.

He glanced at the spot on the ceiling, annoyed such a trivial thing had ruined his bath. The scent of coconut lime washed quickly down the drain as he toweled off and began his bedtime ritual, more irritated than usual.

———

THE STAIN WAS STILL THERE two nights later when he took another bath.

That goddamned stain. It had grown. Zack stood in his tub staring at it. He debated whether or not to get a chair and take a closer look, but it seemed like such an irritating chore. One reason he rented in the first place was to avoid taking care of the minor nuisances involved with ownership.

It was definitely bigger, though. Multiplied. Instead of one spot, there were now three. The original dot had grown slightly, like the ceiling had a suspicious mole, and there were two little brownish-black spots next to it at angles that made the whole constellation look like a surprised cartoon face. The hot water around his ankles splashed as he slipped a little, bracing himself with one hand on the wall, the other gripping the shower rod. The bergamot bath bomb he had used made the bathtub slippery, even as it filled the air with a crisp array of citrus oils.

He reached down and wet his hand, then flicked some water at the spots above his head, trying to see if they would move, or melt, or otherwise be diffused by his moistening them. They remained, implacable.

A flash of alarm shot through Zack as he realized his mistake. If it were some kind of mold, moisture would just feed it. Scowling, he stepped out of the tub and left a trail of wet footprints to his kitchen, where he kept cleaning supplies under the sink.

He opened the cupboard and found his weapon of choice: a canister of spray disinfectant. Instinctively, he shook it, and read the back of the canister on his way back to the bathroom.

"Cleans, sanitizes, deodorizes, blah blah blah... controls odors... kills viruses, harmful bacteria, some types of fungus..." he read. "Good. Fungus. Good."

Grabbing a handful of toilet tissue and a small step ladder from its place in the hall, he approached the tub again. Zack placed the ladder beside the tub and took two steps up. There were now four spots, not three, and he furrowed his eyebrows. "Jesus, how the hell?"

Had he miscounted, the first time? No, he was sure there had been three dots. It had been so facelike, he expected it to wink and ask how he was doing. Zack shook the can vigorously and pointed the nozzle toward the ceiling, unleashing a cone of chemical cleaner. Once the area around the spots was fully saturated, he stood back and admired his handiwork.

Next came a scrubber from underneath the sink. As soon as he felt an arbitrary but ritually important amount of time had passed, he dug his nails into the back of the scrubber and rubbed it ferociously on the ceiling.

The spots remained. Zack tried again, scowling. He wished he had a mask in case there were spores, but the only appropriate safety gear he would have been able to find was a vintage Israeli army gas mask he'd bought at a military surplus store years ago. He tried not to breathe.

"The hell." He stared up at the stain. At least the spots were duller now, less shiny, and therefore, he hoped, less alive. If indeed it was a mold or fungus, it didn't belong in his shower area. Perhaps the substance had actually stained the ceiling. Was this the sort of thing people called a landlord for? It didn't appear to be black mold—the kind he'd read about people in hazmat suits needing to demolish buildings to eliminate. Whatever had been growing there couldn't grow through a layer of Lysol. He'd have to buy some white paint and retouch the stain, covering the evidence of the grime, and then, surely, everything would be fine.

———

NOTHING COULD HAVE PREPARED Zack for the horror plastered across his bathroom ceiling the following morning. Still fighting drowsy brain and rubbing sleep from the corners of his eyes, he was shocked to see the spots had fully bloomed into fractal patterns. Tentacles, delicate like peacock feathers, swirled broadly, almost to the wall and the central light fixture.

It was almost artistic—swaths of patterned waves flowing like the beams of a brown, expressionist sunburst. He called his landlord immediately and watched the stain while the phone rang. Perhaps his disgust could melt it from his ceiling and walls through sheer force of will. The line rang three times and then went to voicemail. Zack left a message, trying to find the right words as he wondered how long he'd be without a bathroom if they had to come in and take the ceiling out. More horrifying than that notion was the thought of the water damage above him leaving such evidence on the other side of the drywall.

It had to be water damage, didn't it? Moisture creeping through the beams, seeping into the nooks and crannies, damaging light fixtures and weakening the structure, so eventually, it would all fall in and crush him while he cleaned himself, burying his naked body, entombing him in his apartment. Zack shook his head. He needed to be rational. Paranoid thoughts wouldn't help.

He finished up his message. "Thanks. Give me a call back. Feel free to stop by or whatever. I'll be home. Okay." His landlord's messaging service emitted a long beep, cutting him off. He had rambled too long.

With sudden clarity, he pictured the basement unit of the building, underneath his apartment. Was his plumbing leaking and causing them similar problems? Or maybe the leak was in the walls. Maybe the very foundation of the building was slowly disintegrating under the lasting assault of ancient plumbing, as it slowly failed and fell apart.

Zack took the stairs two at a time.

The building's bottom floor was compact, but the owner had carved out two apartments, somehow cramming in living spaces out of what little portion wasn't taken up with electrics and the boiler. Old tools and refuse, detached mailbox numbers, and a beaten-up bicycle guarded the hallway beyond the two residential doors, marked respectively with *A1* and *B1*.

He examined the ceiling, taking a moment to orient himself. His apartment was on the west side of the building, which would mean *A1* was below him, although the layouts in the basement differed somewhat from the upper floors. A toilet flush from somewhere upstairs made pipes gurgle overhead, and Zack followed the sound of running water. He glanced down the hall toward the utility area, and gave a quick series of knocks on the door of *A1*. Nobody home. He glanced at his cell phone. It was almost 9:30 in the morning. Surely, his neighbor was at work. Normal people would be at work, now, not staring at the ceiling.

His attention returned to the hallway, and he crossed the threshold of the utility room, hand skimming along the wall and creating patterns in the dust as he floundered for a light switch. His thumb found purchase, and he flipped it. A dull, dingy series of yellow bulbs burst to life, illuminating the space from overhead. An industrial size water heater dominated the room. A pair of large fuse-boxes sat against the opposite wall along with a tangle of cords for cable internet connections and other services. Zack squinted into the shadowy recesses of the exposed wooden beams overhead, but he could see no evidence of any water damage. There was no stain here.

Could the stain really be limited to his apartment? Cursing his luck, Zack stormed back upstairs.

The bathroom was just as he'd left it. He analyzed the stain with suspicion and couldn't ascertain whether it had grown since he'd gone downstairs.

"Doesn't matter," he muttered, stripping his clothes off and leaving them crumpled up on the bathroom floor. This had eaten up enough of his morning, and if he didn't focus, he was going to be late for work. He'd picked up a part-time job showing apartments, ironically, and he made a mental note to look more closely at the upcoming listings. If his landlord didn't call him back soon, and hell, maybe even if he did, Zack wasn't going to live in a place with the stain.

While he showered, he grimly regarded the tendrils of brownish-gray. They reached nearly down to the tile wall of his shower. In fact, one rust-colored smudge seemed to have flaked from the wall and down onto the white, ceramic tile. A thin strand of connective tissue dangled off the drywall above and remained connected to the smudge like an oxygen hose from a space shuttle to an astronaut.

Sneering, Zack reached up to flick it off the shower wall and into the swirling drain below. As his finger got closer, the tendril appeared to move, as though it were made up of a million, tiny creatures—a carpet of life—instead of just a rusty looking filth. He thought of Michelangelo's "Creation of Adam," as he extended his pointer finger to touch the stain.

———

"Come on in, take a look."

The grim, hairy man stepped aside, flipping on the light. The couple, Marci and Doug, huddled in behind him and moved past to stand in the small bathroom.

"How's the water pressure?" asked Marci.

"Is very good pressure. Hot water works well. Long showers, I pay for water. Is good deal."

Something caught Doug's eye as he looked upward, toward the yellowing light fixture. "Looks like you repainted?"

The ragged edges of a touch-up reflected back at them, two shades of white that almost perfectly matched, but didn't.

"Yes, everything is freshly painted. I paint between tenants. Freshen the place up. Walls, ceiling, everything." The hairy man stepped back out into the hallway, crossing his arms, and leaned on the opposite wall. "Bedrooms are back this way, one big, one small. You can use one for office, or make him sleep there when you are angry." He chuckled at his joke.

Marci remained straight-faced, as she turned around, opening a cabinet. "Did you have a leak in here?"

"Past tenant used to wash his dog, I think. Cleaned up, repainted, restored, the whole works. Ready to see kitchen?"

"Was he a problem tenant?" Doug asked, casually dragging his finger over the sink's porcelain surface.

"No, no, just single guy. You know how they can be, yes?" He wiggled his eyebrows, hoping either Doug or Marci would take the bait, but neither reacted. The landlord looked sour, hating to be left hanging. "Place is ready to rent right now. Had everything cleaned out just last weekend."

"Cleaned out?" Marci asked, quizzically.

"Guy disappeared. Just left. Didn't pay rent, call, write, leave postcard, nothing. He told me about some problem with apartment, and I come to fix, he is gone. Tried calling, nothing, checked with his contacts in lease, nothing. He just goes away. I don't know. So, I wait, I am good landlord, I give him month to come, take his things, still nothing. Finally, I can not wait any more. People need place to live, so it comes to you."

Doug glanced at Marci, and they shared a look. "That's weird," he said. "Some people end up starring in their own *Unsolved Mysteries*, I guess."

The hairy man muttered something like "Take your time," and stepped down the hall.

The couple heard him shuffling around down in the bedroom area, obviously trying to speed up the tour. They would not be swayed, however. They had come in with a strategy, and would make sure they checked for the little things that could become big problems later. Things like plumbing. Outlets. Appliances. Things like water damage.

"Doug, honey, look right there."

"Where?"

"Right where I'm pointing. Do you see that?"

Doug followed his wife's pointer finger upward. Almost imperceptible, amid the white-on-white paint job above the bathtub, a small, undefined area, like a passing shadow, placed right in the center of the touch-up. "You think maybe there was a leak?"

"Maybe," said Marci. "But you know what's weird? Doesn't it kind of look like a man's face?"

She was right. It was almost invisible to the naked eye, like the blue black against black shapes when you stare at a bright light and then close your eyes tightly. Just an impression. But it did look kind of like a man's face. And he was screaming. Doug and Marci took note of this and moved on to see the bedrooms. Maybe they'd rent the place, sure, but they weren't going to be stuck with a hit on their security deposit for damage they didn't do.

IN DARKNESS LEFT BEHIND

SPENCER KOELLE

SAM REALLY DIDN'T WANT TO GO INTO THE BASEMENT AT night.

Her girlfriend, Mariposa, remembered friends' birthdays, decorated the row house, and paid the bills. Samantha Pesantubbee was the one who confronted landlords, moved furniture, and killed spiders.

Their roommate Max, after three months of fruitless house meetings, had responded to the thirty days' notice by calling Sam a variety of anti-native slurs, chucking Mariposa's estradiol down the basement stairs, and storming off into the night.

Sam stood at the top of those stairs and flicked the switch, which still did nothing. It hadn't worked since the day after Sam and Mariposa signed the lease.

Well, somebody has to do it. She hung up her flannel jacket and hoisted her Maglite. Upstairs, Mariposa was video chatting with one of her boyfriends to stop her panic attack.

Sam leaned on the rusty railing, inching along the fragile staircase. It was a typical Philly row house basement: unfinished concrete, a clear plastic bag full of old clothes predating the current landlord, moldy cardboard, dank air, and darkness. A detached crimson door with an orange corner rested against the north wall.

The first broad swing of Sam's flashlight failed to reveal the clear orange pill bottle. It could have bounced and rolled anywhere.

Sam examined the nook under the staircase. It hadn't slipped between her fermenting cider and spicy pickles. Something rustled, just audible over distant sirens and arguing neighbors.

The next likely hiding spot was a stack of squashed liquor boxes. Sam nudged it with the tip of her steel-toed boot, twice, before revealing nothing but reddish-brown stains.

The rustling repeated. She'd checked out this place before moving and there were no nibbles, no mouse droppings, no hints of rodents.

The absence was odd, now that she thought about it. No mice at all? Sam was so bad about spreading crumbs that Mariposa didn't let her eat in the bedroom. This old building with its holes and cracks should have presented an ideal home for vermin. A water-stained wooden crate, for example, would make a great hiding spot for rats. It could easily have housed the elusive medicine, too. Sam found neither.

Sam hadn't needed to kill a spider for her girlfriend since moving in. It was as old and leaky as any other West Philly dump, but they'd seen no cobwebs, no cockroaches—not so much as a fly.

The medicine wasn't against the south wall either, as her not-yet-frantic search revealed nothing but dust.

The third time Sam heard the rustling noise, she swung the flashlight in its direction. She saw the door, an empty plastic bag, and a few dust bunnies.

Nothing moved. A car drove by, blasting Drake, but the house was silent.

Sam bit her tongue and breathed in through her nose and out

through her mouth. *This flashlight would make a decent club with 320 pounds of fat and muscle behind it.* She forced herself to bring the light in a wide arc around her, not shaking too much. Again, she saw the sagging crate, old clothes, the red door with the orange corner, dust, pickles, cider, and stairs.

Sam scrambled to the door. Orange plastic glowed in her light. She kicked aside the empty bag and knelt down to retrieve the bottle.

More rustling.

As her fingers closed around the pill bottle, the flashlight almost slid from her other hand.

The empty plastic bag had been full of clothes.

"Hey! Come out!". Sweat dribbled down her chest and her clenched fingers around the pill bottle. Heavy fabric scraped and shuffled along the uneven floor. Sam whipped the flashlight around, hoping to blind—

An pile of old clothes.

Nothing was dragging them. No feral animal emerged. They were just clothes.

The light shook with her pounding heart. She clutched the pill bottle tighter.

A Temple University hoodie, like the one the old leaseholder had worn, stood out along with a midnight-blue dress, a pair of torn skinny jeans, a crunchy Batman sock, a careworn plaid coat, weed-print leggings, and more of the like.

Samantha stepped closer, nudged the mass, and sprang back. Nothing cried out. Nothing scurried past.

Sam tucked the pills into her pocket and bolted.

She stumbled.

At first she thought she'd tripped on the heap. Somehow the jeans and socks were wrapped around her ankle. She tried tugging her leg, but it wouldn't come free. Was she caught on a nail or something? It wasn't until they began shifting and unfolding that she saw the pulsing purple veins joining each piece of fabric.

Sam landed her first punch before screaming.

It was, well, like punching cloth. The winter coat billowed as though to wrap around her. She hammered on everything in reach. She felt veins under her blows, but they didn't rupture.

Sam stopped trying to bludgeon it or break free and focused on pulling it after her. It wrapped more leggings and sleeves around her, but heaved against it. She didn't need to get all the way up the stairs. She grabbed her biggest jar of pickles, lifted it up, and smashed it on the shuddering mass.

It didn't hiss but recoiled from the shards of glass or the stinging brine. Sam scrambled up the stairs and slammed the door.

"Jesus Christ, are you okay? What happened?" Mariposa gasped, crashing into her. "I heard screaming!"

Sam slammed home the latch, dragged the couch over one-handed, and barricaded the door.

"Get my caulking gun, toolbox, spare timber—and the good nails," Sam panted. "Tomorrow, I'm calling Lowe's and the landlord."

The weed leggings were exactly the obnoxious sort of thing Max would wear. And the mass of clothing, she realized, included Mariposa's blue dress and Sam's jacket.

COUCH SURFING

JONATHAN REDDOCH

Today is the day, Dan promised himself in the mirror.
Today is the day Rick leaves my apartment.

Dan got ready for work, same as every weekday morning. The coffee maker beeped. Dave drank two cups and made as much noise as possible as he gathered his computer and accessories.

Rick grunted and flipped over on the couch, mumbling something about a late night.

"Do you have any interviews today?" Dave asked his perpetually perturbed house guest. He already knew the answer. It was always the same:

"Tomorrow."

The apartment only had a single bedroom, so poor jobless, shiftless, homeless, motionless, hopeless Rick surfed the couch. He had surfed it so long, in fact, the couch was reshaping into Rick's oblong form—or maybe Rick was reshaping into an amorphous couch cushion. The longer he remained, ensconced in entitlement the more he became one with the squishy black blob.

"K... wellllll, I'll see you at dinner," Dan said sheepishly.

Dan took a last look at the mass in the dark. It was getting to the point where it was no longer possible for Dan to tell where the couch ended and Rick began.

"Yeah, big dinner," a muffled voice promised from under a cushion.

Dan spent the duration of his rail commute thinking of scenarios that would cause his unwelcome roommate to depart. His idyllic fantasies all ended in Rick voluntarily leaving the apartment after getting a job, a girlfriend, or winning the lottery. None of these seemed remotely plausible.

The thing is, Dan didn't really even know Rick that well when he impulsively decided to let him stay. He was a friend of a friend. Dan wanted to earn friendship points by doing a good deed. And he was bad at setting and holding boundaries. And he was deathly afraid of interpersonal confrontations.

How long ago did he agree to this temporary respite? Weeks? Months? Eons in uncomfortable silences spent binging reality TV with a detestable stranger (Dan loathed reality television).

Want to know the strangest part? The detail Dan was too ashamed to tell anyone about?

Rick was a nuisance who didn't leave the apartment, but he did clean up a little here and there to justify his existence and promised to make home-cooked meals twice a week. Dan had been a remote employee before Rick moved in, and it just so happened that Rick chose to make himself productive when Dan was attending afternoon virtual meetings. Holding up his end of the bargain, Rick would be there throughout those work meetings, cooking loudly, singing to himself, and vacuuming. Their relationship became so strained Dan told his boss he was experiencing problems with his Wi-Fi as an excuse to come into the office.

At the end of another long workday, Dan spent the commute home brainstorming ways to get Rick to depart.

He rehearsed the conversation in his head. "Rick, you need to go. Now get!" The thought of saying it made him laugh out loud in the crowded train car.

Tomorrow, Rick will be gone, he lied to himself, swearing he'd initiate the talk after dinner.

But he never got the chance.

In a strange turn of events, Dan returned to his little apartment to find no sign of Rick. Except for his little pile of grocery bags of clothes in the corner. Even his "borrowed" toothbrush lay on the sink, barely used.

Maybe he went to the supermarket? The bar? He did have an alcohol problem (though he drank Dan's well-stocked cupboard bare). But with what money would he fund his night on the town? He had none of his own.

His wallet, keys, and phone remained in their pile on the coffee table.

Satisfied he was at least gone for now, Dan locked the door and turned off the lights so he could pretend to be gone if and when Rick returned sans keys.

He sat down on the lumpy couch in the dark. When he plopped down, it rippled up and down like waves crashing in the sea.

He heard a murmur below where his butt kissed the lumpy foam.

"Rick?" he whispered.

"Dan..." Rick whimpered from below.

Dan jumped up. He flipped on the lights. He examined the writhing furniture closely, careful to keep his hands free of the lone hand reaching up past the unzipped section.

The garbled speech was coming from inside the couch!

"Dinner time..." moaned the furniture.

The furniture belched as it zipped up tight.

The sofa was satisfied, full, and happy. It would not need to feed again for a while.

After taking a moment, Dan sat down and turned on the TV. He'd finally get to pick the shows he wanted to watch.

His cell rang. It was a friend of a friend. They were distraught.

Dan replied, "If you need a place to stay until you get on your feet, that's no problem at all. A spot on my couch just became available."

HANGING MEAT ON THE BONES

ANDREW KOZMA

Only a few inhabited blocks remain in Marley, a neighborhood that's been destitute for so long everyone thinks it's been abandoned. Despite those residents hanging on in old houses kept up with stubborn pride, the City wants Marley to die. They bulldoze houses as soon as they're foreclosed so squatters can't move in. They cultivate weeds and thorn bushes to eat the remains. City officials want to create a space for rich citizens to visit with pride and a little frisson of fear, their own Central Park, the expanse of tame wilderness every large city needs.

The remaining Marley residents are smack in the middle of that proto-park, their houses rising like a mirage over the potholed roads, hedged in by broken sidewalks and caved-in storm drains. Those residents wave to pedestrians walking the edge of the ruined neighborhood, their arms a comforting clockwork. Their faces are too far away to be seen clearly, but the white teeth and bright eyes stand out like will-o'-the-wisps. Marley's residents always look familiar. Yes, their hairstyles change, heights ratchet up or down a few inches, pounds are slapped on or sawn off, but every silhouette is recognizable, the way you acknowledge that woman who walks her bulldog every morning or the pair of men who jog together every evening, steps perfectly in sync. That is to say, they are recognizable as someone you should recognize, but to ask a name would be admitting your own failure to be a good neighbor.

The road into Marley is a ruin. Cars and trucks break axles over humped asphalt or find their bumpers hooked on twists of rebar. Even construction vehicles get bogged down in rain-bred mires, their abandoned yellow bodies dotting the grounds like skeletons of ancient beasts. The City wants a park, but they're inheriting a graveyard.

Still, Hummers make it through with relative ease. And when the Hummer makes it to the center of those remaining Marley houses, two City bureaucrats open their doors and climb down into a cul-de-sac of a well-lit, if small, neighborhood. They breathe in the smell of cookouts, freshly-baked pecan pies, and honest sweat from yard work. Every lawn looks like a jeweler's show table.

"Fresh lemonade?" a woman from a nearby porch offers. "A slice of pecan pie?"

"Sure," Al says.

"Yes, please," Hal says.

The bureaucrats don't want to be rude. They are here to convince these people to abandon their homes, to go somewhere else and become something new, but that's no reason to be rude. The bureaucrats aren't monsters, after all.

They rest their glasses of lemonade on the high counter of the Hummer's hood and dig into the pecan pie, scraping the ceramic plates with their forks in their eagerness.

Hal wonders how the neighborhood gets its groceries. When he looks back over the road they traveled, fallen trees litter the ground, providing depth to drab mud and tired weeds. There's an abandoned Hummer back that way, vines growing through its hubcaps. The lemonade is sweet, but not too sweet. The pie is equal parts crunch and melt-in-your-mouth.

The eviction papers in Hal's breast pocket are heavy as a miniature Bible. This is not the first time the City has sent eviction papers to Marley's remaining residents, but those residents are still here even if the bureaucrats who carried them are long gone. All around Hal and Al, the residents go about their tiny lives, oblivious to its inevitable end.

But that's not Hal's problem. His job is simply delivery.

And yet what Hal thinks about as he eats the pie is not his job or the way the food tastes like nostalgia or how the houses are sugar-glazed by the fading autumn light or the frantic laughter of the neighborhood children but the way the neighborhood settles onto his exposed skin. Soft waves of heat as from another body, so even with eyes closed he can feel that person's unadulterated happiness.

Hal glances at Al and notes his co-worker's face settling into a languid smile, his eyes closing in contentment. Pie eaten, lemonade drunk, the fork and plate drop from Al's hands to gently clatter on the ground, forgotten props. Long arms reach out from under their Hummer to collect the fork and plate. Hal feels an instinct toward alarm, but peace steals over him like a fleece blanket.

He sets his unfinished pie on the Hummer and pulls the eviction papers from his pocket, holding them out like a talisman. His fingers can't keep hold, and they flutter to the ground. Long arms again skitter out from under the vehicle to pinch the papers between long fingers and drag them into darkness.

"You have to leave," Hal tells the Marley woman, words slurring.

The woman smiles. "You have to stay."

She turns to face Al, who has fallen to his knees. The woman has no back. She is a half-dressed skeleton of trash faced with a veneer of flesh. No meat. Just bones. Radiating warmth.

PART THREE
OUT IN THE STICKS

Getting away from the masses in the city is no guarantee of peace.

M GO BLUE

JOHN BUKOWSKI

THE MONOTONY OF THE BUCKEYE COUNTRYSIDE WAS FINALLY broken by a road sign. "Best tacos in Southeastern Ohio," Bob read aloud. "That's like saying finest bouillabaisse in Arkansas."

"Come on," his wife said. "I'm starving and could go for some good Mexican."

"Which you probably won't find on the outskirts of Youngstown." But Bob dutifully got into the exit lane.

They'd left Detroit early, making good time as they angled south and east. Interstate 70 would take them to PA and then their final destination of Washington, DC. Bob had booked the same suite they'd had on their honeymoon.

This was their first real vacation in twenty years. The new business was finally thriving, and Bob could afford some time off. At first, he wasn't sure if his partner Nate could handle things alone. But Sarah had pointed out that Nate was a good businessman, and that she had bought a new teddy for the trip. His wife knew how to sell just as well as Bob did.

Cocina de mi Abuela was a homey little place a mile down a two-lane road called Danbury Dell, according to the bullet-holed road sign. The outside of the building was yellow, with a sombrero and cactus mural painted by The Little Rascals. The inside looked like a fifties' diner with a bar instead of a counter. But the tacos were good (he'd eaten four), as were the rice and beans. As Sarah visited the ladies' room, Bob waited, leisurely enjoying his coffee. They weren't in any hurry. Days were still long until Labor Day, and they were halfway to the Sheraton. For the first time in a long time, Bob was contented and relaxed. He took a sip then pulled out his cell to check their ETA to paradise.

"You asking for trouble?"

Bob looked up with a start. The voice was not Sarah's. It was low and gruff, and fit the grizzled man in the grease-stained John Deere cap standing before him.

"Um, beg pardon?"

The man lifted a red-flannel arm and pointed. "The sweat-shirt. M go Blue. Them's fightin' words in Buckeye country." His breath held the pungent tang of alcohol fumes.

Bob chuckled. "I can see how you might feel that way, given the licking you guys took last year. But there's always this season."

The man in the tractor cap smiled. His teeth were a uniform yellow, except for the left eye tooth; its darkness stood out like a corpse awaiting burial. "Yeah, pretty funny. I take it you went to school there."

"Yep, I'm a Wolverine. Class of 02."

"Sound proud of that."

"Sure. It's a great school. Harvard of the north, as they say." Bob put down his cell. "What's yours?"

The guy in the Deere cap kept smiling as he studied his scuffed work boots. "I ain't never been to no college. Had to drop out of high to get a job, help the family. Went back and got my GED though."

Bob nodded. "That's...good for you. Congratulations."

The guy's sad smile never wavered but Bob thought it took a

sinister turn. "Got a boy goes to State though, track scholarship. First college man in the *whole* family. A family from Ohio and nothing but."

"Well, congratulations again. Good school."

"But ain't no Harvard of the northland, huh?"

"Um, well, no but..."

Mr. Deere cap thumbed to the parking lot. "That your Lexus out there?"

Bob nodded. "How did you know?"

"Saw the Michigan plates on that red buggy. So, I just figured. Bet she's a *sweet* ride."

"Yes," Bob said, picking up the check. "It's a nice car."

He'd taken the guy for a bar fly that liked to chew the fat. But Bob didn't care for the way he'd zeroed in on their car in the lot. And there was something about the guy's tone that made Bob want to pay and leave. Now.

"Yep. Bet she cost you a pretty penny too."

"Actually, it's a lease through my company." Bob mentally tallied up twenty percent then reached for his wallet.

John Deere man laughed and pounded one skinny leg with a gnarly fist. "Bigshot businessman too. Well, I'll be frickin' la dee dahed."

Bob laid thirty bucks on the table. He wanted to pay and leave in less time than credit cards allowed. He was a gregarious man by nature, but right now he didn't feel gregarious. He felt uncomfortable and ready to hit the road as soon as Sarah returned.

Bob stood. "Well, guess I'll be on my way." His smile felt stiff, which was also unlike him. "Lots of miles to cover today. Nice meeting you, Mr. ..."

"Quebe. Daryl Quebe. From over in Carroll County. But I guess I've driven just about every road in this state. Eastern half, anyway. Lived here all my life." Quebe chuckled. "Hell, I'm kin to half the folks in these parts, one way or another."

Bob cleared his throat. "Well, that sounds interesting. Oh, I see my wife is coming out of the ladies, so I'll say goodbye again."

"Yep. I been everywhere hereabouts. I seen the country folks in their pickups, struggling to make ends meet. And I seen the bigwig northerners passin' through." He smiled. *"Drivin'* through flyover country. Yep, they come in their fancy cars from Dee-troit and Shy-cago. Just passin' through on their way to Floreeda or Virginia Beach."

Bob waved to Sarah. "Well, goodbye again. Have a good..."

"Coming down here with their chests puffed. Shoving their M go Blue in our faces cause our hick kids go to Moo U instead of the Harvard of the northland."

Bob held out his palms. "Look fella, I didn't mean any disrespect. It's *just* a sweatshirt." Bob shrugged. "School pride, you know."

"Thinking they're better than us, them in their Lexi and Meersay-dees. Us in Jimmies and Ford-150s."

Sarah was getting close, but Bob warned her off with his eyes, nodding toward the door. This conversation was going south, and he didn't want her any part of it. She hesitated for a moment, then headed for the exit.

Bob sighed. "Listen, ah, Mr. Quebe. I don't want any trouble. Ohio State is a fine school, but I went to Michigan. So sue me. Now if you'll excuse me, I'll go my way and you can go yours. How does that sound?"

The smile left Quebe's weathered cheeks. An icy glare replaced it. "How about your ass gets acquainted with my size eleven boot? How's *that* sound?"

Bob started to reply, then let it go. More talk would just fuel the fire. Instead, he waved as he turned. An iron grip on his forearm turned him around again.

"Don't you show your back to me, Mr. Bigshot." Quebe cocked his fist.

Bob wasn't much for fighting. That was his nature, and good business. He hadn't been in a scrap of any kind since the service. But the old skills were still there, drilled in by Master Sergeant Anthony Vescuzzi, the base martial arts instructor, drilled almost too well.

Bob's first impulse was a killing stroke, a crushed larynx being the surest way to end hand-to-hand combat. But this was a country waystations, not Iraq. And his enemy was an Ohio cracker, not ISIS. So, he jammed his hip into Quebe's, throwing his opponent off balance, then punched into the breastbone. It was like hitting concrete, but it got the job done. Breath whooshed from Quebe's skinny chest, along with fetid smells of old booze and even older tooth decay. Then gravity took hold, dumping Quebe over Bob's outstretched hip and onto the worn linoleum.

Hands on bent knees, Bob panted down at the grizzled face.

"I said I didn't want any trouble. And I meant it. But keep your damn hands to yourself." Bob's fist throbbed; he tried not to show it to Quebe. "Now, if you don't mind, I'm going to get into my fancy red buggy and be on my way. I suggest you leave it at that."

Quebe glared back, wind gone, pain and astonishment written across his crude features. Bob thought he noted something else there as well, the unmistakable look that said, 'this isn't over, pal.'

Bob straightened. "Congrats again on your son's scholarship. I'm sure he'll make you proud." Then he headed to the exit.

———

Sarah was in the Lexus going through her purse as Bob plopped into the driver's seat and grabbed the wheel. "Son of a bitch!" He shook his hand open, trying to chase away the lancing pain.

"What happened to you?" Sarah said, cupping his hand in hers.

"*Careful,*" Bob said. "I may have busted a knuckle."

"How?"

"Punching a flannel-covered wall."

"What? The guy who was talking to you back there?"

"No, the guy who was ranting at me back there. The same one who tried to take a poke at me."

"What? Why?"

"He didn't like my sweatshirt."

"Huh?"

Bob shook his head. "Never mind."

Sarah kissed his hand. "Want me to go back in the restaurant for a cup of ice?"

"No way." Bob fired up the engine. "I don't want you anywhere near that guy. I've got an insta-cold pack in the glove box."

Sarah reached in and handed the bag to Bob. He started to squeeze it, before bruised knuckles changed his mind. He handed it back to her. "Would you mind?"

Bob heard a pop as Sarah squeezed the activator pellet in the blue and white bag, then gently placed it atop his hand on the wheel.

Balancing the bag, Bob eased over to the gear shift. "Jesus Christ," he grunted as he popped the car into drive.

"Maybe we should take you to a hospital."

"No. It's okay. Once the swelling goes down, I'll be fine. Probably just bruised."

"I don't understand. It's not like you to fight. Over a sweatshirt, no less."

"I wasn't fighting, he was. I just ended it."

"But why?"

Bob angled to the lot exit. "Crazy? Overzealous OSU fan? All of the above? Take your pick."

As Bob turned out of the lot, headed for the freeway, Sarah

leaned over and kissed his cheek. Her lips felt soft and warm. He stopped worrying about his hand and started thinking of her new lingerie.

"Anything I can do for you," she asked.

Bob smiled. "Well, if we were in the hotel instead of the car."

She playfully punched his arm. "Men. Their brains are geared to fighting and sex."

Bob chuckled. "Well, the fighting is over. What else should I be thinking about?"

She punched his shoulder harder this time. "Anything *else* I can do for you?"

"Turn on the radio, please. See if you can get some victory music. Maybe We Are the Champions."

Sarah shook her head and punched the radio. Loud static filled the car until she turned down the volume and searched for a station. "There might not be much," she said. "This is kind of the willawags."

Static changed to a deep stertorous voice proclaiming, "Jesus is the only way."

"Next," Bob said.

More static, followed by the smooth, accent-less voice shared by news broadcasters everywhere. "Soybean futures are down yet again. The department of agriculture attributing the drop to higher-than-expected yields. On the local front, police are asking the public to be on the lookout for Daryl Quebe..."

Sarah made a face and advanced the tuner. Static was followed by country music.

"Go back," Bob shouted, stomping the brakes.

"What?"

"The news station. Get it back. Hurry!"

Sarah shrugged and hit the minus button.

Static seemed to reign forever until the newscaster's voice cut in, "...the murder of his entire family, including his estranged wife and their son who was home from college. Police caution that Quebe should be considered extremely dangerous. Do not approach him yourself. Instead, call..."

An ear-splitting crash threw Bob into his safety harness amidst a shower of pebbled glass. The entire car shook. He braced his hand against the wheel, adding pain from his injured knuckles to the sharp stab of the belt across his chest.

"What the hell!" He turned to Sarah. "You okay?"

His wife nodded dumbly, her face a mask of bewilderment, safety glass sparkling from her hair like gems set in gold.

The car lurched again, this time more a nudge that edged the Lexus forward even with Bob pressing the brake. "What the..."

Bob looked over his shoulder. A large truck grill filled what was left of the rear window, a wrecker's tow arm visible above a rusty-red roof. In between the tow arm and the grill leered the face of Daryl Quebe grinning through a spider crack in the truck's windshield.

"Oh my God," was all Bob could say before the surging whine of a diesel engine cut him off. The air stank of exhaust fumes and burning rubber as the Lexus slid forward. Bob froze, foot jammed on the brake pedal, eyes locked behind at the grinning, black-toothed face. He could almost read Quebe's thoughts.

Let's leave it at that? Don't want no trouble? Well, I'm gonna give you trouble, bigshot. And nothin' but.

The face in the wrecker cab threw back in laughter as if reading Bob's mind.

The Lexus continued sliding to the left. Bob pushed harder on the brakes and slammed the horn button, pain lancing through his injured hand. Another horn answered, this one in front of him. But Bob's eyes were still locked on Daryl Quebe's laughing face.

"Look out, Bob!"

Bob snapped his head around to focus on the road. Their Lexus was now in the wrong lane, a large pickup barreling at them, its brakes squealing. Bob took his foot off the brake and turned the wheel right. The oncoming truck turned left, putting them back on a collision course.

"Do something, Bob!"

But what was left to do? Steering was no good. Braking was no good. Bob punched the gas pedal.

The Lexus lurched toward the skewing Ford pickup. Bob wrenched the wheel left, leaving the road surface. The car bounced and rattled across a farmer's field, corn stalks parting like the Red Sea.

The whine of Quebe's diesel was replaced by the whiplash rustle of plants flogging the Lexus. Bob could see nothing but the sea of corn, smell nothing but its rich chlorophyl, feel nothing but the teeth-rattling jolts of the car. He kept pressure on the accelerator, not knowing what else to do. He snatched a quick glance at Sarah, her terror-filled eyes staring widely into the mass of plant life. He eased his foot off the gas pedal just as the Lexus popped out of the cornfield like a cork from a bottle. The luxury car staggered onto a dirt lane. Bob turned the wheel and followed it.

"What? Where are we?" Sarah asked. "Where we going?"

"I don't know." Bob pointed. "*There*. That farmhouse."

A lone white building rose out of the corn like a ghost on Halloween.

"But, but…" His wife's voice sounded hollow, as if the sense had been knocked out of her. Bob didn't blame her. "What's there?"

"People," he said. "*Cellphone*."

"What?"

"My cellphone," Bob said. "Call 911". He patted down his pockets. "Shit!"

Sarah continued to stare, her pretty blue eyes looking more through him that at him. "What?"

"I must have left it at the restaurant. Get yours."

Sarah blinked repeatedly. "What?"

"Your *cellphone*. Get your damn phone and call the cops."

Sarah nodded vigorously and grabbed her purse. Her hand disappeared inside the cavernous bag.

Bob glanced in the rearview; he couldn't see anything except the road-dust pluming behind the Lexus. "Hurry up."

"I can't find it," Sarah yelled, her hands thrusting about inside.

Bob slowed the car. "For Christ's sake. Dump that piece of luggage and find the goddam phone!"

Sarah threw the bag to the floor. "Don't yell at me!"

"Sorry," Bob yelled back. "But I'm kind of trying to save our lives here. You wanna help me?"

Sarah pointed at the dashboard. "What don't you use Onstar?"

"Because..." Bob stopped mid-sentence. Of course. It came with the lease. "Right." He reached for the Onstar symbol on the instrument panel.

"BAM!"

Again, his body slammed painfully into the safety harness. Again, the car was driven forward by the crunching roar of a diesel engine. Again, a truck grill filled the rearview mirror. This time, Bob didn't bother with the brakes. He just slammed the gas and peeled out in a cloud of dust.

The Lexus accelerated hesitantly, the rear end wobbling with the loud, abrasive noise of tire rubbing against crumpled metal. The dust cloud in the rearview hid any signs of pursuit.

"Who is this guy?" Sarah yelled, tears in her eyes. "Is he crazy?"

"That's my guess," Bob muttered. The farmhouse was only fifty yards away and closing. The rearview showed only dust. "Get ready to run for it." Bob fishtailed the car to a halt amidst a cloud of dirt and gravel. "Now! Run for the porch." He popped his door open.

Fireflies danced as Bob struck his head on the door frame.

Even before the dancing stars had cleared, before the headache set in, his eyes were searching back the way they'd come. Through the drifting dust, he spied the wrecker in the distance. It sat on the dirt road, idling, smoke pluming from the exhaust pipe. Bob didn't get it. Why had Quebe stopped?

Sarah ran beside him, tugging his arm. "Bob. Come on!"

Bob stole one more glance at the idling vision of doom, then ran with his wife.

———

THE PORCH CREAKED and groaned as their feet pelted along wood that was mostly paint flakes and rot. The clapboards were dirty and likewise in need of paint. The doorframe was largely bare wood, more rot visible at the sill. Holes in the screen door had been patched with nylon thread.

The place had the look of desertion: no car in the drive, no lights behind the dirt-smeared windows. *Please let someone be inside*, Bob prayed.

There was no bell, so Bob pounded his good hand against the screen door, jarring it with a clacking jangle of brittle pine and wire. "Hello?" he hollered.

"Hello," Sarah echoed. Her hot breath against his neck smelt of hot sauce and fear.

Bob pounded again. "Anybody there?"

"Anybody?" Sarah pleaded.

Bob raised his hand to pound a third time when he heard footsteps coming slowly toward the door.

"Thank God," he said. The door opened. "Excuse me..."

"Lawd! What's all the commotion?"

A short, blocky woman of maybe seventy filled the doorway. She was dressed in a stained house robe and was smoking a cigarette, a bluish-grey plume rising into beady eyes that squinted at Bob. "What you want?"

"Excuse me," Bob said. "There's someone chasing us. Can we come in and call the police?"

The old lady cocked her greyed head. "Chasing ya? Who's chasing ya?"

"A crazy man," Sarah shouted.

The woman cackled a rheumy cough. "You're the ones look crazy to me."

She started to close the door; Bob pushed it open. "Hey!"

"I'm sorry," Bob said. "He's after us. Quebe."

Now the old lady sounded interested. "Who's that you say?"

"Quebe. Daryl Quebe. The man the police are looking for."

"I know," the woman said. "Heard it on the radio." She looked both ways, as if Quebe might be right outside, then stepped back and said, "Ya'll better come in."

The air inside the farmhouse was ripe with the odors of stale tobacco, fried bacon, and old lady, the latter a mix of Bengay and an ancient perfume that reminded Bob of his Aunt Rose. Although the day wasn't particularly warm, the house was. No air conditioners rattled and no curtains stirred with the breeze of an open window. Furnishings were old and mismatched, a plaid chair here, a threadbare sofa there. A framed sampler on the wall asked God to bless this house. It was quiet except for the tick of a scarred grandfather clock in the corner.

"Get ya'll something? A cup of coffee?"

"Just the telephone, Ms., ah..."

"King," the old woman said. "Coretta King."

"I'm Bob Jackson." He pointed. "My wife, Sarah." He looked about. "Where's the phone?"

"Phone's in the kitchen." Bob started walking toward the hall. "But it don't work."

"What?"

"Damn phone company." The old woman spat a tobacco flake between yellow teeth. "Get a little behind and they cut off the damn phone. Like they don't got enough money; they need to take from us poor folks."

Bob looked right and left. "Do you have a cellphone?"

The woman squinted. "You mean one of them flip jobs? You think I'm made a money?"

Bob looked plaintively at Sarah.

His wife blushed. "I left my purse in the car."

He was about to shout unkind words at his wife for the second time in sixty seconds--a record for their twenty-year marriage. Then c heard the dull rumble of a diesel engine. "Quebe," he whispered, as if the maniac might hear him.

Bob locked eyes with Coretta King. Her lackadaisical manner changed. Her features hardened. Bob thought he saw an inner strength that had been hidden beneath the frowsy house coat. She shuffled to the window, one gnarled hand parting the curtains for a peek. Then she turned to Bob.

"Ya'll better wait in the kitchen."

Coretta tossed her cigarette in an ashtray and strode to the grandfather clock. She opened the scratched door. Inside, beside the pendulum works, stood an old shotgun. She withdrew it with a grunt and snapped open the short double barrels. Bob thought the deed effortless, as if from long practice. Satisfied, she snapped the action closed.

"Go on, now," Coretta said. "I'll handle this."

Bob nodded and tugged Sarah's arm. He felt better than he had since leaving the restaurant.

––––––

THE KITCHEN WAS NICER than the parlor. The appliances were white enamel with rusty nicks --but they were clean. The air smelled better as well, a whiff of baked bread beneath the stronger bacon. There was also the aroma of coffee from an old-style percolator on the stove, a small blue flame glowing from the burner below.

Bob's stomach grumbled.

Sarah smiled and took his good hand. "How can you be hungry after four tacos," she whispered.

He clutched her hand and shook his head. "Nerves."

They both watched the splinters in the hallway door. No sound came from the parlor apart from low murmurs. There was no shouting, no curses, no shotgun blast. Bob realized that he couldn't even hear the rumble of Quebe's engine any longer.

Bob squeezed his wife's hand. "Everything is going to be okay." She smiled and nodded. He looked at his watch: one-forty-five. They'd gotten to the Mexican place around twelve-thirty, then had a leisurely lunch. Now it was only quarter of two.

He looked at Sarah. She raised her brows in return. Bob whispered, "I guess a lot can happen in…"

She raised a hand for silence, head cocked. Bob heard it too.

The front door slamming. Then, long moments later, the sound of a truck door squeaking open outside.

Bob eyebrowed a question.

He must be leaving, Sarah mouthed to him.

Bob's sigh filled the room. For the first time since Quebe approached him in the restaurant, he felt good. Safe. Almost normal. The hairs on his neck weren't bristling. There was no adrenal rush. It was going to be okay.

Bob and Sarah stood holding hands like dating teens. They watched the kitchen door and waited. Any moment now, they'd hear the sound of Quebe's engine rumbling to life. Then, it would doppler away in a cloud of diesel stink. Then, they could leave.

Sarah's cell was sure to be in her purse. They'd call the cops first thing. The sheriff or whoever was the law around these parts would want to ask some questions. They'd file a report, identify a mugshot. It would probably take hours and make it rough to get to DC before dark. But that was okay too. They were in no hurry and motels were everywhere. Bob smiled.

Sarah smiled back and squeezed his hand.

As Bob gazed into his wife's brilliant blue eyes, he noticed an old phone sitting on the Formica table. Bob almost expected to see a rotary dial, but there were push buttons not unlike the phone he'd grown up with. He walked over and slid one finger lazily along the worn, tan plastic of the handset. He lifted the receiver and looked at the business end. In the silence of the kitchen, he heard a click followed by a dial tone.

Bob looked at Sarah.

His wife's eyes asked a question.

Bob spoke it aloud. "What the hell?"

The kitchen door opened, and Coretta King entered, shotgun across the crook of her arm.

Bob held up the receiver and started to speak.

King beat him to the punch. She leveled the shotgun at him and said, "Come on in nephew."

Daryl Quebe entered from behind her, a tire iron in his fist.

King held the shotgun to her shoulder. "I don't think they gonna give you any trouble."

Quebe slapped the iron into his calloused palm and grinned, his blackened eyetooth standing out like a corpse waiting for burial.

THE ANNUAL FAMILY REUNION

CHRISTINA GRIFFITH

"Stay away from there," I whispered, shepherding the toddler away from the water's edge. All children are enticed by a pool of gently lapping water and the tiniest ribbon of dark sand, regardless of the slimy lake weeds and potential for leeches. Cartoonishly large lilies floating not at the whim of winds or current but with some other intention entirely could, in the brash, late summer afternoon, appear beautiful and inviting to the oblivious.

"Yeah, you don't want to play in Lake Salad," Uncle Rocky laughed. He had called it Lake Salad for years. It was a joke to him. It was not a joke to me.

This was our annual family reunion. Nearly two hundred cousins, aunts, uncles, parents, and children gather at the end of every August to catch up with those living across the country or just too busy to make it to the odd Sunday dinner or holiday gathering. If we haven't already, we can meet the newborns, and generally, there are one or two of those every other year.

It was early yet. People were unpacking cars, hugging, slapping shoulders, and ruffling kids' hair. The aunts sat out tablecloths and stocked the soda bar. Cousins broke off and congregated to remember Uncle Vinny, who passed last year; younger kids got reacquainted by yelling and running between adults' legs. The older kids took a hour-long pre-lunch walk, returning giggling and squinting and then making a beeline for the expansive buffet. It's always an impressive spread thanks to passed-down recipes for vegetable lasagna, garlicky meatballs, thick marinara, macaroni salad, chicken thighs simmered in lemony wine sauce, antipasto, arancini, cookies, and cake. "Is there enough?" the aunts—the matriarchs—would ask. There will always be enough, they'd answer each other.

The barn-red clubhouse sat at the bottom of a steep rocky hill face, around which wound the driveway to the fire department sitting atop. In front of the clubhouse was a paved parking lot, and beyond rose a grove of trees and the town recreation area. The two-story clubhouse's white columns supported an overhang in the front and a porch in the back on the upper level overlooking the lawn.

Behind the clubhouse, ringed with great willow trees and a brown strip of sandy mud, waited the lake. Bordered at the far end by a stone dam overgrown with thick moss and Virginia creeper, it was a little less than two acres in size, an irregular oval in shape. The trees kept it mostly shaded, and where the sunlight flickered between their branches, the surface sparkled. The water was dark. On these murky waters floated a patchwork blanket of pond scum, bright green algae, and duckweed crowned with wreaths of water hyacinth. Beneath the blackish-green surface, hydrilla and pondweed danced in the sickly yellowed sunbeams. The lake did not have a name, but Lake Salad had become a running joke.

This toddler I gently redirected was Charlie, named after my older cousin-once-removed who'd passed four years ago. Charlie looked up at me and raised his tiny fist to reveal a rock.

"Here," he said.

I smiled, thanked him graciously, and shoved him a little more urgently toward the clubhouse. The inside was humming with greetings and laughter, shouts, and intense conversations around which aunt's recipe was or should be used.

I slowly moved through the gauntlet of "Hey, so good to see you!" and "Come here, sweetie," followed by a peck on the cheek and the inevitable ask, "So when are you going to get serious with that guy you're seeing, settle down, give Norma some grandkids?"

I chuckled in response—the same chuckle I offered every time. I wrung my hands, clasped them behind my back, put my hair up in a ponytail, took it down, smoothed it out, and put it back up. I looked as painfully uneasy as I felt. There was no hiding it.

Tracking the children was tough. There always seemed to be so many of them, but when I followed each one, it seemed there were precious few. I kept a watchful eye on the kids. They ranged in age from about seven to thirteen: Charlie, Peter, Tommy, Tommy Z, Arthur, Catherine, Emily, Olivia. They became easier to follow after I remembered what it was like to be one of them. At that age, we tend to move in predictable packs.

It was early afternoon, and mealtime was winding down. The food was still out, but the trays were covered. Clamoring voices rose in volume. It was a transitional time when families tended to separate and many smaller conversations began to take over. The stoner cousins took another walk.

One by one, I noticed the younger children peel away from the adults and head downstairs. By early afternoon, the basement was crammed with them. At this age, they didn't have the same freedom to come and go like the older ones but had the agency to escape the embrace of the aunts holding them to their laps, pinching and telling them how big they had gotten. They came downstairs to play video games, try to learn pool, or curl up on the dated furniture to nap.

I was last here twelve years ago and only because I had been forced to come. It was two years after my cousin Diane "went to live with her dad." Before that year's reunion, I'd been arguing with my mother again. I remember that conversation as vividly as I remember Diane.

Mom had stood at the kitchen sink with her back to me, and I leaned defiantly at the table, arms crossed.

"No, you can't stay over Holly's, or Melissa's, or anybody's house," she'd said. "It's our family reunion! We go together."

"Diane won't be there."

"Diane—"

"—Lives with her dad now, I know!" I shouted. It was Mom's bullshit mantra. We followed the same script every time: she tells me I had a traumatic experience and would get over it, nothing happened to Diane, *she just lives with her dad now.*

"Like Denny, right?" I would snap.

Her answer was always the same: "Honey, you don't have a cousin Denny. John-John is an only child."

I knew that didn't make any sense. I was angry. I was helpless. I was a child. The day of that family reunion, I was forced to leave the house, forced to get in the car, forced to get out of the car when we got there. But the moment I opened the door, I could smell it. I could hear it. I could taste it in the air. So, as my parents and sister began making greetings, I hung back and skulked in the parking lot. I wandered off with the stoner cousins, and I didn't come back right away. My dad was angry when they had to yell for me as they packed up the car at the end of the day. I'd spent most of that day sitting down by the road tossing rocks into a ditch.

I remembered Denny. His little hands. His voice. I was barely four years old, but I remember looking for him, calling out as mom and dad were getting ready to go. God, I was so little; dad scooped me up while I squirmed and whined, "Where did Denny go? Why can't I say g'bye to Denny?"

"Shhh," he patted my back. "We have a long ride home. You can sleep then."

And I remembered Diane.

I was eight, and Diane had been two years older than me. She was taller, with rounder features and a fuller figure. She was my mother's older sister's child. We'd see them a few times a year, usually at Christmas and sometimes Thanksgiving or Easter. During the summer we got a weekend or two for the Garlic Festival or the Big E. Her brother Mike and I were the same age, and we'd often butt heads over the same toys.

On that day, we had been in the basement for just a little while when Aunt Tessie's oval shadow appeared in the stairwell. We had spread out on the couch, on chairs, around the rickety foosball table, with a deck of cards on the rust-colored shag rug, with a board game whose box had been periodically masking-taped together in a diligent effort to preserve its life.

"Does anyone want to go out on the boat?" Aunt Tessie announced. "Uncle Patsy said we could use the boat for a while. Who wants to go out? Anthony? Michael? Go on, you all can take turns. Diane?"

"Yeah, I wanna go," Diane said through the lollipop in her mouth and tossed aside last March's issue of *Seventeen*.

"I want to. Can I go with you?" I asked. She nodded, and I rolled to John-John the Hot Wheels I had been tooling back and forth with between my fingers and scrambled up.

We jogged out to the water's edge where Mike and Anthony were already pushing off in the boat. It was aluminum with a short string of numbers down the side in night-glow mailbox letters, very official-like, but I didn't think it was even big enough to require an ID. It sported two wooden planks for seats and relatively new aluminum oars running through metal rings mounted on the sides.

From the deck I heard my mother's voice: "Hey, you kids don't go out too far! Do they have life jackets? Rocky, do they have—"

"Are the oars attached?" Anthony whined. "Don't drop them." The two boys drifted off into the lake as Diane and I watched.

"They have stoppers," Mike said impatiently. "Ugh, it's real weedy."

Their voices became unintelligible, though they didn't seem that far from shore. For a few minutes, they looked stationary, the weeds bunched around them, oars laden with long green fronds. Mike kept pausing to pull them off as he turned the little boat around and returned to shore. Anthony's sneakers stuck in the mud as he climbed out and cursed under his breath.

"Good luck," Mike smirked, sliding the boat over to me and Diane.

Diane climbed in first. I planted my feet on the shore to push the boat in and clambered noisily onto the rear seat. Diane handled the oars, maneuvering us out to the middle of the pond through the clumps of dark weeds and lily pads as best she could. "It's, uh, tough," she giggled, reaching out every few strokes to unwrap a vine from around the oars.

I wrinkled my nose. It smelled unpleasant. The boat felt solid enough, gently rocking, not too low in the water, and just a little damp inside. But I didn't like it. My stomach began to knot. I looked back at the shore, saw our cousins running around with a kickball; our parents standing around holding noshing plates, smoking, or clinking beers. They were all no more than a hundred feet away, but as I watched, the water seemed to stretch, becoming more ominous in its darkness as an animal might do to seem more threatening.

"I don't like this," I said.

"Don't be a baby."

I snapped my head around, I hadn't realized I'd spoken aloud. "I'm not—I really don't like this at all."

Diane rolled her eyes. She again paused to remove rings of leaves from the oars, but this time she looked hard at the green fronds across her fingers. She wrinkled her brow, glancing at me, and then behind me.

"What? What is it?"

"They're moving," she mumbled, then shook her hand over the water, shedding the weeds.

"What?"

"Nothing." Diane, pondering, scanned the surface as we floated in place, and then she took the right oar and began to turn us around. I glanced back to the clubhouse—I couldn't hear them. I couldn't hear two hundred Italians.

"That's not possible," I said, and this time I heard myself let slip something I intended just to think.

"Where'd the birds go?" Diane asked the question but clearly didn't expect me to answer.

I hadn't noticed. I heard no birds, no occasional croaking toad, nor cricket, nor cicada. Only the lapping of the water against the boat, the slosh of movement as the oars cut through the water, sputtering as they came up, bound in stems and wide leaves. She shook the oars, slapping at one or the other as she tried to move faster, but the lake weeds now clung to the edge of the boat and hung there. We weren't moving nearly fast enough—somehow, a great patch of green like an island had grown up from underneath us.

"Hey!" Diane shouted, waving her arms. Uncle Patsy probably had an inflatable raft or float or something he could toss for us to grab and pull us in. I wasn't sure there was enough current, but maybe it was shallow enough to wade out. It was only a small pond, right?

The boat rocked, less gently, as Diane and I both called out and waved our arms again. Our parents were going through the motions of walking, talking, and laughing, as if in a home movie on mute. They had to be able to hear us, but why couldn't I hear them?

I panicked. I stood and yelled, but the movement of the boat knocked me to my knees, bumping heads with Diane on the way down.

"OW! Hey!"

The boat still jostled. As Diane and I each cradled our foreheads, each of us realized the other wasn't rocking the boat. I stood and she screamed. Thick, wet, strong roots with dark leaves the texture of catfish skin wound around my legs. I tore at them with wet fingers; it was difficult to pry them off. The boat dipped hard to one side—I fell into the bottom, Diane shrieked in shock and flailed. Duckweed covered the sides of the boat, blanketing her legs. It dipped hard again, and I slipped into the water as the boat flipped over after me.

The cold rushed into my nose and ears. I pushed with my arms and kicked my legs. My skin felt slick. I'd become helpless moving through the water. It was thick like gelatin and tasted ugly. I couldn't hear or see—the lake roared in my ears and silt blinded me.

I broke the surface, bobbing up right beside the boat, and when I reached out, it was through a thick tangle of weeds. I kicked so hard and so fast, trying to make every movement count, trying to be as violent as I could against the heavy lengths of vine and stem dragging at my sneakers and giving a firm tug at my ankle. A giant lily pad slid over my mouth as I desperately held up my chin, and all I could do was grab it and rip, keep kicking, swing my arms wide, grasp the handfuls of whatever my fingers passed through and bear down with my fingernails, twist, rip, pull, push myself forward, keep kicking—

I heard nothing but the sounds of my cousin and me struggling in the water—splashing and gasping and coughing and screaming, muffled as I briefly submerged, deafening when I surfaced. I was approaching shore now, my toes could just touch the bottom, but I still needed to swim. The milfoil and pondweeds were not as thick here but had still worked their way into my left sneaker, managing to slip it off. I kicked off the other to boost my momentum, churning up thick clouds of sand. I spat grit from my mouth. I was almost able to run through the water, ripping something thick like a branch but slick like an amphibian, wrapped around me like an arm, away from my waist. I beat and yanked at it. Finally, it slid off in one slick motion.

I stumbled out of the water, into the mud, onto the grass, sobbing. My parents appeared beside me, wrapping me in a blanket and shushing me, telling me I was all right, it was okay, and "Don't be scared. You just swallowed some water, you'll be fine."

Diane never came out of the water.

Evening deepened as they comforted me. I was in a change of clothes and a warm blanket on Aunt Tessie's lap. They didn't look for Diane, and when I asked for her, they only said *she's not here, honey*.

It was time to go home, so my dad carried me to the car. "You can sleep on the ride home," he told me, buckling me into the back-seat beside my sleeping sister. "We had some excitement today," he said before he shut the door and hopped in the driver's seat. I remember watching streetlights and sky through the windshield, feeling weak and sleepy, and allowing my eyes to close.

Over time, it changed from Diane *wasn't* there to she was *never* there. And eventually it became *she just lives with her dad, now*.

Yes, I had been here before. In the basement, where they were called to go to the lake. I had to stop it from happening.

Aunt Tessie stood in the kitchen, sorting leftovers into plastic containers. She appeared much older than I remembered. I had seen her every year when I was young. Now, having been away almost a decade, I noticed her age.

"Aunt Tessie, do you need any help?" I ventured.

"Oh no, no, thank you hon, thank you. How did you like the piccata?"

"It was great. I'll take some home if there's another tray."

"Of course there is."

"You know the water is chilly and too dirty today for the kids," I tried. "I don't think they should go out on the lake."

"Oh nonsense," she waved her hand. "They'll have a blast. Go tell Patsy to take the boat out of the shed, would you?"

"No," I mumbled.

She looked at me with a furrowed brow.

"No Aunt Tessie, I don't think they should."

She waved her hand again as though to dispel me like a puff of smoke, and she yelled, "Patsy! Rocco! Get the boat out for the kids, would you? And get your niece a shot—she needs it." Aunt Tess elbowed me with a laugh and moved to the top of the basement stairs.

I wrung my hands, shifting my weight from one foot to the other, while around me, the matriarchs moved about the kitchen as if I were invisible.

A squealing stampede of children moved up the stairs and through the kitchen, accompanied by the aggravated chastising of the adults. Bobbing heads, bubble-gum chewing mouths, and squeaking sneakers bolted past me, ignoring my cries, "Stop! Don't go to the lake! Stay out of the water!"

But I had been here before, too, running outside, playing on the grass beside the lake. They jockeyed for first boat captain. Some scrambled around with kickballs or picked through a pile of water guns before running to the water's edge to fill them.

I couldn't let them go.

Thin clouds filtered the sun. It was a little cooler than usual for the late summer midafternoon lull. Uncle Patsy dragged the boat to the water. Olivia waited there to hop in.

I shouted, "No, it isn't safe! Stay out of the water!"

But they were also shouting, and running in circles around each other, around me—oblivious and careless. Olivia sat with the oars in her hands. Tommy ran past me, and I reached out and called his name. But his little sandaled feet had already slid across the sand, and with a little hop, he now sat behind Olivia. She complained about his rocking the boat and began to row. He complained she was going *too slow*.

My arm still hung in the air from trying to grab Tommy. I watched as they floated away. As I did, the lake surface stretched, groaned, and darkened. I couldn't go after them, and I failed to stop them from going to the lake.

Everything became stiff—everything but the lake was in slow motion. Sounds stretched and muffled. I was confused, disoriented, trying to scream for someone to do something. Nothing came out.

Was this my memory, or was this happening? Time had slowed, but not on the lake. The boat had stopped in silence. No birds, no bugs, no frogs. The children were facing me now and appeared to be shouting, but I couldn't hear them.

I shouted back, but I knew they couldn't hear me.

Olivia raised her arms above her head, waving frantically. I sluggishly turned back around to the clubhouse, calling for help, hearing nothing.

Everyone was so far away from me now. The kickball game had moved around the side of the building, Uncle Patsy was casually leaning by the back door, chatting with Uncle Rocky, a cigar in his hand. My cousins, aunts, and uncles up on the deck took pictures and passed phones back and forth. All in slow motion. No one heard me.

"Don't you see? Can't you understand what's happening?"

And suddenly, I really was screaming. I knew I was screaming because I heard it like a piercing shock, and then a flood of sound followed like a sonic dam bursting. I felt instant terror as everyone paused what they were doing to turn and stare.

"What are you all staring at? Don't you see what's happening?" I gestured wildly to where two hysterical children were begging for their parents. I could hear them now, but no one moved, no one spoke. I was enraged. Balling my fists, I spit out, "You do, don't you? You can all see, and you know what's going on, don't you?"

They didn't answer. The only sound was the disturbingly loud thrashing from the small boat on the lake, children crying out, the hollow thunk of aluminum.

I felt then a rush like water overtaking me, filling my mouth and eyes and ears, but then...an improbable and overwhelming sense of calm, and, even more deeply, understanding.

Of course they know. That's why they're here, in this place. They know what must be done.

I saw it now, too.

It wasn't in the lake. It wasn't even *of* the lake. It *was* the lake. The lake was pulling and grabbing and needing and wanting. It was everywhere. It was taste, touch, smell, sound—great yet formless, grasping and powerful, dark and threatening.

The family are called to the lake, and we give what it needs.

We all come to the feast. Only those of a certain age are chosen for the lake. The elders don't make any selections. Those the lake needs come willingly, eager, and unaware of the purpose or ends they served—ends eternally shrouded in enigmatic waters. The children would take tuns on the lake until one or two of them strayed long enough to let it get hold of them. There were always enough on offer because we made sure of it—to give the lake what it wants.

I understood.

I was still standing on the shore. The boat had drifted back, empty but for a few tattered threads of pondweed. It gently slid onto the sand, coming to a rest leaning slightly to one side.

Someone shouted, "Hey honey, do you think you can take the boat up to the shed for Patsy?"

I didn't answer, but it didn't matter. I'd do it. I stood there for some time, listening to the birds and frogs, watching the weak light of the obscured sun pass over the surface of the lake.

It's about time I thought about starting a family. I should take my relationships more seriously, settle down. That way, there will always be enough.

I'M NOT FROM HERE

J.M. BASK

You look around slowly, holding one hand above your sweaty brow, as if it will somehow magically help you see better in the dim twilight. It does not.

A field stretches into darkness, a blaze of tall purple grass fading to black along the horizon, where storm clouds darken the evening air. Thick flashes of lightning streak across the sky, threads of white zigzagging through the textured cloth of tattered clouds.

There is no thunder, but the hum of electricity hangs in the air, along with a colorless fog of humidity that clings to your skin, seeps under your clothes, and licks trails of sweat down your spine. You suck in a deep breath, and the taste of metal crawls across your tongue.

You pat your shirt and pants pockets hoping for your phone, car keys, a lighter, a piece of paper—anything to tell you where you are and why—but you find nothing. Even pocket lint has escaped this barren place.

At your feet is a faint, rutted track long unused and nearly weeded over. The scene in every direction looks identical to this one, and the heavy clouds have obscured astronomical wayfinders, so you 'eenie meenie miney mo' the two ends of the track until the 'you are not it' at the end has you heading to the right. You begin to walk.

———

You're aware of passing fields, but the landscape is so changeless you might as well be walking on a treadmill for all the progress you seem to be making. Runnels of lightning are the only variation. What could be hours or minutes later, a soft, yellow glow of light appears in the field to your left, a spot of brightness along the horizon.

You leave your narrow path and run toward it.

The glow looks like lamplight–electric, warm, and manmade–that buttery yellow that only comes from bulbs. It's beautiful. You run faster, the thick, bitter air difficult to breathe as you speed through the night.

As you near the light, you see a shape within it—the familiar dark silhouette of a human form. Your legs beat through the grass, the whickering sound of each breaking blade music to your ears, knowing that you are doing something to damage and change this changeless place.

At a distance of twenty yards, a woman's outline becomes distinct beside a low table with something piled on it. She is lit from above, as though a can light with a bright bulb hungs over her. But, other than the brilliance of the light itself, there is nothing hanging above her–no lamp, no bulb, no lantern–just the radiance one would give. You slow to a jog, then a brisk walk. Only ten yards now. Stacks of folded cloth rest on the table.

"Hello?" you call. She must hear you through all this silence.

The words carry, but the person doesn't so much as flinch. She just keeps folding what you can now see are stacks of identical t-shirts. She places them on a low, white, display table, like the kind you would see in any department store. You stop an arm's length from the woman.

A plastic sign on the table informs you the shirts are all ten dollars. The lady's pale face is expressionless as she finishes folding the last shirt, then walks around to the opposite corner of the table.

You wait for her to notice your presence.

Instead, she picks up a perfectly folded pile of clothing and tosses it to the middle of the table in an untidy heap. Reaching in, she plucks a corner of fabric with two careful fingers, and begins folding again.

"Excuse me?" you say, carefully.

The woman looks up at you suddenly, a doll-like grin creeping across her lips, showing neat, white teeth.

You take it as an invitation. "Excuse me, miss. Can you tell me where we are?"

Her shoulders come up in a slow, practiced shrug. All the while, she never stops folding. "I'm not from here," she says.

"So you don't know where we are?"

"I'm sorry, I'm not from here."

"Why are you folding those shirts?" You're trying not to sound frantic, but you can't really help it. "In a field," you continue, "in the middle of nowhere?"

"I'm sorry. I'm not from here." She is still smiling, still folding, her words calm and measured, as a single tear slides from one glassy eye. The woman looks back down at her shirts, the grin still stuck to her face as if you were no longer there.

You back away from the table into the darkness, which now feels somehow safer than the glare beside this strange, smiling woman. When she is doll-sized in a pool of yellow light, you catch sight of another glow, a steady blue-white fluorescence off to your right. You wait until the folding woman moves to another corner of her table, her back to you, and then you run again.

———

THE FLUORESCENCE GROWS CLOSER as you walk. Another person, another shape forming out of darkness. As you get near, your body wet with sweat and humidity and your lungs burning from running, you make out a man at a desk. In front of him stands a stack of paper. Wide, cool light illuminates the man from above. As you approach, you look up, half-expecting to see cold, fluorescent bulbs in a tiled ceiling, but again there is only the light itself and the sky above, no bulb or lamp to be seen.

You edge into the circle of light, but the man pays you no attention. He is hastily filling in blanks on a series of forms. As he swipes a completed sheet into a single black plastic bin on his desk, you realize that the papers in front of him appear to be identical. The only other thing on his desk is a canister of blue ballpoint pens.

You wait until he is scribbling in the last blanks on the last form.

As the man lifts the paper toward the basket, you speak. "Excuse me."

His eyes flick up at you and a smile breaks across his face—one eerily identical to the woman's, though she and he share no similar features. He says nothing.

"Um, do you know where we are?"

"I'm sorry," he says, lifting the stack of paper back out of the bin and onto his desk. He uncaps a fresh pen. "I'm not from here," he says as he starts filling in the same set of forms again.

He is writing the same things, tracing the same words, over and over, the paper heavy with ink. As you back away, you nearly stumble into a wastebasket at the edge of the light, filled to the brim with dried-out pens.

You turn and run into the gloom.

———

Points of light—some buttery yellow, some white or blue, some red—mark the darkness. You find a man standing at a cash register, counting the same stacks of bills and slotting them, over and over again. A woman in a bikini swings around a pole on a tiny, circular stage.

You think about how tired the woman's legs must be as you run into the shadows, and you think about how yours aren't far behind.

A woman lies on the ground by a small yellow car, the make of which you don't recognize, taking off and putting on one of its tires over and over and over. A man stands on a red area rug, pushing a silent vacuum cleaner back and forth. A person stands at a single bookcase filled with books bearing blue covers, pulling them out and rearranging them, despite their sameness. You pull several off and throw them to the ground, where they flop open, their pages blank. You scream the same questions you've asked the others, and as they collect the books, they repeat the same thing the others told you. "I'm sorry. I'm not from here."

And you do the same thing you've always done. You run into the twilight.

———

You aren't running anymore but are weaving through the dark, dewy grass. That electric hum still fills the air and thunderless lightning flashes overhead but never reaches for the ground. Nothing worth reaching for, you guess. You avoid additional pools of light. You can't stand to see another emotionless smile or hear the same words uttered with different voices.

It's impossible to count minutes or hours, so instead you count the lights you pass. You are up to nine-hundred fifty-seven when you see a glow that makes your chest ache with longing. The warm light in the distance reminds you of a welcoming window of somewhere you've been before, but you can't quite place it.

You jog toward it, hesitant at first, your feet speeding and slowing, then speeding up again. Soon, you get close enough to see there is no one in the light, no movement—just familiar objects, waiting for you. You know you should turn and run. Perhaps looking at other people's eternities would be less tedious. But the warm light is so inviting. Maybe it won't be so bad to have a light of your own, a task of your own, especially one you know so well.

Without thinking about it, you step forward and take your place, your hands moving, the light framing your every action. The air feels cooler under the light, and the flashes of lightning seem duller and far away. It's almost a relief to be here, under your light, your hands dancing the same steps over and over.

It won't be the same forever.

Eventually, someone will come and ask—will beg—and you'll get to smile and tell them the only thing you know, with a tear in your eye for the first time in a thousand lights.

"I'm sorry. I'm not from here."

SACRIFICE
BETH KETTE ANDERSON

BETH KETTE ANDERSON

"Look! You won't believe how cool this is," Violet said, pointing up with her flashlight into the corner of the decrepit outhouse. "Check it out, Annie." The beam barely penetrated the cobweb mesh.

Violet scooted to one side of the old, wooden latrine. Annie stepped inside. Deep scratches ran down the outside of the door. That was odd, but I was more interested in what they had found.

These woods were not accustomed to people. I went there as a child for a week or two every summer with my best friend's family. The owners, the Shaws, join us for only a few days. Other than during those visits, the wilderness had its way with the place. Pine trees grew as close together as pine trees could grow, and waist-high salal filled in the rest. Slugs the size of bratwurst ruled the ground.

My flip flops made a sticky sound when I stepped closer to the outhouse, the bottoms of my feet covered with a layer of slug-slime.

"Holy shit! That's amazing!" Annie said. Her luminous, blue eyes shimmered in the light. Her long, blonde hair framed delicate features. She was the most beautiful of the four Russian sisters.

"Russian Princesses," their older half brother called them with disgust. Annie's sister, Violet, had won a Farrah Fawcett look-alike contest earlier that summer. Jan and her boyfriend were homecoming king and queen. The youngest, Margaret, was like me, the neighbor kid—we were chubby rugrats with railroad-track braces.

We poked in our heads to see what treasure Margaret's older sisters had found. The rotten floorboards creaked with our combined weight.

"Where? I don't see anything," Margaret said.

"Let us out and you can look," Annie said as she stepped out of the darkness.

Violet followed. One of her stray strawberry blonde curls slid through my mouth as she squeezed past us.

Margaret and I shuffled into the gag-inducingly horrible-smelling latrine. One of the floorboards sank precariously under my foot. I hopped to the side, remembering that bending board from summers past. I clung to a case of Mountain Bars, candy treats Mr. Shaw paid out for clams we'd dug for him—an incredible deal for a kid rarely allowed to eat candy.

Violet shone the beam of light up to the corner of the outhouse ceiling. Then I felt a shove. The door slammed shut. The chain that secured the outhouse all winter clanked heavily.

Of course.

Once again, Margaret and I were the victims of her shapeshifting sisters. Sometimes the five of us were a gang out for an adventure. Sometimes the older three were our heroes telling us secrets about their boyfriends. And sometimes, Margaret and I were the foil for Annie and Violet's cruel pranks. There is nothing so crucial to the children's social order as the sacrificial victim.

"Very funny," Margaret said. "Open the door."

We both knew that wasn't going to happen anytime soon. We didn't have a flashlight. I breathed out of my mouth. The door being shut meant the combination of latrine chemicals and decades of excrement could knock a person out. Fat strands of jute from what had been a macrame decoration hung down like decaying tentacles. I brushed them off my shoulders.

"Oh, do you need light?" Violet asked. Streaks of light flashed through the slats of the walls.

I could just make out Margaret's eyes, panicked and wide.

Annie howled with laughter from the other side of the wall.

I let out a little giggle. It was pretty funny.

"Have a good night. Look out for spiders," Violet said sweetly. The light disappeared. Footsteps crunched away on the twigs and leaves covering the path leading back to the cabin.

"This is bullshit. I'm going to break this door down," Margaret said. "Look out."

I squeezed into the corner as Margaret threw herself at the door. It didn't budge. She bounced back into me and then fell to the floor. She jumped up and rammed the door again and fell to the floor once more.

A shiver jolted through me just thinking about the floor of the latrine and the permastink soaking into her clothes. We'd have to throw them in the campfire. Except her Alice Cooper t-shirt. Maybe we could wash that in the lagoon. I accidentally inhaled through my nose, shivered, and said my goodbyes to Alice. "Gonna burn baby."

"Marg, stop," I said. "You're going to break your shoulder."

"What do you suggest we do? Live here?" she snapped.

I shook the box of candy. "We won't starve."

Margaret clenched her teeth.

"They'll come back," I said, not fully believing it myself. "Your mom will wonder where we are and come get us."

Margaret offered a guttural growl. "Mom won't even notice. She and Mrs. Shaw are deep in conversation about the ski school, and I heard the martini shaker going when we left." She paused.

We both must have thought of Jan—back at the cabin with the adults, as usual—for next she screamed, "J-A-A-A-A-N!"

Jan had read *Nancy Drew at the Lilac Inn* to us the night before. We could read just fine, but it felt like we were actually in The Lilac Inn when Jan did the voices. She was the oldest of the Russian princesses and fancied herself the grown-up of the group. This could be good when she read to us but also bad when she bossed us around.

"Do you need to use the latrine, Annie?" Violet kidded. The beam of a flashlight accompanied returning footsteps and bounced back toward us.

I knew they wouldn't leave us locked in there very long, but I wasn't sure if we would run out of oxygen before they reached us.

"No, I'm good." The sound of a match scratching across the rough strip on a box of matches.

I smelled the sulfur of a lit match.

They were very close.

A stream of cigarette smoke poured in through the ancient walls.

Margaret grabbed me.

"They're going to kill us," she said.

"The smoke won't kill us. Linda's dad smokes two packs a day and he's fine." The smoke was actually a welcome relief from our toxically stinky dungeon.

"Let us out. I'm going to tell mom you tried to kill us. Beth's parents will make sure you go to jail."

———

Shaw's Cabin sat on two hundred and seventy-three forested acres on Hood Canal. Several crumbling structures stood here and there.

A haunted A-frame stood across the little lagoon and stared at us with triangle eyes. The lagoon, Dead Man's Cove, had a dock with rowboats and canoes tied to it. Almost every night, someone claimed to see lights emanating from different rooms of the deserted chalet across the water. We paddled rowboats toward the A-frame's dock but never stepped foot on it.

Every morning, a stranded rowboat appeared at a different inlet. Moss hanging from tree branches hovered over these places so they were dark and marshy at any time of day. We avoided them at all costs, only accidentally drifting in on the rare occasion we caught a four-inch trout on our drop lines and were too overcome with the thrill of catching dinner to notice our drift.

We would cram into a dusty bedroom in Shaw's Cabin, our sleeping bags rolled out across the floor in an arrangement similar to that which ruled in the brown Rambler Station Wagon that got us there—that the ugliest car I'd seen, until our other neighbor bought one in aqua. Positions in both places were determined according to age. Margaret and I, as the youngest pair in this wild female pack, fell out of the fifth-door with the camping stove, tent poles, and ice chests when Margaret's mother pulled it open. We'd have been packed into this position for hours with full bladders and empty stomachs.

———

"Should we give them the key?" Violet sing-songed.

"Yeah. Probably should," Annie said. "It's right here, Margaret." A shiny, silver glint poked into the back wall between the vertical boards.

Margaret snapped her hand over so fast I didn't even see it. She snatched the key and pulled it inside. For a moment, relief washed over us. The lock was on the outside.

"I hate my sisters," Margaret said. Then she yelled, "Fuck you!"

I didn't know what she meant, but I knew it was bad. Violet had told us that word had something to do with Nancy Drew and Ned Nickerson and that Jan wished her boyfriend would do it to her. Margaret acted like she understood and that I, nine months younger, would have to grow up before she told me.

I heard the sound of two pull-tabs snapping, followed by fizzing.

"I'm really thirsty," Margaret said. "How long can people survive without water?"

"We've only been in here for ten minutes, and you know they're not drinking water. It's gross beer."

"I'm so thirsty I could drink a beer right now," Margaret said, her voice low.

"Oh stop it. You're fine. Want a bar?" I kicked at the case of Mountain Bars on the floor.

"No. I can't eat and breathe through my mouth at the same time."

I agreed.

Outside, Annie laughed so hard she snorted.

"Oh my God, it came out your nose!" Violet yelled.

"Glad they're having a good time," Margaret said. "We are going to get them back so bad."

"What do you want to do?" I asked with ghoulish excitement. She often conjured up the most awe-inspiring revenge plots unique to the youngest child in most families.

"Something worse than this," she said. "Like really scare them. Hmmmm. What if one of us, you maybe, laid down in the rowboat that is always moving around in Dead Man's Cove. I'll cover you with moss and leaves. Then I'll go get them to help me catch the loose boat."

"It would have to be dark out." I knew where this was going.

"Definitely. I'll paddle us under the moss and into the cove. I'll act scared. Then you—"

"Start moaning and moving!"

"And hit them with globs of seaweed! I'll scream like we're being attacked by the Dead Man. They'll pee their pants!"

Something brushed by the side of the latrine.

I jumped, wrapping my arms around myself. "What was that?"

"They're just trying to scare us," Margaret said. "They must have heard me."

"I don't think so," I said, rubbing the goosebumps on my arms. "That was creepy. I felt something."

Margaret stepped slowly to the middle planks with me, away from the walls. "What did it feel like?"

"I don't know. Like a breeze, but with fur." I shivered. Midsummer in the Pacific Northwest can still have a chill overnight. This wasn't the cold I felt, though. It felt alive.

A shrill howl exploded and carried on for a heart-pounding fifteen seconds. We stared, big-eyed, at each other.

"J-A-A-A-A-A-N!" I shrieked.

"M-O-O-O-O-O-M!" I don't think I had ever heard Margaret call for her mother like that before.

Now I was scared. "Why isn't anyone looking for us?" I asked, though I knew we weren't on anyone's radar.

"They're probably singing Kumbaya or something out by the campfire. And Jan won't stop playing The Carpenters on her stupid radio. They'll never hear us."

A chorus of unworldly wails and yips exploded from the thick, black woods. Breezy swishing rushed along the back and both sides of the latrine, a river flowing with the urgency of crashing rapids.

"Wolves!" Margaret yelled.

"Or coyotes," I said. "Or bears."

"Bears don't run in big groups. There must be a hundred of them!"

The crazy shrieks started up again, each continuing and joining the others. I covered my ears and shut my eyes tight. I'd go insane if I let them in my head.

Margaret knew what they were. "Wolves do that when they find prey. They are calling the rest of the pack. They probably killed a deer or a rabbit," she said. "They can't get in here."

"Are you sure?" I whimpered.

"Trust me. That door is locked tight." Margaret rubbed her shoulder.

"At least we are safe in here," I said.

Frantic footsteps scampered up the path followed by frantic pounding on the door.

"Beth, let us in." It was Annie. "Please let us in," she whispered fiercely. "There is a huge pack of coyotes or something circling us."

"Where's the key?" I said, fumbling around in the dark.

Margaret stuck her hand in her pocket, then stopped. "Why should I let you in? You were going to let us die in here."

"Margaret! They are going to get us. We were just joking around." Violet urged, "Hand me the key."

I could see Violet's fingertip run along a warped gap between the wall slats.

Anger radiated from my friend. Did she truly hate her sisters enough to literally throw them to the wolves? This feud was between Margaret and her sisters, and I loved them all. This was one of those rare times when I knew I wasn't family. I was the neighbor kid, expected to keep quiet.

Another war cry erupted. Violet and Annie smacked the door with their palms. "They're closing in!" Annie hissed.

For an instant, Margaret seemed locked in thought before thrusting the key through the opening into Violet's fingers.

The lock shook and rattled. Finally the chains fell loose.

They jerked open the door and Violet leapt in with Annie still behind her. Dozens of night demons were right there, red eyes glowing in the dusk.

My mouth opened wide but no sound came out. I froze.

"Annie!" Violet and Margaret yanked Annie's arm, which was viciously pulled out of their grasp.

Annie and the pack screamed in horrible unison a few yards from the outhouse. The animals snarled and snatched at her pale blue Keds. A big one caught her left wrist in its teeth, and she swung at him. His ears laid flat back on his head. He exposed vicious fangs. Annie got a good punch in, but the beast didn't release her. Drool and blood on his fangs glistened in the moonlight.

If those things were coyotes, they were twice the size of the ones that wandered our suburban neighborhood.

"Annie! Your lighter!" Violet shrieked. She held the door open.

Annie had managed to haul herself up onto a rotten stump, the pack snapping at her flailing arms and legs. She didn't have a chance to use her lighter against the beasts.

Shut the door? Save Annie? Sacrifice Violet? Get us all killed? There were no good options.

"I can't watch," Violet said. She lit her Zippo and ran over toward Annie in the middle of the pack. "Give me something to burn," Violet yelled. She tore off her hoodie and tried lighting a sleeve. It wasn't catching.

"Here!" I opened and dumped out the Mountain Bars, holding out the cardboard box. "This! This! This!" My arms shook as violently as though I were flagging down a plane.

Margaret steadied the box while Violet held the flame to a torn edge. Finally, it caught. Violet faced the voracious animals. There were so many. They were doglike but wild, hungry. She waved the flaming cardboard in their faces. Violet screamed like a warrior, flung her wild curls back and bared her teeth. A few of the creatures stepped backward but didn't retreat.

Mountain Bars littered the floor of the latrine. Margaret ripped the wrapper off of one of the lumpy chocolates and hurled it toward the frenzied pack. Two of the things pounced on it. Sniffed. Growled at each other. One snatched it and it was gone in an instant.

I threw two more bars.

Violet saw what we were doing. She threw the last bit of the burning case at the closest set of fangs. She ran over to us, scooped an armload of candy bars from the floor and threw them machine-gun style at the animals.

We caught glimpses of Annie in the scrum, limp and bleeding, draped over the stump. She was no longer fighting back. Her beautiful face would never be the same. None of us would be the same.

Soon, the chocolate was more of a prize than Annie. The animals fought each other for the bars. We threw the candy farther and farther away.

I had just gotten third place in the softball throw at Field Day, and I felt I could throw five times as far to save Annie. As the bars flew farther from us, the coyotes—or whatever they were—were there to devour them.

At that moment the first one who had eaten the chocolate arched his back and horked up brown chunks. Soon the next one followed suit. Then more.

Seizing the moment, Violet gave us orders. "Margaret, you and I grab Annie. Beth, stay close and keep throwing. We'll get to the cabin. Now! Go!"

I had a handful of bars left. I didn't have to unwrap them now. The animals knew what they were.

We burst out of the latrine and scurried toward a motionless

Annie. Violet shot her arms under Annie's armpits. Margaret took her legs. I saw glints of white on Annie's face. I couldn't reconcile what I was looking at until I realized they were her teeth grinning, exposed through her cheek. I heaved deeply, sucking as much oxygen as I could so as not to faint, and ran sideways throwing those candy bars like the Corn Queen at the Harvest Parade. At least a half a dozen wolves raced behind us nipping at our heels. Wild keening continued in the forest. As we closed on the cabin, the animals shied away from the human noise and light coming from the deck.

Violet and Margaret reached the deck steps with their sister. I heaved the last of the candy into the darkness and scrambled up onto the deck behind them. The pack had disappeared into the trees.

The Shaws, Marg's parents and oldest sister sat around a smoking Hibachi with charred bits of meat stuck in the grates, sizzling. Karen Carpenter's chorus of "Top of the World" blasted from Jan's little purple radio.

Jan screamed when she saw her blood-covered sisters. Their mother leapt into action, returning a moment later with blankets from the cabin.

At this point, Mr. Shaw was yanking down the tailgate of his pick-up truck.

Jan jumped into the bed of the truck. Violet and Margaret maneuvered an unconscious Annie up to Jan who eased her toward the cab. Violet sat on the back of the truck and swung her legs up. Mr. Shaw threw the blankets onto them, got in the driver's seat, and revved the engine. Jan and Violet covered Annie with the blankets and lay on either side of her, tucking her in and whispering things in her ears. Margaret slammed the tailgate shut.

Margaret stood beside me and we watched the truck speed away from Shaw's Cabin.

"Did you see Annie's teeth?" I whispered, my shaky hand over my mouth. The sickly smell of chocolate gagged me.

In the night, Margaret's dilated eyes were wide as owls' as we watched the truck turned down the dirt road, quickly enveloped by the pitch black forest.

"Yeah," she whispered back. "Cool."

THE MORNING AFTER

WILLIAM WANDLESS

Serena had hoped for more: more compassion, more consolation—hell, even more fireworks. But her world had come to an end with a pitiful whimper.

She had told the truth, and the editorial board had not found the truth amusing. Mr. Patel, bored and unsmiling, had repossessed her laptop and handed her off to security. And Marty, the kindly guard who greeted her at the front desk every morning, had led Serena on a walk of shame through PopStop's bullpen. Her assembled officemates, her comrades and confidantes for the past three years, didn't even look up from their screens as she passed, engrossed as they were by their media feeds.

She took the 2:30 train back to her tiny apartment, stuffed four suitcases with everything she cared to keep, and drove north from the City toward the Faradays' house in Vermont. Serena stopped only once during the six-hour trip, eating a Happy Meal in a parking lot in the middle of Massachusetts, scattering the last of her fries for the pigeons, and admiring the plum-colored supermoon that already loomed in the twilit August sky, as lovely as it was unnerving.

Serena arrived well after dark, just as August ended and September began. She lugged two of her suitcases inside and played with the dog until it remembered her scent. She trudged upstairs with the cats curling between her feet, texted her mom and Alyssa to say she'd arrived safely for house-sitting duty, stripped down to her underwear, and collapsed on the bed face-first.

Serena was dreaming of bees when she woke to the buzz of her iPhone, which was sandwiched between her pillow and her face. She peeled it away from her cheek and rolled onto her back, squinting at the bleary slab of alerts that had trickled in overnight. Even half-asleep, nestled in this strange bed in this strange room in this strange house, she could feel a habitual rhythm taking hold, a pattern and a prison. She took a deep, deliberate breath and released it evenly, intentionally. "Not today," she said to the gathering morning light. "Not anymore."

It took an act of will to leave her glasses on the nightstand, another to turn her phone entirely off. Serena dropped it on the bed beside her and pushed it out of reach. Bear, the bigger of the two cats, crept up from his post between her feet, sniffed the phone, and jammed his head beneath her empty hand. Bean, the littler, jumped up on the bed with a myowlp and started making biscuits on her hip, claiming a spot of his own. In seconds, she had both tabbies purring, and for a few drowsing, blissful minutes she forgot all about her phone, the City, and the life she was leaving behind.

Serena allowed herself to rest—to genuinely rest—for the first time in years. She stretched her legs, indulging in the cool friction of the clean sheets, and smiled. Today there would be no scramble to throw together some semblance of a healthy breakfast, no attempt to set a new record for getting ready, no sprint to catch the 7:20 train. Today she wouldn't dream up clever things to tweet, check the web for new job prospects, or let herself get pissed off or petrified by clickbait about the Helheim Glacier. Today she wouldn't attend any meetings, answer any emails, or let the PopStop calendar app tell her where she had to go or what she had to do. Today she would do her best to simply exist.

"I'm not getting out of bed for anyone but me today," she informed the cats, and Bear rested his paw on her hand in feline solidarity. As if on cue, however, she heard the telltale ticking of toenails on hardwood, and a white-muzzled Retriever ambled into the bedroom, wagging her tail so happily that she could hardly keep her balance. "Well, anyone except my good friend Daisy," she added, climbing down and submitting to a round of sloppy canine kisses. "I'm sorry I was rude to you all last night," she told her housemates, "but I'll make it up to you." Serena grabbed her glasses, claimed Friday's tee shirt from the floor, and headed for the bedroom door. "Let's see what we can make of this beautiful day."

Serena led Bear, Bean, and Daisy downstairs and into the kitchen, filled their bowls, and watched them tuck in. While they were preoccupied, she fired up the coffee maker and rummaged through the cupboards. Several times she caught herself resisting the urge to snap pictures—of light the color of pink champagne flooding the kitchen and dancing on the marbled countertops, of steam rising enticingly from an ombre stoneware mug, of the three adorable creatures lolling at her feet as she sipped her coffee at a shaded table on the railed patio between the house and the pool. She wanted to post to Instagram, to humblebrag about the sweetness of this house sitting gig, to fish for a few likes and retweets to start the weekend. Instead, she drained her mug and went back inside, determined to go at least one day without those low-grade jolts of dopamine.

All three animals watched Serena as she visited the bathroom and savored a half-hour shower, as she dried her hair and brushed her teeth, and as she slipped on her leggings and a tank top and loaded the rest of her clothes into the guest room dresser. They escorted her as she snooped around the house, imagining what it would be like to live as Jamie and Alyssa did. And they attended her as she eased her way through a yoga session by the pool, letting her body remember the poses, letting lingering tensions evaporate. When she finished, she realized a pair of squirrels had been watching her from the side railing, and she smiled and bowed to them.

She found a container full of nuts and birdseed just inside the door, and she slipped back outside, scattered some on the patio, and left two extra handfuls in small heaps at either end of the railing. The squirrels, which had darted away at her approach, instantly reappeared. "It's okay, babies," Serena cooed. "I know I'm not your usual mama, but I'll feed you just the same."

She made smooching sounds to call Bean and Bear inside, but the squirrels didn't seem to mind them and began to eat. A pair of jays appeared and claimed their share, and a robin joined them, pecking at the seed perhaps six feet from Bean. Bean, oblivious, started grooming himself while Bear climbed into an overflowing splash of lavender in a big terracotta pot. Serena settled by the sliding door with Daisy at her feet, hands on her hips, feeling like Snow White.

Serena went back inside and finally read the note Alyssa and Jamie had left. She imagined they must have already landed and were aboard the boat that would take them around the southern tip of Greenland and up to the heliport on the eastern coast. From there they would fly over the fissure where the Glacier had split and see whatever had been hidden underneath the ice all this time. She sighed—it had only taken about three weeks for entrepreneurs to turn a natural disaster into a tourist trap. The Faradays had left her the number for their hotel in Nuuk, but they would be hard to get hold of until Wednesday. "Our offer's still open!"

Alyssa had jotted at the bottom of the page, adding a smiley face. "We'll chat when we get back!"

And Serena wondered if she had somehow manifested all of this—if her intentions and visualizations and daily affirmations were making these changes happen, if this was the path the universe meant for her to take.

She puzzled over the prospect as she misted the houseplants. On one hand, she knew there was nothing mystical about most of the pieces that had fallen into place. The rent on her studio apartment in the City was going to climb out of reach at the end of the month, and she had already decided she was going to let her lease lapse. Getting fired from PopStop hadn't come as a surprise, either. In the span of a week, Serena had authored two pieces that had gone over poorly with Mr. Patel, even though they'd done great numbers. Hipsters loved her quizzes, but "Which Nepo Baby Are You?" had rubbed readers in a few key demographics the wrong way. And "Real Talk: How Screwed Are We?"—her column on Helheim, a listicle summing up the worries of some of PopStop's go-to scientists—had been too frank for most readers to stomach. No one wanted to hear about rising sea levels, polluted coastal ecosystems, or prehistoric viruses drifting up from the fissure and entering the atmosphere and water supply. It wasn't the sort of upbeat fluff advertisers wanted, and she'd known that when she wrote it, but snark and doomscrolling were reliable commodities.

Serena wasn't spacey enough to see the Law of Attraction in any of that. But the fact that she'd bumped into Alyssa and Jamie in the City last summer at a coffee shop she'd never visited that had opened up this house sitting gig? Or the fact that the gig just happened to coincide with the end of her lease and career as well as with a vacation she'd scheduled months ago? Or the fact that Alyssa had brought up the job offer Jamie mentioned in passing at Christmas, an offer that came with a spot in the front office of Faraday Farms and a deal to live in their carriage house for a fraction of her City rent? It all seemed too good to be true, as if forces of nature really were bending her way.

Serena spotted Bear pawing at the patio door, and she slid it open to let both cats inside. She stepped out to grab her coffee mug while she was at it, and beside it she found a surprise: Bear or Bean had left a well-chewed catnip mouse on the table, and the squirrels had brought her a walnut from a tree almost fifty yards away, where the spirea hedge ended and the woods began. Serena beamed. "Aren't you just the sweetest?" she called to all the animals in earshot. "Thank you!"

A chunky squirrel chittered to her from the apple tree next to the patio, and a crow cawed from the pergola beside the pool. She scanned the patio, but all the peanuts and seeds were gone. "Sorry, bud—we're all done with breakfast," she said, waving to the crow. "But we'll be serving elevensies soon!"

Back inside, Serena rinsed out her mug and checked out what her friends had left in the fridge, trying to decide if she should make the five-minute drive south to Cavendish to have brunch at the café. Alyssa and Jamie had unsurprisingly stocked the shelves for her, and they'd given the leftover sushi from their Friday night dinner pride of place. "That settles that," she said to Daisy, who was begging unsubtly beside her. She gave Daisy a rawhide chew from a box on top of the fridge, then grabbed the sushi tray, soy sauce, and chopsticks and headed back to the patio. Bear had curled up on the sofa, but Bean came outside with her.

When Serena had settled back into her chair and popped the lid off the takeout tray, she reached for her phone, realized it was still upstairs, and sighed. She tried to remember where she'd read that it took three weeks to break a habit—just the sort of trivia she would normally Google on her phone. "This is going to be tougher than I thought," she said to Bean, but Bean was busy. He had adopted a stalking posture, his shoulders low and his butt wiggling. She looked to see what he was hunting, and his quarry caught her by surprise: an assortment of junk had been strewn across her yoga mat—a foil gum wrapper, a bottle cap, and a short strand of Christmas tinsel. Bean pounced on the tinsel and gnawed on it, and Serena rose to get a closer look at the curious collection. She scanned the lawn for squirrels, then remembered the crow.

It was still perched on the pergola, and it cawed to her. Serena laughed. "I'm sorry, bud!" she called. "I almost forgot we had a date!" Though she felt a little silly doing it, she picked two unagi rolls from her tray, placed them on the lid, and set the lid on the railing. "Here you go!" The crow watched her and cawed again, but it didn't move.

She sat back down, popped a slice of spicy tuna roll into her mouth, and considered the little hoard of shiny treasures. She'd written a piece about the intelligence of crows once, about how they could use tools, solve simple problems, and remember their friends and enemies. She knew a bit about similar social phenomena in the animal kingdom, too—how squirrels will bring the humans who feed them nuts and acorns to help them get ready for winter, and how cats will bring their owners dead mice and birds because they assume they are crummy hunters—but Serena would have to ask Alyssa and Jamie if they had trained a crow to trade with them when they got back.

As she was entertaining the idea, the crow swooped in, landed with surprising grace, and helped itself to her offering. "Well, I'll be damned," Serena whispered, grinning at her guest. It didn't take long for him to finish, and as soon as he was done, he cawed once and flew off over the pool, heading to the south.

After brunch, though the thought of binging on trashy TV seemed awfully tempting, Serena decided to keep her no-tech momentum going and plunged herself into the work of keeping house. Alyssa and Jamie hadn't asked her to do any chores, but she figured staying busy was the surest way to avoid lapsing into old habits. She took Daisy on a long walk and, when they got back, settled her in the shade under the porch swing with a fresh bowl of water. Serena then uncoiled the hose and washed her car, which she hadn't done by hand in years. She almost broke down and pumped Spotify from her phone through the Bluetooth speaker she'd seen in the kitchen, but she doubted she'd have enough willpower to turn back once she started down that path, so she sang to herself instead—a little Lizzo, a little Nelly Furtado. She kept on singing as she watered Alyssa's flowers and filled the bird-bath, and a group of juncos flew in to take advantage before she had even finished rolling the hose back up. Their flapping and splashing was all the inspiration she needed.

Serena returned to the kitchen, drained a glass of water, and looked out at the pool, which sparkled in the midday sun. She took a few steps toward the guest room, trying to remember where she'd packed her swimsuit, when a wicked impulse struck. She peeled off her clothes, dropped them in a heap by the patio door, and scampered for the pool barefoot and naked, pausing just long enough to let Bear and Daisy outside. Serena was waist deep in the water before she remembered she still had her glasses on, obliging her to wade back, scale the stairs, and leave them on the patio table.

And then Serena swam. She moved sleekly through the water, starting with a half dozen brisk laps and ending with a tranquil float in the deep end, relishing the contrast of the cool water beneath her and the warm sunshine on her face. Had she applied sunscreen she might have stayed in longer, but after twenty or thirty minutes she reluctantly kicked back to the stairs in the shallow end and left the water behind. She stood and stretched, letting herself dry in a soft September breeze, feeling utterly unlike the woman who left the City just yesterday. On Friday she'd been churning out listicles, quizzes, and columns of frivolous copy; today she was embracing change. She felt brazen, wild, free.

Serena put her glasses back on and looked out over the pool, sure that the life that was meant for her was coming closer.

And as Serena walked back toward the house, where Daisy, Bear, and Bean were waiting for her, something spongy squelched beneath her foot. It was an ear, a human ear, a silver hoop earring hanging from the lobe. Just past it, arrayed on her yoga mat, were an assortment of shiny new treasures: a nickel, a keychain, a barrette trailing hair and a bit of bloody scalp, the ragged stump of a finger with a ring still on it.

Serena turned back and saw the crows, ten or twelve of them now. One of them cawed a question, and Daisy barked an answer. Bear and Bean snaked between her feet, refreshing their scent on her skin, claiming her.

Down beyond the walnut tree, a fox screamed. Somewhere past the spirea hedge, a coyote yipped. In the woods, in a string of calls and responses that seemed incredibly close, something barked, something howled, something roared.

MOTHER'S DAY

VANESSA REID

Linda eased her Chevy Vega off the interstate and into the parking lot of a nameless Shell station, relieved there was gas available. They were almost on empty, and it was getting late. She didn't relish sleeping in the car on the side of the road with her 10-year-old son, even if Stevie would think it was a grand adventure.

"Wake up, buddy." She glanced in the rearview mirror at her dozing son as she stopped next to the only working pump. Back in Atlanta, there would be a five-car deep wait. *Thank god for small towns where nobody goes anywhere.*

Stevie grumbled lightly from the back seat. He hadn't slept well the night before. The Starry Night Motel was noisy through the thin walls, and he had woken up with another one of the nightmares that started when his father left them. Stevie dreamed of a man with an ax chasing him through the woods, and right before he woke up, the man had caught him.

Fuck you, Dennis. Asshole.

Linda reached back and gently jostled her son. He clutched

the Luke Skywalker action figure her parents gave him on his last birthday, and she felt a slight squeeze in her heart. Losing her parents to a car accident six months later had nearly destroyed her, but what hurt more was that Stevie was so young he would only remember a fuzzy picture of Bonnie and Burl and his Luke Skywalker action figure.

She hated to drag Stevie from the only home he knew to an unknown future, but the job in Bangor and a high school friend who lived there were all she had. A small part of her, the once optimistic girl, felt a flicker of hope for their future, but the road would be hard. They had almost nothing.

"Where are we, momma?" Stevie asked.

Linda grinned, "No idea whatsoever."

Stevie smiled and looked out the window. "Man! There's a store. Can I get a Coke and a Zero bar... please?"

"Get me a Tab and you have a deal!" Linda reached into her purse and handed Stevie her wallet. "Make sure you get the gas, too." Stevie scampered off happily as a battered pickup truck waited for him to cross and parked next to the air pump.

Linda stepped out of the car and stretched her aching bones. A late October breeze tossed her blonde curls, which she twisted to keep out of her face. She opened the gas tank, slid the nozzle in, and began fueling, watching the dollars accumulate.

Linda's hair came loose again, and she piled it on her head with one hand as she listened to the ticks of the pump. Another breeze circled her, and she closed her eyes, enjoying the crisp feel of it on her neck.

We're going to be okay.

As the breeze faltered and died, a strange quiet settled around her. That's when she felt it. Someone was watching her. She opened her eyes and looked around. Stevie was still in the store. She could see him through the window talking animatedly with the clerk. He was like his grandmother; Bonnie never knew a stranger.

Linda felt the source of the gaze and looked at the pickup truck. A grimy man in a plaid shirt squatted by his back tire, topping off its air, but he wasn't watching the gauge. He was watching her. He seemed to squint blindly at her in the glare of the setting sun. Though she couldn't see his eyes, she felt his gaze as if his filthy hands stroked her neck, her shoulders, her breasts.

"Well, hello, little lady."

Linda broke their stare, jerked to replace the pump, and fumbled with the gas cap. Then, she strode toward the shop to find Stevie and to put as much distance as possible between Plaid Shirt Man and herself.

She opened the glass door covered in ancient stickers: We Like and Will Stick with Ike & Dick, Don't Get Bit at Everglades National Park, Kilroy Was Here. A bell jingled, and she glanced at the clerk behind the counter—no Stevie. "Excuse me, have you seen a little boy with curly hair? He talks a lot."

The pimply-faced clerk, maybe only a few years older than Stevie, nodded politely. "Yes, ma'am. But he left. Probably went to the bathroom or something." He stood, staring.

Linda blinked, "Where is the bathroom?"

The clerk blushed at the pretty woman speaking to him. "Um, it's around back. You can go through there, though." He pointed toward a dimly lit hallway "On your left."

"Thank you," she called over her shoulder. An ancient Coca Cola cooler's sickly flicker provided the hallway's only light. Linda glanced inside in hopes Stevie found her Tab there, but the cooler's only contents were spatters of icy black mold and what must have been deer meat wrapped in newspaper. Linda shuddered and hurried on.

The passageway was longer than she'd first thought, and the

flickering neon light faded as the space grew darker with each step. A sour mold scented the air. *What the hell am I doing?* She was about to stop and turn around when she finally bumped into the door in the darkness. Shit. She felt for the doorknob and shoved open a heavy wooden door. Golden sunlight enveloped her. After the dark of the hall, even the fading afternoon light was blinding. Linda's eyes focused, and she looked left and right. No Stevie.

She found the paint-chipped door to the men's room and knocked. "Stevie? Stevie!" No answer. She even tried the women's room next to it in case he had walked into the wrong restroom but, again, no response.

A snaking threat of an anxiety attack rolled through her stomach. She ran around the building to the front and found Stevie standing by their car, talking animatedly with Plaid Shirt Man. Her pressing anxiety gave way to anger. What was this stranger doing so close to her son? She marched over to them and stood between the man and Stevie, who promptly sidestepped her.

"Hey, mom," Stevie said. He turned to Plaid Shirt Man and continued, "So what I am saying is that the best ship is, hands down, the A-Wing. The TIE fighter is cool and all, but the A-Wings are more agile and adaptable."

Plaid Shirt Man grinned. Even in her unease, Linda could see he may have once been handsome under the dirt, grease, and what she assumed were wrinkles from years of smoking. A pack of Kools in his hand, he regarded her with soot-black eyes even as he spoke to Stevie.

"No way, son." Linda started at his familiarity with the boy. Son? "The Empire made the best ships, hands down. I mean, look at the Death Star. Now that's a ship!"

Stevie frowned and looked skeptically at Plaid Shirt Man. "But the Death Star isn't a ship. It's a battle station." Stevie cocked his head and looked carefully at Plaid Shirt Man. "What do you think of the first ship? You know, at the beginning of the movie?"

"Aw, that old Millennium Falcon? That's a hunk of junk." Stevie frowned.

Plaid Shirt Man turned his attention back to Linda. "So, little lady. I hear y'all are traveling up north. Where are you headed? I can give you good directions. I drive a truck when I'm not fixin' cars. I can tell you the best backroads." His gaze bore into her eyes, expecting an answer. Linda pursed her lips, thinking carefully about her reply to this stranger, but before speaking, his gaze again slipped down to her breasts, and she wished she'd worn a bra under her thin Ramones t-shirt. She felt naked and small under his dirty stare.

Linda grabbed Stevie's hand. "No, thanks. We're good. Let's go, Stevie." She pulled him to the car and slid into the driver's seat, turning over the engine before the boy could close his door.

As she peeled off, she heard Plaid Shirt Man call, "Be careful out there."

As soon as they hit the highway, Linda accelerated over the speed limit for ten minutes before she realized the gas meter was already starting to dip. She wanted to put as much distance as she could between them and Plaid Shirt Man, but she slowed when she realized they would need more gas before they got to the next county if she wasn't careful.

"That was weird, Momma."

Linda tensed. She didn't want to scare him by sharing her discomfort about plaid shirt, man. "Stevie, I didn't want to be rude, but we were in a hurry and—"

"No, I mean, that man said he knew everything about Star Wars. He saw my action figure and started talking to me about it. He said he knew everything, but he said the first ship in the movie was the Millennium Falcon. But it wasn't. It was the Tantive IV."

Linda relaxed, "Oh, honey. People can be fans and not know everything about the movie."

"Yeah, maybe. But a real fan would've known."

She glanced back at him. "Hey! Did you remember my Tab?"

"Oh yeah," he smiled and reached into the plastic bag he was clutching, taking out her Tab and opening it for her before handing it forward. Linda took the can and took a long sip.

"Thank you, buddy."

"Oh! And I have something else for you."

"You do?" She heard him rustling in the bag.

"Here!" He stuck his hand out next to her, and she glanced over to see a plastic yellow rose. "Happy Mother's Day, Momma."

She took the flower and looked at him in the rearview mirror. She had forgotten it was Mother's Day. "Oh, Stevie, it is lovely! Thank you, buddy."

"It's not real, though." She grinned. "I know you like real flowers, but this was all they had. And besides, it'll last forever!"

Her eyes filled with the hot sting of tears. "Yes, it will, buddy. And I will cherish it forever." She glanced back at Stevie again, his earnest face so like his father's but softer and kinder. She choked back a sob but realized she wasn't sad. *It's going to be okay.* Maybe that girlish optimism, the way she used to look at the future as infinitely possible, was not completely gone. It was sitting in the back seat. "Okay. Time for some tunes!"

"Yes!" Stevie agreed.

Linda searched for a rock station. When they landed on Thin Lizzy's "The Boys Are Back in Town," they sang at the top of their lungs.

———

Darkness settled in for the night, and Linda looked back at Stevie to see he had fallen asleep again, Luke Skywalker resting on his chest.

"Stevie?" When he did not stir, she slipped a Virginia Slim out of her purse and pushed in the car lighter. Stevie hated it when she smoked, and she planned to quit, but her nerves were frayed.

She lit the cigarette, inhaling deeply, and rolled down the window. With each inhale, she unwound, and the soft glow of the dashboard lights and Simon and Garfunkel tenderly singing "Bridge Over Troubled Waters" smoothed her nerves. One day, she would be mellow—one of those confident women who doesn't worry about every little thing. Stevie would be proud of her, and he could stop saying, "Momma, don't worry so much. We're alright." One day.

As she tossed her cigarette and rolled up the window, she noticed headlights in the distance behind them. She hadn't seen a car since they left the gas station. Its right headlight flickered erratically.

The car at first seemed to trail at a steady distance, but then it closed the gap. The guttural engine complained as the vehicle shifted gears to accelerate. It sounded like the combine—a metal monster—from her parents' farm, the one that ate everything in its path.

As the truck drew up behind her, it tailed her so closely its lights blazed into her rearview mirror. Jeez, what a jerk. She slowed to let the driver pass, but it met her speed and remained on her rear. Linda's anxiety returned in intolerable waves.

She sped up and held steady. The other car met her speed but held back a bit so that it was no longer riding her tail. She heard the gravel-eating engine chug again, and the driver slid into the left lane and continued accelerating.

Linda eased her foot off the gas to let the other car pass more easily, but instead of passing her, it pulled up beside her and held pace. She glanced at the driver of the battered pickup truck. The Plaid Shirt Man grinned at her.

Linda was plunged into icy water. Her heart pounded, and nausea rose in her belly. She glanced at him again, and he grinned, stretching his thin lips over yellowed teeth, saluting her with his right hand. He shouted something and gestured for her to roll down her window.

She rolled her window down a couple of inches but kept her hand on the crank.

"Y'all doing okay out here? Know where you're going? It's not safe out here at night, little lady. I can show you where to go. Why don't cha pullover?" He winked.

Linda frantically rolled up her window and hammered the pedal, leaving the Plaid Shirt Man behind as her old sedan reached its top speed. The truck's headlights receded in the darkness.

"Momma?" Stevie rasped, emerging from his heavy nap. She realized then that she still had the accelerator on the floor, and her leg was trembling with the force. She eased off the gas.

"Sorry, buddy. Just trying to make good time."

Stevie sat up and regarded his mother in the rearview mirror. "Geez, Momma."Don't get us killed," he laughed.

"I'll try not to."

"Momma?" His expression changed. "Are you okay?"

Her eyes met his in the mirror. "I'm okay."

Stevie sat up and scooted behind her seat, wrapping his thin arms around her neck. Linda inhaled his sticky sweetness. Coca-Cola, candy bars, and perspiration. She held onto the moment as he gently patted her cheek. He wouldn't be ten forever, and although she suspected he would always be kind-hearted, he wouldn't hug her like this with both of them knowing the other, bonded by the fresh pain of his father leaving and the horrible years before the bastard finally did. She wished she'd left Dennis years before so Stevie didn't have to think that's how a man should treat a woman or his boy, but he knew. He knew too much for a 10-year old.

"Momma?"

"Yes."

"Will you call me Stephen? Please? I'm not a baby—not a Stevie anymore."

Linda hid her surprise and pang of sadness with a smile. "Sure, buddy. Stephen, it is."

"Thanks," he squeezed her and sat back. Maybe him growing up is happening even faster than she realized. "How much longer to the hotel?"

"Uh, about thirty minutes, I think. We're close. Getting hungry? How about we find a McDonald's when we get to town?"

"Yes! Can I have a Big Mac? And fries? And a milkshake? Please?"

"You can have a milkshake and a small hamburger and fries. It's late, and we don't need more nightmares because you ate a big meal late at night, buddy." When he didn't complain, she glanced back over her shoulder and saw him gazing out the window. "Stevie?"

"Momma!"

"Sorry! Stephen?"

"Yeah?"

"You okay?"

"Yeah, I'm okay," he replied, his eyes not straying from the starless night.

———

Linda's eyes fluttered as fatigue overwhelmed her. Alarmed at how close to falling asleep she was, she sat up straighter, shook her head, and reset her grip on the steering wheel. A glance in the rearview mirror showed Stephen had fallen asleep again, stretched out on the backseat, Luke Skywalker in hand. His brown curls lay on his forehead, damp commas circling his brow, and boyish heat flushed his cheeks.

A flicker of light reflected in the rearview mirror, and she studied the image. Permeating the inky black, two headlights shined pinpricks in the distance. The right one flickered.

She slammed the gas. The old car accelerated slowly, growling a low purr against the engine's pressure. She couldn't pick up speed fast enough. Panic overtook Linda as the truck and its hideous lights crept closer.

"Come on!" she hissed, jamming her foot on the gas pedal. "Come on!"

"Momma?"

"It's okay, baby," she said, her voice breaking. "Just trying to get to the hotel quicker."

Stephen sat up and rubbed his eyes. He followed her worried glance and turned to look out the back window. When he turned around, he sighed, "He's back."

"I know," Linda said, realizing Stephen hadn't been asleep when the truck gave her a scare earlier.

Linda looked for a road sign, gas station, or anything that gave them a way to get off the highway and to a place with people, but only darkness loomed. She eyed the truck. He had cut the distance between them and couldn't be more than a hundred yards away. Her old Vega couldn't outrun Plaid Shirt Man.

Now, he was coming up behind her. He slowed only inches from her bumper, headlights reflecting in the mirror and into her eyes. The right one blinked like a sickly strobe.

Linda jerked her car into the empty left lane and snatched her foot from the gas, slowing quickly. She watched Plaid Shirt Man's look of surprise as she dropped behind him and he sped away. For a moment, he maintained his speed, and she prayed he would go on. Just leave them alone. Maybe he'd had his fun. But then, his brake lights flared a red warning, and he slowed until they were again side by side.

His window was down, and he again grinned at Linda, all

yellow teeth. His grin was unbearable. It promised dark things, and he would smile as he did them. A scream built in her belly, but she held firm. She didn't want to scare Stephen, her baby.

As a last effort, Linda hit the accelerator once more. She couldn't stay in the left lane even if there was no oncoming traffic and would rather be in front of Plaid Shirt Man than behind, so she urged her car forward, pushing it until the heap sputtered in protest. The old girl persisted, and Linda passed the truck. Instinctively, she signaled right and then realized how preposterous that was. A mad laugh bubbled in her throat.

"Momma? We have to get out of here."

"I know, baby. I know. I'm trying." She took a deep breath to steel her nerves. I cannot lose my shit now.

"I think I saw a sign back there for a town. 'Havendale,' I think it said. Maybe we are close?"

"Maybe." They had to be.

As they headed north, the terrain had become increasingly hilly. The road edged east, and a sliver of moonlight pierced the darkness, revealing the vast drop below, only inches from the passenger side of the Vega. She'd have to be careful, she thought as she looked out of the window at the tree tops dotting the night sky.

She heard the groan of the truck. Plaid Shirt Man pulled up next to her again, still smiling that awful smile. He indicated for her to roll down her window as he shouted something at her she couldn't make out.

She shook her head no and looked ahead.

He yelled something else, his tone shifting to anger. He was no longer smiling.

He eased his truck to the left, and for a moment, Linda thought he was slowing down, but then he veered back and into her car, slamming his truck into the Vega. She swerved wildly but righted herself, fighting to keep her wheels on the road. The deep embankment to their right yawned, empty and black.

Plaid Shirt Man was smiling again. When she met his gaze, he flicked his snakelike tongue suggestively. Then he slammed into her again. This time she felt the Vega's back right tire spin off the road, catching and spraying rocks into the wheel well as she struggled to keep them on the road.

At this instant, she noticed Stephen standing on the rear-passenger-side floor, his arms wrapped tightly around the headrest in front of him. He stared unblinkingly at the man in the truck.

"Stevie!" she yelled. "Sit down and put on your seatbelt," as she pulled her own around her and slid the clasp until it clicked. "Stevie!"

He stood in a daze, holding on for dear life. This wasn't his actual nightmare come true, but he was there in it, as if it was happening: a man trying to kill him.

"Stevie!" Linda screamed at the top of her lungs. "Sit down and put on your damned seatbelt!"

That broke Stephen's trance, and he looked wildly into her eyes and nodded. He sat and fumbled for the seatbelt.

"Hurry!" She heard the clang of metal on metal.

"It won't lock, Momma."

"Stevie, hurry!" She could see the truck veering again and feared he would hit her this time with all he had. "Hurry, Stevie!"

"Momma! It won't lock!"

"Stevie!"

The truck rammed the smaller car, and Linda held tight to the wheel, willing to keep them on the road even as she felt the car sliding, the tires slipping off the pavement. As soon as the wheels left the highway, the vehicle slid steadily for a moment until it reached a deep terraced drop. Then, it tipped and flipped, tumbling down the embankment and landing hard against a copse of trees. Before she could even register the sharp violence of the fall, Linda dreamed of shattering glass and moaning metal, wrapping around her in a jagged tomb. *Stevie.* Then came nothing but blackness.

———

"Momma. Momma! Wake up!"

Linda started, inhaling savagely. It took her a moment to understand what had happened. When her head cleared and panic gripped her again.

"Stevie!" The door pinned her on her left, but her right hand was free. She unlatched her seatbelt to turn and check on her son, but the impact had crumpled the nose of the car. The force had pushed the steering wheel into her, holding her body against the seat.

"Stevie?" Silence.

She checked the rearview mirror, which had twisted crazily, and it reflected only the car's ceiling and a tree branch that had broken through the glass of the passenger side window and missed her head by inches. She reached up and adjusted the mirror to see the back seat.

Stevie lay stretched across the back seat as if napping and this whole experience had only been a nightmare. But he wasn't napping. His matted hair shimmered with shattered glass and glistened with blood. The liquid pooled near his ear and ran down his cheek in a sick stripe of bright red, dripping silently onto the car's floor. His eyes were half open, but Linda knew he would never see anything again.

Linda screamed. "Stevie? Wake up, baby. Wake up." She frantically reached between the seats to shake him awake, but she couldn't get to him, and his empty gaze never wavered. "Stevie!" She stretched madly with her free hand, desperate to touch him.

As dawning understanding seeped into her mind, she felt the tendrils of anxiety slip around her, growing into thick, black vines, squeezing her. Stopping her breath. The world slipped away into a whiteness where she felt nothing. No time. No reality. Just void. For a moment, nothing existed, and she didn't care if she ever returned. But then, her own raging voice dragged her back to awareness, and pain filled her, shaking her awake. Alive.

Linda dropped her hand and sobbed, lowering her head onto the steering wheel, screaming a wild, desperate prayer into the night.

"Well, hello there, little lady," the Plaid Shirt Man called from the embankment.

Linda looked up, confused by the absurdity of his voice at her moment of fathomless grief. Anger mixed with her madness, and her senses awoke.

"You really should have let me help you, you know? This is no place for a pretty lady to be out driving by herself," he grinned, panting wildly. "But don't you worry now. I'll be right down to help. I'm going to go back a piece. It's too steep to climb down here. I'll get you out, and we can really have some fun. I promise you that." He turned and walked to his truck, which she could hear puttering in the middle of the road. The gravel sprayed as he spun the truck and took off.

Linda leaned back. *I'd rather die.* She looked at the cracked glass of the review mirror and pulled a triangular piece from the frame. She held the glass up for a moment and looked at her son's reflection. I'm coming, baby. I'm coming.

Linda's left hand was pinned between the door and the steering wheel, but her wrist was exposed. She pressed the sharp point of glass against her flesh, took a deep breath, and...

"Momma!"

Bang, bang, bang.

"Momma, stop!"

She looked up at the sound of Stevie's voice, but it wasn't

coming from the back seat. Her precious boy stood next to her car door, pounding on it.

"Stevie? You're okay! Oh, baby. You're okay."

"Momma!"

"Baby!

"Momma, we don't have much time. You have to go."

"Me? I—" Linda considered her son. His cheeks flushed, and his sweet curls now dry. There was no blood on him—not even a scratch. Linda glanced at the shards of the rearview mirror. Her son still lay on the back seat. Confused, she turned to the boy standing by the door. A dawning understanding brought fresh sobs. "Oh, god. Stevie!"

"Momma." Stevie's tone was firm. "There is no time for this. You need to be big and strong and face this," he said, as she'd say to him when he was avoiding something hard. He pulled the car door open and held it for his mother, freeing her from the metal tomb. He took her elbow gingerly and helped her slide out to stand shakily on uneven ground.

She looked at her boy as tears rolled down her cheeks. He smiled softly and said, "It's okay, Momma. It's okay" He embraced her.

She could smell his sweetness and feel his warmth as she held him tighter until he pulled away. "Stevie."

"Momma, it's Stephen. Remember?"

She brushed his cheek with the back of her hand and smiled sadly.

"That town is not far. A mile or two, maybe. Keep following the road but stay hidden in the woods. Do you understand?"

"Come with me, baby."

"I can't, Momma, you know that. Besides, I have something to do."

Linda looked at him, puzzled.

"I have to make sure he doesn't follow you, but you have to go.

He'll be here any second. Take this." He handed her his Luke Skywalker action figure. "It's yours now. It's gonna be okay, Momma," he said, confident. "Now, hide!"

He pushed his mother into some bushes, and he waited.

Then, he heard the sure, heavy footsteps of Plaid Shirt Man lumbering through the woods from the other direction.

"Hang on, little lady. I'm almost there," he singsonged.

Stephen smiled and said, "Don't worry. I'll take care of him, Momma. I'll take care of him. He won't hurt us anymore, Momma. Happy Mother's Day."

PART FOUR
ALONE

Hell can be something we find on our own, too.

IMPACT

JOHN MAHONEY

The collision still reverberates throughout the few parts of my body not light-years away from sensation. My hand cannot detect the presence of the smartphone. My burning eyes inform me it is partially crushed, the rambling text I'd been tapping out vanquished by dark, spiderwebbing glass. Doesn't matter. Were the device pristine, it wouldn't connect to God, and nothing short of the Almighty could remedy this. I cough, and blood bubbles up, tasting of metal, perhaps like bent steel.

My children are home. Whatever may happen beneath the glare of the twisted streetlight, they will not bear witness. Zoe has already begun primping for some jock at school—his identity must rate seclusion with the golden hoard of Fort Knox. Kevin's tattling is my only evidence of the boy's existence because any observation of Zoe's unnecessary glances in every mirror and surge of selfies is somehow a violation of her constitutional right to privacy. The tamer of plastic horses I used to rock to sleep during thunderstorms is becoming a woman and is lying to my face about it.

Kevin has pillaged and burned my quiet sanctuary of unbelief in mental illness. When not instigating screaming matches with

Zoe or redefining the word "Fragile," my son can be relied on to pepper me with variations of the same question. How often I've been tempted to provide, if only once, not the answer he wants but the one he asks for: "Daddy left us because of you."

I smell gasoline. According to Hollywood, crashed cars explode. Michael Bay doesn't direct my life, but I'm not certain he's unfit for the post. A quick boom and fireball don't leave much time for suffering.

My head is angled just so. I can see into the Honda. Unmoving, the husband slumps, chest caved in by the steering column, his lower half draped by a deflated airbag. His wife is yards away, barely captured by the streetlight's flickering corona. I don't know why my brain insists they are—were—married, or why it matters. Death has parted them.

Raised by a fair-weather feminist, I recall my mother declaring I could do anything because women are stronger than men. Helplessly, I watch the catapulted wife prove her right. Heedless of the squarish chunks of windshield that had accompanied her flight and still lacerate her flesh, she crawls toward what remains of her vehicle. Her mouth opens and shuts, and my mind supplies pre-rendered moans and whimpers my ears can't hear.

There's a cliché that liars will eventually believe their own deceits, given enough repetition. If I spoke the words, "She's bloated" or "She's overweight" a trillion times, I'd remain hard-pressed to forestall memories of my own pregnancy. Not that she doesn't have a lot on her plate right now, but I feel a mad yearning to warn the ejected wife her instincts are false. Genetic hogwash. Husbands are fickle deserters. Kids are a thankless torment. She is clinging to life for the wrong reasons.

She sees me and lifts her hand, a majority of her fingers bent to more points of the compass than nature intended. Her pleas reach me no better than her oblong, fluttering grasp. She sags to the glass-strewn road and then lies still. As I watch, blood oozing from dozens of wounds slows.

Again, my son and daughter hijack my thoughts. Despite all my sacrifices and toil on their behalf, our little family is crumbling. I can't envision how Zoe and Kevin could survive without me. Their father is as likely to return as the husband in the totaled Honda. They face foster care, drugs, crime. And that may be a best-case scenario. My children need me.

In prostration before the altar of self-serving fiction, I subscribe to the deceit. I cannot let this be the end of me. I have to be there for my kids.

I do not put the smartphone in my pocket because its GPS records my location, and I couldn't bring myself to call for help. I turn from the woman in the street, not because I can't look upon my deed. My car still functions, and I painfully squeeze into it, already calculating a route to the nearest car wash. A deer, I will say. It isn't a fear of prison conjuring the story now unspooling in my head.

I am thinking only of my children. I don't have to utter the lie even once to know I will never believe it. I am silent as I shift to first gear and bear down on the accelerator.

THE GRAVE OF THE QUIET

NIGEL QUINLAN

I knew I shouldn't have done it, but sometimes knowing isn't enough. And sometimes knowing is enough, if knowing and doing go together. I shouldn't have used the shovel, for a start. You'd think a sturdy implement designed to cut through soil and root wouldn't have been too much bothered by a fella's head, but after what was, in fairness, a few hefty blows to start the job, a few hefty more to finish the job, and a final hefty few whacks, stabs and slicings to make sure the emotional catharsis of the act was fully achieved, the bloody thing broke.

Literally bloody, that is. The handle snapped, three quarters of the way down, leaving a long sharp splinter gleaming out clean against the layers of graveyard muck.

"Well, bugger me," says I to meself. We only had the one spade due to budget cuts. Mind you, the long, sharp splinter put me in mind of a stake, which is what I should have used to pierce the old vampire's rotten heart.

Ah, well. It was a crime of passion, you might say, done in a moment of heated excitement. Though of course I'd also been planning it for years. A premeditated crime of passion, so it was.

Now you might be thinking to yourself, there's no better place for killing a fella than the middle of a graveyard, especially if you do it at night. But that was the stickler, you see. No way could I suggest, persuade, trick or force him to come to the graveyard at night. We were gravediggers after all, not grave robbers. Grave robbers would complain if the gravediggers turned up to ply their trade during the working hours when they were plying theirs. Complaints would be made and notice would be given.

So, in the end, and what with one thing and another, I bashed out his brains with our only spade in the middle of the graveyard in the broad daylight with more than a few visitors wandering around. Dragged out to a graveyard in the middle of the day as if they had nothing better to be doing by emotional blackmail exerted from beyond the veil. Some of them in dirty clothes standing around staring at the sky.

So now I had a dead body, a broken spade, and a grave to dig for a burial at two. I should at least have waited 'til after the grave was dug. I could have hefted him in and covered him a bit, then the coffin would be lowered on top and the grave filled in. A perfect crime, courtesy of the auld ghost of the staircase, thank you very much, but that's crimes of passion for you.

You see, I worked with the man for years, and he never said nary a word to me. Not hello, not goodbye, not how's she cuttin', not soft day thank God. In sunshine and in rain. In fog and in snow. Side-by-side we labored day in and day out. Not one single word. Digging graves is a special vocation. It's not an ordinary job. When you think about it, we're like that fella with the girl's name who ferries the souls across the river Sticks, while they drink the water of forgetfulness. The holes we dig are the river. The coffins are their boats. And the thick, heavy, smothering clay we rattle down on them is the total obliteration of thought and memory. I said as much. I told it to him, over and over again. Did he so much as mumble an agreement? Mumble he did not.

So I ask you this: was year after year of nagging, superior, ignorant, arrogant silence any way to treat a brother Ferryman?

We started together on a cold April morning, were handed our shovel by that officious desk-bound donkey from the Council department that ran the graveyard. We were shown our workman's hut and our timesheets and the maps of plots full and to be filled and the weekly schedule that would always be waiting for us first thing every Monday. From that moment, standing side by side trying to work out which of us would take charge of the shovel, to the moment I hit him a clatter with that very self-same shovel? Not. A. Word. Not. A. Peep. The hundreds of graves all around us weren't as silent.

I had to do the talking for both of us.

I talked and I talked. I filled every hour of every day with words and words and words. I discoursed on every subject under the sun. I sang songs and recited poetry and chanted ballads and lays and ancient epics. I talked 'til my throat was raw, then I talked 'til it wasn't. A thick layer formed 'round my tonsils, tough as a rhinoceros hide. All the time I talked, I waited for him to comment, to interject, to respond with so much as a shake or a twitch. Nothing. He was a void into which I cast all my words, and they vanished forever down that unfillable bottomless pit. Even a beast of the field will answer when called and can be trained to respond, but not he.

And so I stood there over his cooling body, his lifeblood drying on the gravel of the grave and the black shiny marble of the headstone. They like their big marble headstones 'round here, black-and-white, with elaborate gold lettering, each telling a story of a life. Carved with pictures of cars and phones and hurleys and horses that might have been hints of their deaths. No more would he ignore me and act as if I weren't there.

But that wasn't right, was it? Now he would continue to ignore me for all eternity, and I'd have to do his share of the work. What a fool I was.

No! I was happy he was dead, happy to have murdered him, for all that. It was a grand and terrible tragedy. I'd finally succeeded in cracking him open and seeing inside, and if it wasn't a pleasant sight, it was still a miraculous one. The stuff splattered and sprayed all around that shrine to some dead joyrider is the self same stuff that goes into making us living, breathing, talking human beings. If that isn't a miracle of the world, I don't know what is.

Well, so much for my reasons for clattering the fella in the head until the shovel broke. They weren't much help to me now. I was left with a body in a graveyard in the middle of the day. "If only I had a coffin," I said to myself, for all we'd cursed and mocked the polished finish and shiny brass fittings, all to be left rotting in the ground. Well, I mocked them I suppose. He had kept his opinion on them to myself, the way he kept all his opinions to himself. Despite my precarious position, the thought made me oddly wistful. Could it be I'd miss him, just a little? The hut will be emptier, lonelier. Granted, I could keep talking away to equal effect now that he wouldn't be there, but it wouldn't be the same.

This was no good—no taking this back. Nobody knows better than we gravediggers: the slumber of the dead goes on unbroken, cannot be disturbed, will endure without surcease, and all that. The only business left was the disposal of the remains.

Unless the grave robbers get you.

We knew there had to be grave robbers, because we would be finding dug up empty graves every couple of mornings. What could it be but grave robbers? Let them at it. They had their job to do, same as us.

Right, so.

I went back to the hut, leaving the body where it lay. There wouldn't be much difference between him being found alone and him being found with me standing there, gormless.

In my mind I was thinking I might get a nice bit of tarpaulin and the water hose and the wheelbarrow, all of which would start me on my way to making the mess more presentable and less shocking to the public eye. But once inside, all sense of urgency fled, and instead I opened the grate of the stove, threw in a few pieces of wood, and put the kettle on to boil for to make myself a cup of tea.

I sat down in my chair and I looked around. I had nothing to say, and no one to say it to. I thought about how I had sent all those letters to the donkey at the Council, detailing my grievances about my work partner. Eventually he turned up himself, looking flustered and annoyed and told me to cut it out. That I should be as proud as himself of their policy in hiring people with disabilities, and at as much as half the going wage of whole people. Hadn't there even been a piece in the paper about this, with all those photos of us and everything?

I just shrugged. Maybe so. But if he was really deaf and dumb, how come he'd never said a word to me about it? Isn't that what simple common courtesy demanded? The man from the Council just looked at me as if I'd grown an extra head and warned me I'd be docked pay for every letter I sent from here on out, and that was the end of it.

I fished out a replacement form for the shovel from under a pile of old newspapers and blank timesheets. I licked my pencil and held it over the empty boxes and lines. Oh God, though. If I sent this in, I'd never hear the end of it. The auld bugger would probably take the cost of it out of me pay. I threw down the pencil and tore up the form. Then I picked up the pencil and put it back behind my ear because you never knew when you'd need a pencil.

Outside, the screaming and yelling had started. I huffed at it.

It's only a dead body. Sure aren't we surrounded by dead bodies? Isn't the whole point of this place to be filled with corpses? I shook my head, crossed my arms, hooked one leg over the other, and while the caterwauling went on outside, I decided to wait for night to fall and then go see if there was ere an opening with the grave robbers.

AMBROSIA

C.R. LANGILLE

I WAKE TO THE CLICK-CLACK-CLICK OF SOMETHING TAPPING nearby. Darkness surrounds me, wrapping its icy embrace around my body like a wet blanket. I can't breathe.

Whenever this happens, I am instantly transported back to when my grandfather used to cover my mouth and nose with his calloused hands, all the while laughing and saying, "Oh no! It's the Smothers Brothers."

He found it incredibly amusing. I did not.

Fortunately, the moment passes as quickly as it came. However, the click-clacking persists, wearing away my nerves.

A low chuckle comes from the darkness in front of me, and the clicking picks up in intensity and speed. That's when it hits me. Fingernails across a table. No, not a table. Its resonance is lighter. Maybe a plate?

"Who's there?" I ask.

"Who I am is of little importance. It is who you are that piques my interest as well as that of my brethren."

Strange choice of words. Was I at a Renn Faire or something?

The voice is low. Not quiet, but deep. It vibrates in my chest and travels through my body to my fingertips and toes.

"Where am I?"

Another laugh, this time stifled, although not well. The click-clacking stops and the undeniable screech of wooden chair legs across hardwood fills my ears.

"That is the question, isn't it? There is a simple answer. Well, easy for me, I suppose. Please forgive me, but let me answer your question with a question of my own. What is the last thing you remember?"

I don't like questions for answers, but it seems I cannot do anything about it. The last thing I remember…

"…Well, I think I was driving. I remember my hands on the steering wheel."

And I do remember that. The wheel was sticky as it sometimes gets in the heat. It was my old Pontiac Grand Am… no, that was my first car. Was it the truck? I think it was the truck. The wife and I bought it as a treat for ourselves. Brand new Dodge Ram. But was I driving that? The memories are fuzzy, overlapping and hard to sift.

"Good," the voice says.

Good? I'm not sure how it could be good. It doesn't answer anything. To make matters worse, my head hurts. Like a migraine from hell. Did I crack my skull or something? It would explain the weirdness of the situation. I still can't see in all the darkness, either.

"Am I blind?" I ask.

The voice across from me laughs. Genuine, full of mirth this time.

"No, you're not blind. Not that it would matter."

Cryptic as fuck. But okay.

"Then why can't I see?"

The chair across from me creaks as whoever occupies it shifts their weight. The click-clacking picks up again.

"You can't see because it isn't yet time to see," the voice says. "Patience. We'll get there."

If his answer is supposed to comfort me, it does the opposite.

"What does that mean? None of this makes sense. Where am I? Who are you? Where is my wife?"

That last question gives me pause. It's the first time I've thought of her since waking up. The thought turns my stomach, but I can't figure out why.

That chuckle again.

"Excellent questions. Don't worry about your wife. You never have to worry about her again. As for where you are and who I am... in time."

What in the flying fuck does that mean? "Never have to worry about her again..." doesn't make a lick of sense.

"Is she... dead?" My voice cracks. A part of me wonders why, and the very thought makes me want to curl into a fetal ball.

"Back to the question at hand. You remember you were driving. Good. What else?"

Again, my head hurts. A nail driving into my skull. Maybe it's better it's dark in here, as I'm sure lights would make things worse. Once this migraine is under control, I'll be able to think straight again and then I can—"

"Focus and answer the question, please."

Screaming. There was screaming.

"There was an accident."

Click-clack-click. Click-clack-click.

"Tell me more," the voice asks. Is there a hint of desperation this time?

I try to focus, but the memories are fuzzy.

"Someone hit us. No... that isn't right. We ran off the road, I think. Swerved to avoid hitting a deer. Or was it a fox? Damnit!"

The images flash through my mind, jumbling, mixing and

making it impossible to figure out what is real. I rub at my temples, but it does nothing to soothe the pain or clear my memory.

"Close. But not quite. Something else was happening before that. Concentrate."

I focus on the moments just before. There is still screaming. She is screaming.

"She's scared."

The clicking stops again, and the mysterious person scoots even closer to the table. I get a whiff of something now. Garlic? Maybe some sort of broth. It smells good. There's something else behind it all. An aroma causes me to salivate. But it dissipates quickly, leaving me to wonder if it had been real.

"And why is she scared?"

"I don't know."

A lie, even though I can't conjure the details to fill in why it's a lie. It's just a feeling I know to be true.

"Where is she?" I plead.

The clicking starts back up, and the wood of the chair across the table groans as whoever is across from me shifts their weight.

"We've been through this already. You don't need to worry about her."

"Bullshit."

"Indeed. Like much of your life."

My face flushes. This person doesn't even know me!

"What?"

"Your life. It was a farce. Meaningless. Well, not entirely. You will yet serve a vital purpose."

My mind jumbles the words as I try to generate a retort. All that arrives is a cliché.

"Do you know who I am?"

"Yes. I know everything about you. Michael Richard Stevens III. Named after your father, who was named after his father. Michael, because of the archangel." He chuckles again as the name slides off his tongue. "You were born in a tiny town in Alabama named Pluck, population a measly 235. You didn't finish school, but found your calling, becoming a pastor for the Baptist church. Quite noble." He places a hefty amount of sarcasm on the word noble.

"Not a religious man, I take it?" I try to hide my derision but fail miserably.

"Oh no, quite the opposite. I find it quite useful for producing a quality specimen such as yourself."

"I've had enough of this. I want to see my wife and get the hell out of here now. Do it, or I'll call the police."

Sirens in the distance. More screaming. My wife, screaming. A memory flashes. We're in the truck, racing down the highway at night. The cops aren't too far behind. Their lights twinkle like Christmas decorations. My wife screams, telling me to let her out —to let her go. But I can't do that. I can't let her go. She's mine. She must obey me. If I can just get it through her thick skull.

Divorce is not an option. It never was.

"Good. You're starting to remember. Those kinds of memories add a certain... *je ne sais quoi* to the whole thing," he says. "A fun aftertaste, if you will. Spicy. Layered. Complex."

"What are you talking about? Did you not hear me? I'll call the cops, have you arrested, and you can spend the rest of eternity locked up."

He laughs. Hard this time.

"You're funny, you know that. Most people are crying and pleading for their soul at this point. Quite impossible but amusing all the same. But not you. I like that."

Something about the way he says this sends a shiver up my spine. More doubt crawls into my already broken mind.

"Where is she?"

I already know the answer. Tears well up as the memories flood back, crashing into my skull like a meat tenderizer.

"Yes. Continue," he says.

The cops are chasing us. There's blood on my hands. Her blood. She's in the backseat crying for me to let her go. She's dying. Well, it's her fucking fault for wanting to leave me. We had a nice thing going. A divorce would make me look bad to the congregation. It would ruin me. Especially if the reason for the divorce were to slip. A pastor must be faithful.

"She had it coming," I say. "I told her to shut her fucking mouth. But she kept yakking and yakking, and then she said she wanted a divorce."

"Couldn't have that, could you?"

"No."

"Did what you had to do, didn't you?"

"Yes. What!? No!"

"Your kind is so easy to manipulate. A nudge here. A twist there. A pretty redhead there. A fox in the road..."

The sound of far-off screaming licks my ears. At first, I think it's my wife. But it isn't just one person screaming.

It's thousands.

A ruby glow appears behind me, and I turn. As I do, I find I am not in a room at all but in a basin of black stone. In the distance, a giant volcano erupts, spewing red-hot magma high into the sky. The explosion shakes the very ground.

Dark storm clouds send lightning chains through the sky. Mountains stretch into the distance, higher than any I have ever seen—shadowy winged shapes flying as though a murmuration of starlings dancing in the sky. Yet these are not birds. They are much larger.

But it isn't these things that make me want to pluck my eyes from my skull and run screaming into the bloody darkness. No, it's not the impossible landscape defying everything I know. It's the people. The screaming people—and the things that devour them.

"I'm in hell."

"Not quite, Michael. You see, there is no heaven. No hell. There is only this waiting for each and every one of you. Your kind provides my brethren and me eternal life. You are cattle, cared for and manipulated to bring about the best taste in the cosmos. The soul of a sinner parading in sheep's clothing really is the best."

Strewn across the landscape are large cauldrons, bubbling with soup and people. Hundreds per vat. And the things that eat them...

"Look upon me, and be not afraid."

I don't want to turn and look, but I can't help myself.

As I turn, I find a smaller cauldron. One just for me. The liquid inside is lilac and just starting to simmer. My mind cracks as I put a face to the voice.

It isn't the many eyes that make me piss myself. It's the infinite rows of teeth.

HOME COMFORTS
ROB FRANCIS

I scale the mound of rubble, fragments of brick and concrete shifting underfoot and threatening to drag me into suffocating brokenness. It's a relief to reach the peak, to view the surrounding wasteground with its splintered shells of old factories and workshops nestled amongst piles of debris. Sunlight glints from shattered panes of glass hanging in gaping windows like jagged teeth. The old industrial estate is forgotten, abandoned. No developer will build on it while the recession rages. It's a ruined landscape, a barren place. Except for the house.

I dig my feet into the slithering detritus to gain some stability, dislodging old dog-ends, singed fragments of porn mags, and empty lager cans. The scat of teenage boredom. Perhaps I'm not the only one to stand here and watch the house, wondering why it exists intact amongst so much desolation.

Wondering why the old man still occupies the place.

The house stands at the edge of the estate, its territory marked by black iron railings, front and rear gardens choked with waist-high grasses and small trees. Yet the building itself is well-maintained, each window intact and clear, roof-slates neat, the wooden door and window-frames painted a cheerful yellow. Cultivated ivy cloaks the walls. A thin plume of woodsmoke drifts from the chimney, dipping across the brick frontage and over to where I stand. Its scent awakens something in me, a curious mix of anger and longing. Reminds me of Liam, a little.

I light a roll-up and raise the binoculars.

The cigarette burns down. The wind nods the heads of the garden weeds and a half-dozen magpies come and go, but nothing moves in the house even as the evening shadows gather and the day slowly dies. My legs burn but I stand my ground until at last the back door opens and the old man appears. He is dressed in the same smart brown suit as before. His hair and beard are trimmed. He is smiling, and once again he stands at the threshold and lights his pipe, contemplating the ragged garden with a look of contentment.

Five days I've watched, and each day the old man performs the same routine. Once each morning he opens the door to admire the blasted wilderness around him before vanishing inside, only to return to the doorstep again in the evening. When it gets dark, the lights come on, and around midnight they go off one by one. I've not yet seen the man leave or anyone come to visit.

Pipe done, the old man vanishes behind the closing door and I allow myself to sit. This is what I've been waiting for.

There is always a moment between the lights being switched on and the curtains drawn when the living room is visible. The room and all its valuable contents. Paintings and ornaments, silverware and glass cabinets. Leather-bound books on tall bookshelves, the kind only well-to-do arseholes have. The old man's rich. Too rich.

Which isn't fair. The elderly don't need much. They're almost done. They've had a lifetime of hoarding, and now there isn't enough for everyone else. Until they drop dead, and sometimes not even then. The likes of me have lives to build, and making good costs money. But old bastards like him have it all.

The lights are on in the living room. A dark wooden dresser laden with ornaments. Oil paintings on the walls. A bookcase lined with leather volumes. Objects of value. Almost certainly there are drawers of jewelry—perhaps cash. A lifetime of accumulated treasures. Things worth looking at. Things worth sharing.

I light another miserable roll-up and settle down again.

Not long now.

———

THE LIGHT of the pen torch is feeble, but I make it to the back door without stumbling or scraping my old boots along the overgrown path. Close up, the house bears small signs of weathering and neglect: paint peeling from the window sills in places, bird shit on the glass. The door is locked, but the frame is pitted and riddled with woodworm. It's no effort to slide the end of a screwdriver between door and frame and push, leaning until the bolt pops out. I pause for a long moment, breath held, waiting for any sign of movement from inside the house.

Nothing.

The room beyond is empty. More than that: dilapidated. Old kitchen cupboards and drawers slump against stained walls, mounds of dust and the detritus of decay lie in the corners, covering every surface. My feet scuff against hard wooden boards. In one corner lie an old rucksack and a cardboard sign on which is written, in thick black letters:

BUT FOR THE GRACE OF GOD

It doesn't make sense.

I cross to the sink and turn the tap handle. No water flows. I flick the old brass light switch by the door. Nothing. I curse under my breath at the absurdity of it all. How can the man live like this but hoard all those things in the living room?

The house is silent.

Beyond the kitchen door is a hallway leading to the front door. Another door to my left is ajar, opening onto what must be the living room, while to my right a bannistered staircase leads to the upper floor.

I poke my head into the living room. It's empty, the wooden floor buckled, holes like gaping eye sockets in the plaster of the walls and ceiling. Against one wall a few small wooden crates have been stacked as if to create a makeshift chair. There is no sign of cabinets, or bookcases, or oil paintings.

Faint footfalls sound from above.

I creep up the stairs, my feet rustling through ribbons of peeled wallpaper that snake across the steps. It reminds me of Christmas when I was a kid. Wading through the remains of wrapping paper with Liam, long gone now. My hands clench at the memory.

Mustiness and neglect hang in the air.

"Oh! Oh, hello."

I stumble and grab at the bannister rail to steady myself, and it rocks beneath my grip.

An old man stands on the landing, jogging trousers and a tattered flannel shirt loose on his near-skeletal frame, a ragged beard hanging almost to his waist. An erratic halo of white hair sprouts around his head like dandelion down. Fine silver dust covers his clothes and skin as if he's been asleep for a few decades.

But this can't be the man I saw taking his leisure on the doorstep. That man stood tall and manicured. The figure in front of me is barely a shadow.

He licks his lips before offering a nervous smile.

"I haven't had a visitor before. Have you come to see me?"

Saliva thickens in my mouth.

The man's smile fades, the loose skin of his face sagging.

"Unless..." His eyes boggle. "You're not here for... No! You can't have it. It's mine. It was meant for me!"

The man lifts thin, trembling hands and lurches towards me, face contorted in panic. His fingers seize my shoulders, his sudden weight atop me, bearing me down a step. "It's—for—me!"

I grab the man's wrists, thin bones sharp beneath the skin. I twist so my back is to the wall and push, and there is an odd rush of shock and satisfaction as the rotten railing breaks and the man tumbles, head smacking against the far wall before he crumples to the floor. Blood spreads, soaking into the dust.

I sit on the stairs, heart racing, acid heavy in my stomach. Killing the old man wasn't the plan. I don't regret it, though. I can admit that much at least. I need money to make a new start, whatever the cost.

But where are the treasures? And where is the other man, the one I've been watching these last few days?

The house is quiet. Only the faint sigh of air from an open window reassures me the world outside still exists.

I consider fleeing back into the filthy embrace of the wasteground, but the old man's body is in the hall and I don't want to go near it yet. Instead, I hurry upstairs, determined to see what is there and to confront the other occupant. I need answers.

Upstairs is just as decayed as below. A bathroom stands at the top of the stairs, with three other doors ajar on the landing, each leading to a small bedroom. Everywhere, the surfaces are layered with the same silver dust that had covered the old man, shining in the torchlight like powdered aluminum.

Two of the bedrooms are empty, apart from a pile of ceiling plaster and crumpled wallpaper in one corner, and some odds and ends of moldered clothes. The third contains an old mattress looking like it has been salvaged from landfill. There is no-one else in the house after all.

I turn to leave, but a glimpse of something on the wall gives me pause.

A small photograph has been tacked to the wall over the mattress. My penlight illuminates an image so familiar that for a moment I can't breathe. It's an old photo taken by my parents, before the accident. In the picture, my ten-year-old self looks up at the camera from my father's knee, little Liam at my side. Mum stands behind Dad, arms around his neck, smiling. It's the only photo I'd managed to keep through all those years at the children's home, then the many months sleeping rough and breaking into houses. I'd held onto it until HMP Dartmoor, where it vanished from my cell one day while I was at rec. I never saw it again.

Until now. What was the old guy doing with it? And why put it on the wall?

I reach out trembling figures to brush the creased surface, and as I touch it the light in the room changes.

The walls brighten. The torn wallpaper is gone, replaced by an ivory emulsion reflecting the soft light now spilling from the ceiling lamp, which moments before was dull and dark. The bed is fresh, clean, the scent of lavender floating up from the plush duvet and pillows.

Here is the house I saw through the windows.

I step out onto the landing and look to the bathroom. It's like something from a show home; the pearlescent enamel of the sink and bath is radiant in the light, while the cool blue of the wall and floor tiles bathes me in calm. I keep walking, the strange reverie of the house pulling me onward.

The stairs are richly carpeted, the bannister intact, the walls painted in bright shades of white and yellow. I head down the steps. The old man is gone, and there is no blood. Although I can't quite bring myself to walk across the spot where he lay, I move down the hallway and into the living room. It too is no longer derelict, but neither is it as it was when I observed it through binoculars: no wooden dresser, no oil paintings, no leather-clad books.

But there are stacks of paperbacks, the kinds of crime novels that kept me sane during long years of anxiety and solitude. A TV and DVD player sit in one corner, dozens of films piled next to them. I catch a glimpse of some of my favorite titles: Amores Perros, Un Chien Andalou, Kes, Vertigo. A dartboard hangs on one wall, and a leather armchair in the corner screams comfort.

Then comes the kitchen, equipped with a huge fridge, cooker, microwave, kettle, and toaster. Everything anyone could need. I open the fridge, and it is crammed with food. Cheese, ham, salami, chicken, half a dozen varieties of jam. Bottles of soda and beer.

I take out a beer—a craft stout, just my taste—and cross to the drawer by the sink, where I would have kept the bottle opener if this were my house. And there it is, nestling amongst some fine silver cutlery. I open the beer and drain it in one go. When I return to the fridge, a new bottle has replaced the old, and when I look at the empty in my hand, I find it has vanished.

I take another beer and retreat to the living room to think. The padded leather armchair welcomes me as I sink into its depths.

This isn't real—it can't be—and yet I am certain it is. No wonder the old man was keen to defend it.

I finish the beer and close my eyes as a wonderful lethargy takes hold. When I open them, I half expect everything to have returned to its dilapidated state. But all is the same. All is perfect.

Someone is watching me from the corner of the room.

Startled, I jump from the chair, but it is only a mirror. I move closer, hesitant, unsure of what I'm seeing. The reflection follows my movements, but I don't recognize the face in the mirror's bright surface. Or do I? Yes, there are the too-wide ears and oft-broken nose, the pale grey eyes that have always made me look half-blind. But the skin is wrinkled, the hair white. It is the face of a seventy-year-old, not a man in his twenties.

I push my fingers into the loose skin, massaging it. I roll up my sleeves to see the hairs on my arms. In the reflection of the glass, they too are white, a forest of pale stalks covering liver spots.

So. I'm old, and the house has given me... what? Shelter. A place to feel safe and secure. All the food and drink I could want. Entertainment to last a lifetime.

A home.

Nonsense. I dismiss it all and turn to leave but find myself hesitating. I need to think. If it were true—if it were possible— would it be worth the trade? A few more years to live, another decade, perhaps more. But living in comfort and ease. It might be worth staying. Or I could leave, and maybe things would go back to normal.

But I find I don't want to. Not yet. I want to enjoy the house for a while.

I get another beer—the fridge is full again—and settle back in the armchair. Sleep creeps up, and I welcome it.

———

THE DAYS PASS with delicious laziness, each evening and morning drifting by. The sun rises full and bright every day, so I go to the back door to look out at the garden and the view of woodland and fields beyond. There is no wasteground now.

A small table stands by the back door, with a box of Cohiba cigars on it. While I admire the vista, I smoke and think about nothing at all. I know I must be dreaming, and I don't care.

There is plenty to occupy my time. I'm content, and never bored. The kitchen offers me whatever food and drink I want whenever I want it. I watch whatever I feel like on the TV. There are always films to enjoy, whatever I'm in the mood for—movies I've seen and love, and plenty of others that are new to me. Likewise with the books: favorites that remind me of fleeting hours of happiness lost in stories, and new tales I've never read before.

Sometimes I long for company, but within minutes, it fades, and I am content to read, or watch, or stand in the garden, or just sit and dream. The dreams are blissful, and at night I sleep better than I ever have. Since the accident, at least.

The memory is the only thing that intrudes on my bliss. Even the house can't keep it away all the time, so that, without warning, I find myself starting to wakefulness and it is as if I am a boy again, the smell of smoke and petrol heavy on the air, being dragged from the car just in time.

Just in time for me.

The house can't help me forget that. Not completely.

———

THE DAYS MERGE INTO ONE: a glorious, unending, sedate dream. I am truly happy, or as close as I've ever been.

As I stand at the back door one morning, smoking and dreaming, a wasp buzzes at my ear. Its persistent, ringing hum tickles my spine. I reach up to swat it away, but find myself grabbing it instead, holding it in the cup of my palm.

It stings me, a pulsing agony stabbing into my finger. Then again, another finger, my palm, and my thumb.

And as the pain rushes through me, the sunlight dims, and I see the waist-high weeds again. I see the confusion of the garden, the piles of rubble in the wasteground, the abandoned, broken buildings.

My gaze falls on the metallic powder that covers my skin and clothes, as if I have been smothered in ash. The tiny silver motes almost seem to be moving.

There are kids playing in the wasteground, skidding their

bikes down the slopes of brick and stone. One of them stops his descent in a cloud of dust to stare across at me.

I open my hand and the wasp flies free. My emaciated, dust-smothered fingers are red and trembling, just for a moment. And then they are normal and the pastoral panorama has returned, the sun burning bright, birds singing somewhere nearby.

I need to go back inside, where it is comfortable and safe. Doing so is such an easy decision to make.

The house welcomes me with a fresh box of cigars on the little table by the back door.

———

SOMETHING WAKES ME. All is silent, but I have a half-memory of breaking glass.

I slip out of bed and to the landing. The sweet scent of woodsmoke drifts from below but as I stand there the odor changes to something harsher, more offensive. A horribly familiar smell.

Petrol.

Light flickers in the hallway. Somewhere, something is hissing, like an animal in pain, desperate to release its fury.

The peeling wallpaper returns, the filthy carpet, the layers of rippling silver specks that cover my body. I take a few shaky steps downstairs.

The old man lies where he fell, his skin tattered, his clothes a slough of moldered fabric. Behind him, fragments of broken glass shine in the light of the fire that races up the walls and across the floor.

There comes a child's laughter and I see Liam once again, screaming and burning in the wreckage. Fire blocks both the front door and the back. The hallway is an inferno.

I head back upstairs. My bedroom window overlooks the garden, and I rush to open it. I grasp the rotten latch and push, but before I can swing the window outwards the floor beneath me gives and I'm falling into the flames.

I hit the floor hard and roll, and as my skin and hair ignite, the world shrinks to a tiny core of incandescent, unbearable agony.

I scramble to the back door and burst through into the garden, crawling, rolling, desperate to stop the burning.

Something wet and dark enfolds me. There is the stench of rot and damp. I'm not burning, but pain still radiates through me. I don't think it's ever going to stop.

The darkness lifts and I realize I'm wrapped in an old carpet, some detritus salvaged from the wasteground. A pale, hooded face hovers into view—one of the kids I'd seen the morning the wasp stung me. His cheeks are wet with tears.

"I'm sorry! It was supposed to be a prank; I didn't know they were going to do that. I'll call an ambulance." He pulls a phone from his jacket, the screen lighting as he taps it.

I shake my head, the movement sending shockwaves down my spine. "Don't. Just go. Stay away... from the house."

After a moment's hesitation he leaves, his bike tires crunching on stone and gravel as he rides away.

It's just me and the house, perhaps neither of us long for the world.

There is a high-pitched whine carrying on the wind, and I imagine the house screaming as it burns.

I feel nothing. It's as if I have been lying here all my life. Liam lies nearby, his broken body burning too. I feel his fingers grasp mine. We are together, side by side, where we should always have been.

I watch the stars as clouds of scorched silver billow across the night sky.

THE GOD OF THREE-FOUR-TWELVE

G. GORMLEY

I met an old god on the playground. He stood between the oak tree and the swing set, his smile clean and perfect. He didn't look like the gods I had heard about before, the gods of lightning-in-hands, flesh-on-tongue, of eucharist and bacchanal. He looked like the satisfaction of palms scrubbed clean, the crisp lines of white linen.

Nobody else could see him. The other children out for recess were still running and hollering, throwing themselves down the slides with all the energy of second graders who would soon be made to sit still again. The teacher monitoring us leaned against the side of the school and surveyed the lawn, giving no indication of alarm. Not even the sun noticed the god in its midday summer heat. It fell through him without leaving a shadow.

Nobody else could see him, but I couldn't see anything else. He was so clean and perfect, I instinctively examined my own hands. Dirty, with wood chips clinging to them. The ugliest things I had ever seen.

I smeared the dirt against the bottom of my T-shirt, trying to wipe them clean. Trying to make myself half as perfect as the god in front of me. The first prayer of a newborn convert.

"They're still dirty, child," he told me. His voice was the reassuring weight of closing a door, the thunk of a lock falling into place. "And now your shirt, as well. When you touch your face, that will be dirty. Children spit in this dirt. Dogs piss and birds shit in it. Look."

And he showed me. A boy puking after getting off the slide. Chunks of peas spraying with the vomit, rolling away caked in goopy yellow. Seagulls spattering the wood chips white. Spilled food, tomato thick and syrup sticky and saliva and snot and bacteria teaming and festering and rotting and crawling up my hands into my skin into my blood.

I shuddered, looking up at my old god. My hands were stiff in front of me. I couldn't move them—couldn't move any part of myself from the fear. If I moved, the fabric of my shirt might brush my elbow, might spread the filth. Hands might touch my face, as good as if I had let sickly yellow vomit pour into my mouth.

"You'll be alright," he hushed before I could begin to cry. "Come with me."

He walked me into the schoolhouse, down the hall, and into the bathroom. He led me to the sink, and the water spilled clear and cool over my hands. Relief like a balm against a burn. Terror subsided, nausea receding. My fingers stopped shaking.

He was a kind god. He showed me how to wash my hands until they were raw and bleeding at the knuckles. And again. And again.

And again.

"Four times," he taught me. "Three, four, twelve. Those are my numbers. They'll keep you safe. I'll keep you safe."

The sharp smell of cheap school soap was cleaner than any honeyed flowers that Elysium could have gifted me, holier than any offering of Jerusalem. When my skin cracked, it burned, and the burn meant I was clean, inside and out.

The god of perfect things walked home beside me.

———

ALL GODS HAVE RULES. There weren't so many to start out with.

Wash your hands twelve times. Brush your hair four times. Don't touch anything that's been near someone's mouth. Don't let food mix together. Check four times that your name is on your paper before you turn it in.

I did what the old god asked, and I was clean.

Wash your hands twelve times. Then twelve times again. Then twelve times again. Then twelve times again. Brush your hair twelve times. Don't touch anything that's been near someone's skin. Don't eat food if your mom didn't make it, if you don't recognize it, if the texture is dirty-infected-contaminated-filth. Write your name twelve times on your paper. Each side, each piece. Staple it twelve times.

All gods have rules. Old gods have so many rules they can eat you right up. But I knew that if the rules didn't eat me, the infection would, and I knew which one was worse. Besides, the rules were there for a reason. I was glad to have my old god. He lived in the back of my mind and the corner of my eye, and he kept his promise. He kept me safe.

I was eleven when he said, "Someone will come through the front door tonight."

I had been lying in bed, but I sat up to look at him. In the night, the shadows looked strange falling through him. They didn't touch him any more than the sun had.

"Someone you don't know," he elaborated, "will come through the front door tonight. They'll be inside this house with their shoes and their hands and their saliva. Everything clean, ruined. Infected. And your family. You'll never see them again."

And he showed me. A tall man, fingers sticky as he touches the doorknobs. Shoes tracking dirt over the carpet. Quiet footsteps. A pillow pressed down over my mom's mouth, her limbs jerking and twisting and breaking. My dad shouting, red spilling, vile over the floor. My baby brother with his small hands and soft curls going pale, pale, pale. My sister facedown on the bathroom floor. The dog barking and then whining, straining to scamper away.

I swallowed hard, trying not to cry. My stomach was a ball of dread, panic making my lungs convulse. I didn't want to see the things he was showing me, but he kept them plastered over the insides of my eyelids so I couldn't blink without seeing the blood that was congealing in a puddle under my sister's head.

"Unless," he said, "you make sure the door is locked. Unless you let me protect you."

He didn't need to convince me to follow him. I kept my footsteps soft, working to keep my sniffling contained as hot tears threatened to spill. My mom was a light sleeper, and I didn't want to wake her.

The night was black and cold on the other side of the sliding glass door, a mass pressing against the house. The family room was alien in the dark, the house huge all around me. Something shifted, and I nearly jumped out of my skin before I saw the dog curled up on the carpet, her breath heavy with sleep.

I pressed my hands against the door's cool glass, reaching in the dark until I found the shape of the latch. I lifted it up, letting it fall back into place with a heavy thunk. My hands cracked with the motion. It had been a long time since they were anything but raw and breaking apart. But my hands were clean, and the house was safe.

"Not yet," he told me. "You need to make sure. Twelve times."

I tapped my index finger against the lock. Three sets of four. Three, four, twelve.

Twelve times. That was his number. That was how he protected me.

I returned to bed. I lay on my back.

My dad shouting. A pillow over my mom's face. I jolted up again, looking at the old god who stood in the corner.

"It might have come undone," he told me. "Check again."

"Twelve times?" I asked.

"Twelve times," he promised.

And again. And again. And again.

It was three in the morning by the time it was done. Limbs heavy, eyes sore and drooping as I finally went to sleep. I didn't mind, though. My family was safe, and the house was safe, and everything was clean.

When night came again, the god of every creeping terror smiled and said: "Someone will come through the front door tonight."

After that, I was tired every day. Exhaustion pounded a staccato beat inside my skull. Four-taps-and-four-taps-and-four-taps, and four-taps-and-four-taps-and-four-taps, and four-taps-and-four-taps-and-four-taps, and-four-taps-and-four-taps-and-four-taps.

My hair was coming out in clumps from twelve brushes, twelve brushes, twelve brushes. My hands cracked and bled and cracked and bled.

And cracked and bled.

———

Here's what they don't tell you about following old gods: the old gods follow you back. Even when you don't want them to. And the rules build up and the skin breaks down, and eventually you will want it to stop. Eventually, you will look at your hands and you will not feel holy or clean or perfect. You will feel like your body is coming apart around you.

He watched me drink the glass of water, watched me see that there was a speck of dirt swimming at the bottom. So small. So insignificant. But my mouth was an open wound and the water was rot flowing into me, bacteria swimming down my throat with fish feces-infection-filth, runoff from cattle farms. My hands began to tremble as my skin begged to be scrubbed clean, panic clawing me to pieces.

He fell into step beside me as I rushed to the bathroom. Stood behind me, over my shoulder in the mirror as I brushed my teeth twelve times, twelve times, twelve times. Tears blurred my vision, and I could not see his face. I didn't know if he had ever had a face.

"You're still dirty, child," he told me, and it was difficult to breathe. I wanted to pull my hair out four times-four times-four times. I needed to get away from the contamination of my own filthy saliva inside my own infected mouth.

"The skin itself," he guided me. "You need to remove the skin itself."

Revelation. This is what they write psalms about: the mad search through bathroom drawers until hands close around a nail file wrapped in plastic. This is the work of the muses: dragging the file over lips and tongue until all is raw as a wound, raw as my hands, clean and perfect once more. Impurities scraped away. This eucharist tastes more like blood than the wine they pour in churches.

The rest was easy as he led me through it, a priest leading a prayer. Wash the blood away with hand soap. Hand sanitizer, disinfect the site of the contamination. Clean and safe and perfect. No holy temple could ever make someone so pure.

And then it was done, and the panic began to fade.

He whispered how clean I was, how clean and safe and

perfect. And my mouth was still a wound as I walked back towards the glass of water, still sitting where I had left it.

There was no disease inside the cup. No crawling rot.

There was only a speck of black.

When I turned the cup, It stayed in place. A smudge on the table.

———

SOMETIMES, a clever person can trick an old god.

Old gods speak in precise words, and you have to stay inside them. But there are many ways to follow a precise set of words.

"You said when I brushed my hair I needed to do it twelve times and twelve times and twelve times," I explained as I pulled the blanket over my face to sleep. "But I'm not brushing my hair, so I don't have to."

The god of many rules looked at me.

"That's true," he finally said, "but it will tangle."

But there were never any rules against tangled hair—only about what one needed to do to prevent it. I let my hair tangle and snarl and clump, and when my mom complained, I let her shear it clean off.

"Your alarm," he reminded me when I lay down to sleep. "Twelve times."

"Three alarms. Four checks each," I explained. "That's twelve."

He didn't say anything, because he knew there was nothing to say. The rules had been followed to the letter.

If you can't trick an old god, sometimes you can outlast one.

"It might have come undone," he said. "It might have come undone."

"I already checked the lock," I told him. "Twelve times and twelve times and twelve times and twelve times. It's safe."

"It might have come undone. It might have come undone."

I lay there for hours until the sun was beginning to rise, light pale through my bedroom window. The old god stood in the corner.

"It might have come undone."

"It's morning now," I told him. "It's important that the door is locked at night."

Sometimes a clever person can trick an old god. Sometimes a patient person can outlast them. And there is not much sleep, but the hands bleed less. Sometimes, he even looks a fraction smaller.

Usually, the old god wins. And the hands crack and the hair comes out. And it is two in the morning and I am checking twelve times, twelve times, twelve times.

So IF YOU meet the old god
    who knocks three times at your door,
    calling out your name
    in sets of even four:
    don't lock him out, don't let him in,
    pretend he never came
    and if you check the door again
    he's already within.
    He's the sickening infection
    And the terror that compels,
    he's every false perfection—
    The God of Three-Four-Twelve.

CONTENT DISCLAIMERS (SPOILER WARNING)

For those ISO "trigger warnings," you've found them.

If you don't want anything that might spoil stories, please direct your eyes elsewhere at this time.

I'll wait...

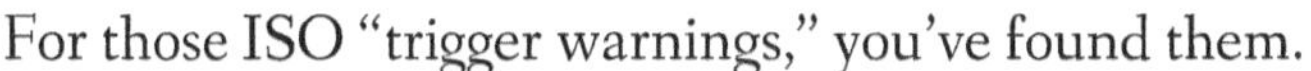

Okay! Here we go, story by story. Please forgive us if we've missed something; we're doing our level best.

SECTION ONE: THE SUBURBS

Incident with the Barqueleigh Square Court Homeowners Association: Gore, depictions of violence against children, HOA member deaths described in intimate detail

The Physical Impossibility of Love in the Heart of Someone Wanting: eye gouging, violence, dismembered body parts

Watching Over Her House: grief over personal loss of a loved one, old furniture

One, Two, Three: incidence of crashing aircraft, trains, etc.; wanton wishing of mass death on the part of a character

Hoodlums: presence of a Karen, youth struck by motor vehicle, possible racism or classism (implied, not explicit)

Off Label: lycanthropy, auto accident, references to alcohol abuse and domestic violence

Decorations: gore, body parts, dismemberment

Shadows in Renovation: partner abuse, child endangerment, stabbing, corpses packed into tight places

Everything is Fine: negligence of corpses, mild scenes from apocalyptic plague, child death, mental illness

Just Checking In: child of protagonist is harmed (off screen)

A Sacred Place: HOA member murder, implied religious violence

Sounds of Summer: child harmed (off screen)

Idols of Godless Men: cult-like emotional abuse

Just Being Neighborly: bigotry, anti-semitism, kidnapping

The Geese of Bronson Boulevard: goose-on-human violence, force feeding

SECTION TWO: CITY LIFE

Creepy Crawly: crawling insects

The Scream: claustrophobia, panic attack triggered by claustrophobia, child witness to panic attack

The Customer is Always Wrong: customer-to-server verbal abuse; brief mention of sexual assault

If I Go Missing: isolation / loneliness, despair, alcohol, mention of kidnapping / implied murder

The Humming Refrigerator is Almost Purring: psychosis

The Stain: spooky bathroom stain

In Darkness Left Behind: monster in basement-type stuff

Couch Surfing: couch-on-roommate violence (off screen)

Hanging Meat on the Bones: gentrification, urban blight, gore, implied poisoning and violence

SECTION THREE: OUT IN THE STICKS

M Go Blue: car chase, hillbilly-on-city-slicker violence, particularly strong sense of impending doom

The Annual Family Reunion: lake-on-child violence, helplessness, child death

I'm Not From Here: isolation

Sacrifice: bullying, gore, (creature / non-human) violence against children

The Morning After: it's a mood (isolation)

Mother's Day: misogyny, car chase, child death, ghost stuff

SECTION FOUR: ALONE

Impact: graphic depiction of aftermath of catastrophic car wreck, including deceased or dying bodies described in detail

The Grave of the Quiet: gravedigger-on-gravedigger violence, violence against someone with a disability

Ambrosia: eternal one-on-human violence, domestic violence, death

Home Comforts: isolation, possible psychosis (or is it supernatural in nature? You decide.), wasps, death, violence, house fire, death in car accident

The God of Three-Four-Twelve: obsessive-compulsive disorder writ large, vomit, intrusive thoughts, self-harm, paranoia

For those ISO "trigger warnings," you've found them (they're above this message), story by story.

If you don't want anything that might spoil stories, please direct your eyes elsewhere at this time.

CONTRIBUTING AUTHORS

Summer Alexis is a graduate of Northern Arizona University where she majored in English and Women's and Gender Studies. She received the Charles E. Bull Creative Writing Scholarship for poetry, her literary analysis has been featured in Magazine Americana, and she has fiction featured in *Parhelion Literary Magazine* and *Dark Mirrors: An Anthology of Horror*. Summer enjoys reading and writing horror and thriller stories and lives in Minneapolis, MN, with her two cats.

Beth Kette Anderson placed in the Top 25 New Writers for *Glimmer Train*. Since then, she has had stories published in *The Saturday Evening Post* and numerous anthologies. Beth lives with her husband at the very end of the Puget Sound in Washington State.

Abby Andresen started writing horror after discovering the work of Shirley Jackson, Patricia Highsmith, Charlotte Perkins Gilman, and other women writers of dark fiction. Since publishing her darkly comic novel, *An Inappropriate Crush*, in 2017, she's had stories published in three horror anthologies, most recently in *Land of 10,000 Nightmares: Minnesota Tales of Terror* (Glint Media, 2023). Previously, she wrote articles and essays for several Minnesota publications, including *Minneapolis St. Paul Magazine*, and worked as a Minneapolis-based standup comedian. She tries to mix a little humor into her horror, when appropriate. She has an MFA in Creative Writing from American University.

Robert Bagnall was born in Bedford, England, in 1970. He has written for the BBC, national newspapers, and government ministers. Five of his stories have been selected for the annual *Best of British Science Fiction* anthologies. He is the author of sci-fi thriller *2084: The Meschera Bandwidth* and two anthologies, each of which collects 24 of his eighty-odd published stories. He can be contacted via his blog at meschera.blogspot.com.

J. M. Bask lives in the suburbs, which are a horror unto themselves, the greatest terror being the nonstop moan of leaf blowers. When she is not writing, she is doing typical suburban things to blend in, such as raising children and petting people's dogs. She has been previously published in *Allegory Magazine* and is currently working on a novel.

Melissa Bobe is the author of *Season of the Witch*, *Nascent Witch*, and *Sibyls*. Her collection *Electric Trees* won the 2023 New York Author Project. She has recently published fiction with Intrepidus Ink, Bards and Sages, Urhi Publishing, Wyldblood Press, and World Weaver Press. After years of teaching college English, Melissa now works as a librarian. You can find her on social media @abookbumble and abookbumble.com.

Tiffany Michelle Brown is a Los Angeles-based writer who once had a conversation with a ghost over a pumpkin beer. She is the author of *How Lovely To Be a Woman: Stories and Poems* and cohost of the *Horror in the Margins* podcast. Her fiction and poetry has been featured in publications by Black Spot Books, Dread Stone Press, Death Knell Press, Hungry Shadow Press, and the *NoSleep Podcast*.

John Bukowski was previously a researcher and medical writer with professional publications ranging from journal articles to website content to radio scripts. In fiction, he has two novels and seventeen short stories in publication. He's a native of the Midwest but currently lives in eastern Tennessee.

Rob Francis is an academic and writer based in Bedfordshire, England. He mainly writes short fantasy and horror, and his stories have appeared in magazines such as *The Arcanist*, *Apparition Lit*, *Metaphorosis*, *Tales to Terrify*, *Cosmic Horror Monthly*, and *Weird Horror*. Rob has also contributed stories to several anthologies, including *DeadSteam* and *DeadSteam II* by Grimmer & Grimmer books, *Under the Full Moon's Light* by Owl Hollow Press, and *Alternative War* by B Cubed Press. He lurks on 'X' (formerly Twitter) @RAFurbaneco.

G. Gormley (they/them) is a writer based in Washington state. Their short stories have appeared in magazines such as *The Chamber* and *Rural Fiction Magazine*, and their novels *Sing The Angry Children* and *Weep Our Wretched Land* were published under the pen name Celia J. King. They enjoy writing everything from sci-fi to gay rat poetry.

Christina Griffith is a journalist and freelance writer living in Philadelphia with her dog, two cats, and her significant other, a human. She digs music, sci-fi, and cooking, and is originally from New York's Hudson Valley.

Kay Hanifen was born on a Friday the 13th and once lived for three months in a haunted castle. So, obviously, she had to become a horror writer. Her work has appeared in over forty anthologies and magazines. When she's not consuming pop culture with the voraciousness of a vampire at a 24-hour blood bank, you can usually find her with her two black cats or at kayhanifenauthor.wordpress.com.

Tyler John Kasishke lives and writes in Portage, MI, where he is a student of creative writing at the Kalamazoo Institute of Arts. His work has been published in *The Horror Zine's Book of Monster Stories*. You can find him lurking on Twitter @TKasishke.

Jordan King-Lacroix is a Jewish writer from Sydney, Australia, via Montreal, Canada. His first book, the non-fiction *Ugly: A Bikie's Life*, was published by Penguin-Random House in 2021, and his short story "The Last Chosen", in the *Jewish Futures* anthology (Fantastic Books, 2023), was well-received by critics. When not writing, he can be seen gigging around Sydney in his punk band The Limited.

Spencer Koelle is a stressed bisexual living in the City of Brotherly Love. He shares his row house with a partner, a roommate, and four orange cats. His website is spencerkoelle.com and his twitter handle is @KoelleSpencer. He enjoys fake meat, red wine, and scary movies. He also loves feedback from readers, so feel free to drop him a line!

Andrew Kozma's fiction appears in *Apex*, *Factor Four*, and *Analog*, while his poems appear in *Strange Horizons*, *The Deadlands*, and *Contemporary Verse 2*. His first book of poems, *City of Regret*, won the Zone 3 First Book Award, and his second book, *Orphanotrophia*, was published in 2021 by Cobalt Press. You can find him on Bluesky at @thedrellum.bsky.social and visit his website at andrewkozma.net.

C.R. Langille spent many a Saturday afternoon watching monster movies with her mom. It wasn't long before she started crafting nightmares to share with her readers. She is a retired, disabled veteran with a deep love for weird and creepy tales. This prompted her to form Timber Ghost Press in January of 2021. She is an affiliate member of the Horror Writers Association, the DEI Chair for the League of Utah Writers, and she received her MFA: Writing Popular Fiction from Seton Hill University in 2014.

Jon Lasser lives in Seattle, WA with his wife and two children. His stories have appeared or are forthcoming in *Lightspeed*, *Analog*, *Interzone*, and elsewhere. He's a graduate of the Clarion West writers workshop. Find him on the web at twoideas.org and on Mastodon as @disappearinjon@wandering.shop.

Daniel Lumpkin is from Georgia. He currently teaches college English Lit and Comp courses at Shorter University. He loves being a husband and dad. You can reach him at nonprofitstepbystep@gmail.com.

John Mahoney is a writer living in one of New Jersey's less cheerful locales. His short stories were published by *The Yard: Crime Blog*, *Pinky Thinker Press*, *Etched Onyx* magazine, and *That is SO Wrong: An Anthology of Offbeat Horror*. *Highlights* magazine published a joke he wrote before he knew Santa Claus wasn't real.

Lena Ng lives in Toronto, Canada. Her short stories have appeared in publications including *Amazing Stories* and Flame Tree's *Asian Ghost Stories* and *Weird Horror Stories*. Her stories have been performed for podcasts such as *Gallery of Curiosities*, *Creepy Pod*, *Utopia Science Fiction*, *Love Letters to Poe*, and *Horrifying Tales of Wonder*. *Under an Autumn Moon* is her short story collection.

Gevera Bert Piedmont is a neurodivergent cyborg swamp witch living on the edge of a frog pond in Connecticut with her spouse, cats, and an impressive collection of rubber lizards. She is the author of *The Maw and Other Time-Traveling Lizard Tales*, the Mickey Crow paranormal series, co-author of *Airesford* (the other author is an actual zombie), editor of the *Necronomi-RomCom Cthulhu Mythos* duology and co-editor of *Horror Over the Handlebars*, an anthology of Connecticut horror. Her short stories have been published in *Love Beyond Death*, *The Fellowship* *of the Old Ones, Doomscrolling, Wicked Sick,* and others. Her novel *Fat Monster* will be published by Nightmare Press in 2025. Bert has an MFA in creative writing and belongs to HWA, Connecticut Authors and Publishers Association, and New England Horror Writers. Connect at facebook.com/geverabertpiedmontfac, geverabertpiedmont.com, obsidianbutterfly.com, or her Amazon and Goodreads author pages.

Stephen S. Power is the author of the novel *The Dragon Round*, and his new novel, *Safe at Last*, a story about a traumatized woman trapped in a smart house, is currently under submission. His short fiction has appeared most recently in *Unorthodox Stories* and *The Arcanist*, *Dark Recesses*, and *Dread Machine* and will soon appear in *Heathen*, *Lightspeed*, *Stupefying Stories* and the anthology *The Growers: The Best of NewMyths, Volume 5* as well as on the podcast *Creepy*. He lives in one of New Jersey's more cheerful locales, his site is stephenspower.com, and he skeets at @stephenspower.bsky.social.

Nigel Quinlan has written two books for children, and several short stories, published in the collection *This Way Up*, as well as in *Ember Journal*, *Albedo 1*, *The Caterpillar*, *Slant*, and *The Book Smugglers' Quarterly Almanac*. He lives in Ireland.

Jonathan Reddoch is co-owner of Collective Tales Publishing. He is a father, writer, editor, and publisher. He writes sci-fi, fantasy, romance, and especially horror. He has been working on his enormous sci-fi novel for over a decade and would like to finish it in this lifetime if possible. Find him on Instagram: @JonathanReddochAuthor.

Vanessa Reid is an English teacher in Atlanta who writes about the human monsters that haunt us. You can find some of her stories in *Georgia Gothic* and *The Fourth Corona Book of Horror Stories*. A member of the Broadleaf Writers Association and the Horror Writers Association, Reid lives with her adorably macabre family, an evil cat named Moreland, and a dog who tries to avoid his wrath. For more information, visit vanessareidfiction.wordpress.com.

Michael Allen Rose is an award-winning writer, musician, editor and performance artist based in Chicago, Illinois. His stories have appeared in *The Magazine of Bizarro Fiction*, *Heavy Feather Review*, and *Tales From The Crust*, among other periodicals. He has published several books, including *Jurassichrist* (Perpetual Motion Machine Publishing) which won the 2021 Wonderland Award for best bizarro novel, and *The Last 5 Minutes of the Human Race*, winner of best collection in bizarro fiction 2022. He is the host of the annual Ultimate Bizarro Showdown at Bizarro Con in Oregon. Michael also releases industrial music under the name Flood Damage. He lives with an awesome cat named Dr. Light, and enjoys good tea. You can find more at www.michaelallenrose.com.

Jesse Rowell (he/him) is an award-winning science fiction author whose work explores naturalism, technology, and the human condition. He can be found at jesserowell.com.

J.D. Simpson is a Kentucky teacher and author currently based in Barcelona. Under his pen name "John Beardify," he has written campfire-style horror stories that can be found via the *NoSleep Podcast*, Blair Daniel's *Halloween Horrors* anthology, and other publications. His work is based on the folklore of places he has lived and worked during the past decade, including Japan, the Republic of Georgia, and Appalachia. In his free time, he enjoys hiking in the Pyrenees with his family.

Katlina Sommerberg (xe/xyr/xem) is living xyr best queer life in a menagerie of stuffed animals. Xyr work has previously appeared in *Zooscape* and other places. sommerbergssf.carrd.co.

Michael Subjack was born in a small town in Western New York and has since relocated to Pasadena, California. He's published two short story collections, and his work has appeared in the anthologies *101 Proof Horror*, *It Calls from the Forest*, *Trigger Warning: Curses*, and *Heavy Metal Nightmares*. He's also had a story read on an episode of the horror podcast *Chilling Tales for Dark Nights*. Most recently, he had a story published in The Horror Tree's *Trembling With Fear.*

Elizabeth Suggs is the co-owner of the indie publisher Collective Tales Publishing, owner of Editing Mee, and is the author of a growing number of award-winning published stories, one of which titled "Into the Dark" part of the *Collective Darkness* anthology was Amazon Bestseller, and another was selected for second place in the Quills Short Story Contest "Technicolor Tears." She is also a book reviewer (EditingMee.com), popular bookstagrammer, and cosplayer (@ElizabethSuggsAuthor). When she's not writing or reading, she's traveling the world.

William Wandless teaches English by day, and by night he writes speculative fiction. His latest work can be found in *Bourbon Penn* as well as the *Hidden Realms* and *Home Sweet Horror* anthologies. He can be found on Bluesky as @billwandless and on Twitter as @ArsGoetica.

Sam Weller is a two-time Bram Stoker Award winning writer of fiction and nonfiction. His collection of supernatural gothic stories, *Dark Black*, was published by Hat & Beard Press in 2020. Sam is the authorized biographer of the late and legendary Ray Bradbury. His book, *The Bradbury Chronicles: The Life of Ray Bradbury* (HarperPerennial) was a national bestseller. Sam lives and writes in Chicago. You can follow him on X @Sam__Weller or learn more on his website: samweller.net.

Angela is a biochemist-turned textile artist who listens to scary podcasts while walking her dog through the deep, dark woods of the Canadian Rocky Mountains. Occasionally, she happens across an abandoned cabin. She always goes in.

ABOUT THE EDITOR

Founder of Whisper House Press, Steve Capone Jr. is a Utah-based writer hailing and longtime educator, origin:Rust Belt. While his short publications have mostly been in horror, his first book length publication was in YA historical fiction, *Max in the Capital of Spies*, which he released after a successful Kickstarter in 2024. His second, *Jimmy vs. Communism*, is due nationwide from Gibbs Smith in 2026. He's got more in the chamber, but works in development are in game literature and horror.

You can find Steve's short fiction in anthologies including *We Are Dangerous* (LUW Press, 2023), *Darkness 102* (Collective Tales Publishing), *This Isn't the Place* (Timber Ghost Press, 2024), *Write Where You Belong* (LUW Press, 2024), and elsewhere. His short screenplay, "A Cure For Creativity," was a selection at the Oregon Screams Horror Film Festival in the fall of 2024, and his first Sundance rejection arrived back in 2023. He's a fanboy, and he's going to keep trying.

Steve received his B.A. from a small liberal arts college (Washington & Jefferson College) that offered exactly what he needed: a close community and plenty of supportive instructors. He then earned an M.A. from the University of Chicago in the highly lucrative field of Humanities with an emphasis on Kant studies—and then an M.S. in the even more highly profitable area of Political and Social Moral Philosophy (foci: Egalitarianism, Manners & Social Graces).

On a more personal note, Steve is also a staunch pizza advocate (you can find a how-to on his @stevecaponejrauthor YouTube page!) and dog helper with Arctic Rescue in Utah.

Steve lives with and is shaped by several invisible disabilities and believes it best to #recoveroutloud wherever possible. If you're in need of help with mental health and / or drug addiction / alcoholism, there's help out there. He's not an expert, but he's found support in a 12-step fellowship; maybe that'll work for you, too.

You can find Steve's personal incorporeal footprint on his website at www.stevecaponejrauthor.com or his linktr.ee at https://linktr.ee/stevecaponejr. He welcomes your communiques at editor@whisperhousepress.com and would be happy to take a few runs with you at Alta or Solitude in the Cottonwood Canyons.

———

Affiliate Member: Horror Writers Association and member of its very fine Utah Chapter

Member of the League of Utah Writers, Screenwriters Guild chapter and Salt City Genre Writers chapter

———

facebook.com/SteveCaponeJr

instagram.com/author_steve_capone_jr

goodreads.com/steve_capone_jr_author

tiktok.com/@steve_capone_jr_author

youtube.com/@WhisperHousePress

ACKNOWLEDGMENTS

A massive "thank you" is due to the contributing authors, all of whom jumped on board this relatively homespun project and dug in to make the collection and its launch as strong as possible. Many even sat for interviews, and for that, I owe an additional acknowledgment and expression of gratitude. Many contributors also offered advice in layout and design, answering questions here and there throughout the process. They've by and large been much more involved in the publishing process than most writers are asked to be in other projects. If you're thinking about joining the crew for a future collection, expect that open and inclusive cooperative community.

I owe a debt of gratitude to the League of Utah Writers, whose members have been integral to my continued growth in writing and publishing. The same debt is owed to the Horror Writers Association and its Utah Chapter.

I wish to acknowledge and thank independent bookshops and libraries—The Printed Garden (bookshop in Utah), the Salt Lake County Public Library, and Salt Lake City Public Library in particular.

Small publishers like Timber Ghost Press and Collective Tales Publishing have in direct and material ways made this book better and perhaps rendered it possible. You and other small publishers: Thank you for leading the way.

Horror authors in general and HWA members in particular: You are the most supportive group of creatives I've come across.

From the least-known indie writer to the best-known award winners: Thank you.

Thanks are also due to the 50+ Kickstarter backers who supported the production of this book with nearly $1800 in funding. Folks didn't much seem interested in being named individually, so please let this stand as a collective acknowledgement of my appreciation.

And as always, the largest debt—the one I will never be able to repay—is due to my family, who have encouraged me from the start and continue to pay the majority of time- and money-related costs to this weird obsession with writing and stories that I keep pushing to the next level. My wife Sara in particular is unwavering; thank you for your persistence and support.

I am grateful to anyone who's picked up this book to check it out. I hope you find a story in this collection that speaks to you and I hope you grab our next one: *Dread Mondays*. It releases in October 2025 and is likely available for pre-order as you're reading this page.

Steve

Salt Lake City, Utah
    May, 2025

WHISPER HOUSE PRESS

This is Whisper House Press's first publication. If you've read and enjoyed it, please pretty please leave a positive review on the usual places and tell your local library and booksellers about us.

The publisher is releasing ***Dread Mondays: A Whisper House Press Horror Anthology*** in October of 2025. If you like this collection, please consider picking up the next. We thank you for your support.

Writers, be on the lookout for submission calls for future anthologies. We anticipate the following themes will show up: *family squabbles, airports and train stations*, and whatever other terrifying minutia the editor-in-chief cooks up. Future calls will be posted in all the usual spooky places: HWA social media, HorrorTree, The Submission Grinder, Reddit, et. al.

We're also always looking for 200-1000-word shorts. Check our website.

Small horror presses and agents working in the horror genre should consider reaching out to this publisher in the interest of building a new horror publishing consortium of strategic mutual support, the Independent Horror Publishing Consortium, or IHPC.

Please stay in touch by following along at www.whisperhousepress.com and subscribing to the editor's newsletter, which is linked from his linktr.ee @ www.linktr.ee/stevecaponejr.com.

9 798989 391936